Moonrise Falling

A Modern Gothic Tale

By Adrian L. Jawort

Moonrise Falling: A Modern Gothic Tale

Moonrise Falling: A Modern Gothic Tale

By Adrian L. Jawort

Copyright © 2018 by Adrian L. Jawort.

Printed in the United States of America

Published by:
Off the Pass Press LLC
2224 US Highway 87 East #43
Billings, MT 59101
www.offthepasspress.com

ISBN-13: 978-0-9863810-4-1
ISBN-10: 0-9863810-4-7

Edited by Todd Barselow

For my brother on the other side.

We did this together.

"In the middle of the journey of our life I found myself within a dark woods where the straight way was lost."
~Dante Alighieri, *Inferno*

Contents

1. Into the Vortex   9

2. Blissful Ignorance   25

3. To the Stars!   43

4. Value Menu   53

5. Karma   69

6. Just a Kiss   91

7. A Daymare   95

8. All-American Immolation   101

9. Mind Blown   111

10. Moonlight Drive   127

11. Crazy Content   139

12. Buckshot Elvis   151

13. Sunny Elixir   155

14. To the Clouds   167

15. Dead Flowers   173

16. The Diary of Dusk   181

17. Paper, Rock, I Win!   187

18. Iconoclast   207

19. Diana Hades   213

20. Late Charges   225

21. Greener Pastures   235

22. Rave D'oeuvre   243

23. Indecent Proposals   247

24. Date Rape   257

25. Sweet Dreams Are Made of These   267

26. So Opiate!   277

Chapter 1—Into the Vortex

IN THE DAYS RIGHT PRIOR to the dawn of heavy cell phone use and a half an hour or so after dusk, the daylight's previously near intolerable heat still very much lived inside of the concrete sidewalks and blacktop roads. Not that I really cared, since I was sitting inside an air- conditioned house in a spaced-out meditation of sorts before someone broke my lack of thoughts and offered me a drink.

"No thank you, kind sir. I need a level head."

"Level head...what the fuck ever, dude! You need your head examined is what you need," my roommate Eric said, obviously irritated. He took a slug out of a half-pint of whiskey. "So, you *really* gonna do this, huh?"

"Why not?"

"Because...you fucking know why the fuck why! I mean, you have shit going for ya!"

"Such foul language from a lady," I said. "Fuck you. Smart ass," he laughed.

"Look, I don't have a dime to my name. That's what's 'going for me.' Hitherto, I have two dollars to be used for alms for a 40 of frosted malt liquor later and that's my...uh...life's current amassed investments. Henceforth, I must venture into a risky business venture to seek profit for such aforementioned reasons. This town's easy for that. Simple."

"A trip to prison, that'll be the return on your 'risky business venture' to increase your 'life's current amassed investments.' You know, you ain't a juvenile who's gonna get a slap on the wrist. 'Henceforth? Hitherto?' Honestly, who the hell says shit that? You're fucking weird, man."

I heard footsteps approaching the door and got up.

"I think so sometimes. Anyway, it is done," I said and waved him off. I opened the door. "Ah, you have zee merchandise, Herr Cedric?"

"Yes, I have zee merchandise, Herr A.D. Hah hah! What the hell does that mean, 'Herr?'"

I shook my head as to make him ignore my trifled 'Herr' response. He sat down and pulled from his inside coat pocket a small, silver, .380 caliber handgun with an extra clip rolled up in a bandana.

"Hot, so...I haven't seen it...ever," he said seriously.

I grabbed it, wiped it off, and checked to see if there was a bullet in the chamber. There wasn't. I pulled the slide, chambered a round, and grabbed the extra clip. "Those other things?"

He reached into his other pocket and threw me a pair of black leather gloves and mumbled something like, "Operate," as I put on a pair of latex surgical gloves before them.

I had a bandana around my neck, a hooded sweatshirt, a stocking cap, and baggy cargo pants over my normal ones. All of the clothes were black."I got a bad feeling about this, bro," Eric said.

I was hopping around like a boxer warming up and barely heard him. I rolled my neck a few times and put on my dark sunglasses.

"I'll be back," I unoriginally said like The Terminator before leaving the house.

The house we were in wasn't mine, Eric's, or Cedric's. It belonged to another friend of ours named Ray who was currently working at his job at the restaurant. We always hung out there and he never minded as long as we kept the place tidy and at least saved him some food if we ate there.

My name is Abidan Dominic, and people call me A.D.—just like 'anno Domini.' I never liked my first name much, so I just combined it with my middle initial. As for my last name, forget it. Unless you're German you'll screw up the pronunciation, although it's not all that long. It was early summer, I was 19, and would be 20 later that fall after I was to go to college full-time as an art student. I had a scholarship and everything to do so. Artists are known to have peculiar habits, but I think armed robbery was for the more extremely eccentric or the seriously starving ones. I think I qualified for the former and latter of those reasons. I suppose most artists with this habit slightly worse than smoking would eventually get caught and sent to prison where they'd really have time to practice and hone their drawing skills, amongst many other not so intriguing prospects, such as maybe giving out prison tattoos and envelope letter art in exchange for cigarettes and gang rape leniency.

Me? I wouldn't get caught. Of course, that's what they all think and say right up until they do. Unlike they, however, I had a brilliantly conceived and original back up a plan: they'd never take me alive! Well, maybe it was pretty rudimentary come to think of it, but I tried not to think about that aspect as it seemed slightly discouraging and, well, defeatist.

What was my plan? I guess I was just winging it; on a 'jack mission' as they say back in the 'hood. Whose 'hood says that I don't know for sure, but I heard it from somewhere. I blame gangster rap music. I would trek to my house, pick up my mountain bike, go somewhere, do a stick-up, and then have the perfect getaway. So at least I had that general aspect of the problem worked out. I personally thought the bike was a fairly innovative idea— who'd ever think a bike was a getaway ride?

I lived approximately two miles away, and had plenty of time to think of a place I might rob during the walk. I knew it'd probably be one of the many machine-play

11

casinos lurking about because those dens of inequity had a surplus amount of money that would make the effort worthwhile. This one dope fiend once owed my friend an unhealthy drug debt, and he came back after like an hour with nearly all of the $600 he owed in five dollar bills—he'd definitely cashed out one way or another from one of the casinos. A bar was probably overly crowded on a Friday night, so I'd have to wait until near closing time, and I didn't want to wait and risk chickening out in the meantime. *Excuses, excuses.*

A convenience store looked like the option if I were to get it over with quickly, although the last time I didn't profit well hitting one of them. I remember practically sprinting a four-minute mile before I saw a patrol car with its lights on drive directly towards me in an alley. I ducked into someone's backyard, and seriously almost pissed my pants while hiding behind a fence and hedge on that rainy night. When you got to go you got to go; plus the steady rain drop sounds and—never mind. I felt the patrol car's spotlight beam above me like a laser burning across my back and thought I was finished. What a scary rush that had been. I had experienced something while hugging the musky smelling leaves, dirt, and mud that hardly any normal sane person could ever fathom or conceive—not that they'd want to.

A smile crossed my face as I thought about yet another time I'd committed such a felonious act. The target had been a bar, but I honestly didn't know it was a gay bar at the time of the 'alleged crime.' We'd made jokes about how witnesses 'would easily pick my ass out of a line up.' Oh, and suddenly my friends said it was 'A.D.'s favorite bar,' like it was a damned trucker code or something when referring to it from then on.

What the hell was wrong with me? Theoretically, I was a good, respectful student, as my teachers and elders had said. They'd encouraged me to go to college, and had full faith that I could make it far when they wrote their recommendations. No one would ever suspect me of doing something as stupid as what I was doing just then. Besides, like Eric had mentioned, I was no longer a juvenile and I was way too pretty for prison. *Just lay down and relax, and eventually you might start to like it. Egad!*

Hence, the theoretical saving of the last bullet so I wouldn't suffer, but what were a few shitty years compared to death? With such craptastic options to potentially consider if worse came to worse, I promised myself this would be the last time I'd ever do such a thing, no matter what kind of senseless maniacal rush I got out of it. It was not worth a couple hundred bucks. Like doing it without a condom, I should've pulled out right then and no one would've cared but my pockets, but the distorted comfort of knowing I wouldn't ever do it again made sense for some odd reason, as if that justified everything.

I turned into an alley and began walking with a calmer, more confident step. *Breathe...steady.*

After a quarter-mile or so I saw a few tough looking young ruffian thugs drinking on a back porch point at me and talk amongst themselves as if I were somehow trespassing on the public sidewalk, and I realized I might be in slight danger as the neighborhood wasn't exactly suburbia. I grew up in suburbia, so to speak, with the two car garage houses, picket fences, a friendly dog, perpetually mowed lawns, and this area was not that (although there were still ugly chain link fences and uglier snarling dogs). This was the so-called ghetto of the small industrial city I lived in just east of the Rocky Mountains, if you could call an area that in Montana. Everyone else in town that's probably never been to a bigger city said it was, at any rate.

I was gone as soon as they saw me, however, and if they wanted to be meddlesome you could say I was ready for them. I'd practiced shooting all kinds of guns for hillbilly fun plenty of times, and I was an extremely proficient shot, but it would've been so un-cool right then to pull a gun on wannabe gang bangers trying to prove their bravado and lose-lose for everyone.

I turned right and jogged up a new alley to distance myself quicker.

An intuitive feeling came over me, and I glanced behind me with the gun half-drawn. A blur shot back into the alley where I'd just come from. *Just a cat*, I thought. *Yeah, right. Big cat.* I knew I was paranoid of those hoodlums following me for hypothetical trespassing, but they couldn't have come up the street that fast without me hearing them. My senses were attuned.

"Damn CIA spooks trailing me again," I said to myself out loud as a personal joke to ease the tension.

Fate happened two blocks later when a dark-blue nineteen eighties Regal pulled into the alleyway one block ahead of me. The cat was in the bag. Something was either very right or very wrong. I hugged low to the wall up to the street, ran about 20 yards down to the right, and crossed straight towards the alley with the Regal. I peeked around, and with a quick half-second scan I took in everything I could through the car's tinted windows.

With the help of a dim streetlight I saw two people in the car: the male driver and most likely a female passenger judging by their outlines. I also noticed that the license plates were from out-of-state, which sealed the deal of the unfortunate victims just because I felt like being ironically hospitable during their vacation or business stay. Judging by the area we were in, I presumed they were dropping off drugs or had money from doing so based on the known drug house location. They weren't selling Girl Scout cookies or magazines, that was for sure. A rising apprehensive feeling in my chest threatened to make my head light as I put my sunglasses on and pulled up my bandana like an old, wild-west cowboy outlaw.

I slipped into the alley, crouched behind a large dumpster, and noticed the windows were rolled most of the way down. Stupid! You have to keep going! I counted three breaths, and looked at the gun to double-check and make sure the safety was off. I heard a female voice.

"Well, hurry up this time. This shit is—baby!"

I was in his face with the gun. "Get out the car, now!" I yelled in my scariest sounding police voice, although in all black and with my face covered I think he hardly mistook me for a cop. I could've looked like a one man swat team though.

The guy almost got a shot off on me after he grabbed a gun next to him. I caught him in the shoulder and chest area with a bullet, and he dropped it. "Ah, shit!" he yelled. "You fucking bitch!"

I pulled open the door, and with a mighty pull the heavy set Hispanic looking man fell to the ground, cursing me through heavy, forced, wheezing breaths.

Pop! Pop! Pop!

I peppered him with three more bullets—two to the chest and one to his forehead—and a mist flew up on my glasses. Maybe it was not right to shoot him thrice more, but I knew he would've likely died anyway, and he should have gotten out of the car peacefully. I had my eye on the female passenger and noticed her actually reach for the discarded gun on the floor. I aimed at her and said, "You really that fast?"

She wisely let her hand move away from the gun and put her hands up. At least she's not screaming. Shall I shoot her if she does?

"That's better," I said while digging through the dead guy's pockets, barely even looking at him. I didn't want to. I found a fat wad of cash in his back pocket and thought fast.

Getaway!

I wanted to run right then, but I was in unsafe

territory and would've had to go a half-mile just to get to some sort of safe house like my place or Ray's. I knew a few people here and there, but no one I wanted to get in trouble for harboring me if the trigger happy Gestapo coppers started shaking down the neighborhood and the police dogs closed in. So I hopped in the car, threw out the other guy's gun, and told the lady to stay put as I did not want a witness right at the scene literally screaming bloody murder. I knew people were shooting off fireworks and firecrackers all the time, so maybe the gun shots would pass as that for a few seconds or even minutes. The immediate area had started stirring by then, so I pulled out at a normal pace so as to not arouse further suspicion.

I felt a sickening gurgle creep into my chest after feeling a speed bump that I knew to be the back wheel of the car rolling over the dead dude's leg. The severity of the situation struck me with full force when I glanced at the lady. Dude, I have an actual hostage!

"You gonna kill me?" she asked without the slightest hint of panic in her voice. Her body said otherwise.

"Probably," I said. "I mean, just don't do anything stupid, all right? Like talk to me."

I had gotten a good look at her through the blood-spotted sunglasses and noticed she was very good looking. She had blond braided hair extensions, and she may have been part black or Hispanic—or both. Her short, tight blue dress showed off her scrawny but curvy body well. I took another long look at her nylon covered legs, and I noticed it took some of the intensity out the moment and helped the gurgling feelings in my chest go down.

She must have noticed that too as she looked at me nervously. "Don't," I said. She looked straight ahead. I started screwing with the radio, as there was a violent rap CD playing and I wanted to take my mind off of that.

I found one of the many local country music stations

and left it. George Strait's "Fool Hearted Memory" was peculiarly soothing. I left it on.

Think.

I figured out the new phase of my plan as I cruised on a main road. First and foremost, I was going to go to the warehouse district and simply ditch the car, as it was a huge piece of evidence in the murder case that was about to be built. I had no use for it as I knew of no chop-shops where I could unload it. I couldn't even remember the last time there was a carjacking in town, so there probably weren't any chop-shops anyway. I cruised into the warehouse district, and kept my eyes on full alert although the only people usually about in the perimeter at this hour were winos. I saw no one.

I pulled into a cornered, tree-filled area and reasoned the vehicle would not be found for at least a day or two since it was the weekend. I got out and told the woman to do the same.

She started crying as she noticed the isolation around her despite me telling her to shut up. "He was an asshole anyway," she said. "We just came up to drop off some stuff and I helped him drive and—"

"Whoa, whoa, woman," I interrupted her. "You got any more 'stuff?' This is important. Tell me anything that you have. Now!"

She immediately calmed down. "Um, there's some weed under the seat, it's probably up in there really good, but I know it's there."

"Good, good. What else we got in the pimp mobile? Unless you want to die protecting that dead dude's shit."

"Uh, some crystal. Not a lot though. I don't know how much he had left. Mostly personal and the stuff we were dumping off."

"Hmm," I pondered. "So...what the hell you want to do? Get the hell out of here or what?"

"Yeah," she knew she had to make her answer right. Technically, I was stupid for not killing her as she was the only witness to a murder, but she hadn't yet seen my face. The bandana and stocking cap I wore suddenly seemed way too hot and sweaty. "We were leaving tomorrow. Tonight we were just dumping off the rest of the stuff, going to the club, and then leaving. The other money is at the motel. I won't tell anyone, I swear!"

"Whatever," I said. She'd answer to someone, because in my pocket was already a fat wad of money that would have to be accounted for. "Shit!" I yelled just for the sake of cursing. "Grab the rest of that stuff or whatever and the weed under the seat, and please hurry. The hell with the motel, the cops will be rolling up there any time now. Hurry, hurry!"

"It's under the front bumper, the crystal," she said as she walked toward the front of the car and stopped. I nodded that it was okay.

She pulled a small container out that must have been attached by magnet to the car, opened it, and produced two rounded, soap-sized packages. I took them and shoved them into my pocket. I knew by the lumps I felt that both mini-bricks were full of 'rocked-up' methamphetamine. She proceeded to go to the driver's side to get the weed. I watched her very carefully, which was in fact easy to do. Lurid thoughts of violating her crossed my mind. Who'd ever find out? I even had a condom on me so no worry of leaving behind evidence or catching anything she might have. *No, not a time to get caught with one's pants down. Gee, that was lame. At least touch those legs and act like you're patting her down.*

But that just was not me, not my style. I was naturally reserved as it were.

She handed me the marijuana and my eyes lit up. The weed was practically glowing in the dim darkness it was so green.

"This it?" I said and aimed the gun at her head.

I should have known what the reaction was going to

be. "Yes! Yes, it is! I swear! I just wanna to go home and leave this place. Oh God, I'll never do any of this stuff again, I swear!"

"Well then, you got any money?" I said.

She pulled out a clip from her bra and tried to hand it to me.

"I thought you said that was it. Never mind, keep it to get the hell out of here. If they catch you, they'll keep you here in jail for questioning for months—trust me. You go back to that motel I guarantee they'll nab ya there and you'll be suspect numero uno. The hick town cops here would like nothing better than a bad cop, good cop, witch hunt interrogation ...whatever. So get the hell out of here, call a cab, get on a bus, and ride whatever direction takes you the farthest away from here the fastest, or you will have an extended vacation in this town. Got it? Make yourself invisible, although it may be hard in that outfit, come to think of it."

"Yes, yes."

I actually threw her the car keys, convinced she'd avoid the police at least for the immediate time being. She knew the game and probably figured the police would be a waste of time other than to harass her and waste her time.

I took off running in the areas that would leave minimal—if any—footprints and that was it with her. Why I didn't kill her is anybody's guess. Executing a woman would have haunted me probably. But she never saw my face and complied with my instructions, so I guess she was on her own. I don't know if the cops would have kept her if she talked to them, but I do know in her line of business it would've been wise to leave town ASAP unless she wanted to catch a potential federal drug case lest she turn snitch.

She learned a fresh lesson courtesy of me about the lucrative fallacies of the business she was in and the not-so-fringe benefits. Drug dealers from the west coast and southwest fed towns like mine had all the addictive substance they could handle and then plenty more—especially methamphetamine. Dealers like them raked in wealthy profits running for more hardcore connected mafia-type dealers, and this burgeoning trade spread out like a rude boulder smashing ripples in a placid mountain pond that affected even the most rural of areas. The dealer I had shot was obviously a middleman runner, and I was not Robin Hood, as I'd stolen this money from the ghetto rich and would only sell the dope back to the poor. I looked at the wad and nearly choked. There had to have been at least fifty one-hundred, fifty, and twenty dollar bills in the rounded roll. I had second thoughts about not going to that motel room they stayed in, but that would have been foolish in a not so big town with every cop out to be the hero in what was sure to be front page news.

From my starting point I could run on foot a great distance without being seen or until I was out of breath. There were numerous train tracks and I could run alongside of until I got back into a more populated area. If I kept to the back alleyways, no one would notice or think anything of my presence. I was nearly home free!

A block after reaching the first houses, I sat down casually by a large garbage can and yanked off my baggy black pants, hooded sweatshirt, and stocking cap to reveal the normal clothes I had on underneath. Just your average denizen I was then. The clothes found a secure place in separate dumpsters as I zig-zagged throughout alleyways toward my final destination, Ray's house. I figured the whole deal must've taken less than an hour and I'd cashed out more than I'd ever fathomed, but it came at an onerous cost to my conscience.

While walking, I had casually stashed the methamphetamine under the back opening of someone's shed while keeping the weed. The meth was an automatic felony or federal offense if I got searched and had it on me, the weed was a misdemeanor. I had no criminal record except a minor in possession of alcohol charge, but that didn't matter if you were caught with a sizable amount of meth. You were fried lest you went with the 30 cent bail program many druggies used to get out of law trouble: drop a dime (snitch) on three and get out for free!

By then more people were out cruising and enjoying the night. Cops were abundant as well—no doubt as a result of the mess I had caused—so what I did with the meth was not altogether stupid or overly cautious in my opinion. The gun and car keys found an extra secure spot in a garbage can inside of a cereal box, just in case some bum noticed something shiny while digging for beer and soda pop cans to recycle.

As I got closer to Ray's house I became giddy and stopped worrying so much. I even had a drink and quick chat with some winos after they offered me some cheap MD 20/20 wine. I sort of knew them as I usually had them buy me beer and such in exchange for a couple bucks. That night they were returning the favor to me, I suppose. Before leaving, I gave them my previous last two dollars I was feeling so well.

I was at Ray's house at last and walked in triumphant. "What up kids! What's up on dem drizzinks and ho's, yo? I got me like some mad cottonmouth, word!"

I was being a facetious moron and they knew it. I wasn't lying about being thirsty, however, as the main reason I drank with the winos was that I truly was dehydrated after hurrying those few miles or so.

That and I was an alcoholic. Ray was the first to greet me. "Ah, what's up?" He shook my hand and patted my shoulder. "Thought you were dead by now! Just playing. I just got off work and this guy here said you were doing what? You better not be bringing that drama around here. I am a respectable citizen, like Citizen Kane, unlike some people in my circle. So you get some or what?"

He meant money. I nodded happily.

"Hey dude, you got something on your brow there," Cedric said.

It was just Cedric, Ray, and I.

"Really?" I rubbed both brows and on my left hand I noticed a small red smear. The blood inside of me suddenly became thicker, ungraciously slamming me back to reality. "Oh, man. I gotta like...shower and stuff. Where's Eric?"

"He's at some party we're going to at Tito's," Ray said. "Took off with some preppy chicks."

"Bastard. But I didn't know dude was having a party."

"You know how it is, everyone has to go somewhere and whatever," Cedric said. "So, you gonna tell us or what?"

"I'll tell you, but I got to use the bathroom first, shower and whatnot. Feels like I'm gonna faint for reals! Everything is spaced-out suddenly, like a dream. You got any extra clothes, Ray? Ugh. Need water."

After making sure I was feeling alright, Ray gave me some extra clothes. We were the same slim build and six-foot height so they fit me well. Nothing fancy. I took a crap, shaved my goatee, and started taking a long, hot shower. The drain in the tub seemed to rise higher and become closer as I watched the water swirl hypnotically. The shower became louder as I bowed my head into the spray, and the rest of the world became mute. I wished my sins of that night would go down in that drain as well. What have I done? Although I felt like a hypocrite doing so, I genuinely prayed to Jesus that He'd wash away my sins of the night right then and there, even as the blood of the dealer I'd shot disappeared down the drain. I knew how to pray as I'd grown up going to church. Having let the pretty girl live was my only consolation. I was certain that I could not and would not even remotely attempt something like that again. I choked out a sob and my tears became lost with the rest of the water. *Please, Jesus, just this once let me get away with this...please, Jesus.*

Chapter 2—Blissful Ignorance

I LEFT THE BATHROOM feeling somewhat refreshed with my eyes clear of any tears. I just wanted to go to Tito's party and blend in. They'd rolled a blunt with the weed I'd giving to them for just that purpose, and I put it in a cigar box.

"Well now, we all set?" I asked my friends who were in their own conversation. Cedric and Ray were actually cousins.

"Yeah, yeah," Ray said. "So what'd you do?"

"I'll tell y'all in a minute."

"I mean, in the bathroom, bro. You took like forever!"

"Hah, hah! Did I? I was praying for forgiveness."

"Forgiveness for what?" Cedric laughed. "Oh shit, never mind!"

"That took took me a moment—the, 'oh shit' part— but I was praying for forgiveness for *this*."

I pulled out the wad.

"Damn!" Ray said after looking at the wad. "What'd you do, rob a bank? I thought they were closed at night!"

"It was a stagecoach."

"I'm either your new best friend, or stay the hell away from me!"

We laughed. Feeling fully rejuvenated, I put on my baseball cap backwards and lead the way out the door, hopping all of the front porch steps in one leap.

I told them my tale animatedly on the walk over to the party. Cedric, Ray, and maybe Eric would be the only ones to ever know what I'd done. The more you blab, the bigger the chance you had of getting caught. It was common sense. These people, I knew I could trust them as much as you ever could fully trust someone. Cedric once accompanied and drove getaway on one of my cash liberating 'missions' downtown.

I lit up the blunt on the sidewalk, and started puffing away as a cop drove by.

"What the hell," Ray was all serious. "You trying to get busted?"

"Sorry man," I handed the blunt to a laughing Cedric. "Cops don't care. They think it's a cigar or cigarette. Besides, they got bigger fish to fry tonight. Notice how they're all tweaked-out?"

"Hell yeah they are," Cedric said. "You bashed a hornets' nest with a bat, that's for sure. Oh, man!"

"The 'fish' meaning you. All the more reason to fuck with us," Ray said looking around all paranoid, but puffing on it anyway.

"Okay," I said in a neutral tone, not wanting to debate it.

The party house came into view. I felt my chest sink comfortably at last at the anticipation of relaxation, and thought the night might get better after all.

***

TITO GREETED US AT THE DOOR and shook our hands. I handed him the rest of the blunt and said, "Keep it."

He looked at it, and after noticing the smell took a drag. "Geez A.D., walking down the street with this thing. You're nuts."

"I know," I said. "'Nuts' to Gestapo Nazis! But cops are just doing their job—out looking for real criminals tonight. See them swarming all distraught like?"

"Yeah. It's making me curious...them being so...'distraught,' I guess. You're a geek sometimes, I swear. Sounding all like a Vulcan and shit, yo!"

"I feel like I'm on the Enterprise. Anyway, I have a feeling something went down...something big."

"Probably," he said. There was no point in telling him. I didn't want him to become paranoid and ruin the party for him. He was from 'back east,' and was a very cool cat based on the couple of years I'd known him.

"Well, anyone here I know?" "Eric is here."

"Blah!"

"Tom's here too, sitting there playing DJ with gangster music no one likes! What's up with you and Eric?"

"What are we, a couple? Nothing," I said. "Just that I see him already every day!"

"That's right! I forgot. I saved you a forty in the freezer, kid. I know how you like 'em slushy practically! The rest are in the normal fridge."

"Cool, dude, you. Thanks."

***

I MADE MY WAY IN after handing out some choice buds of the cannabis to my friends to smoke at their leisure, and eyed all the people. I was very unpopular outside my own circle, kept a low profile, and could've been described as infamous at best. I was a bit of a loner who rarely made public appearances. I took a seat on the couch across from Tom, who was fixated on the lights pulsating with the rhythm of some Memphis rap group on the large stereo in the living room.

"What's up?" I said.

"How art thou on this glorious evening?" he yelled over the music.

"Pretty good, pretty good," I said. I pulled out the weed and handed him a bit of it. "Roll one up."

He got happy and started breaking up the bud on a CD case. I told him to hold it a minute after he rolled it as I made my rounds. I saw Eric, of course, and he introduced me to his female acquaintances.

"Why hell-loo!" said a girl named Jessica—just call me 'Jessie'—as she shook my hand and laughed with her friends. She did nothing to hide the fact that she was attracted to me. "This that friend of yours, Eric?"

Eric looked at me with a sly grin on his face. "Yeah, this is him. You guys should get to know each other."

I knew he thought it was funny, hooking me up with some preppie girl without even the slightest notion of consent from me or even a warning. Oh well, what was I to do, complain? It was all right because she'd be a pleasant distraction from the morose disposition of my world at that current moment. He probably knew I hadn't been laid or even tried to get laid in a while, and maybe thought a female would help soothe what he rationally figured was a disturbed mind-state fueled with an overabundance of unused testosterone. Whatever, I thought and took the girl's hand and led her into the living room to get high with Tom. I was usually shy around girls, but for some reason I was confident with Jessie and I couldn't have been nervous right then if I'd wanted to be.

Jessie was on to me well. Perhaps the hard liquor smell on her breath gave her an extra bossiness, as she forced me down in an unnecessarily playful way on the couch, and cuddled close. Tom looked at me funny. "You got that ready yet?" I said.

"Of course," he said, and displayed the perfectly rolled joint. "I had it ready like ten minutes ago, don't you know?"

"You cool?" I asked Jessie. "Sure, I'll take a couple hits."

She did, and I told Tom to keep it after smoking it to about half way down. I was already blazed from the blunt. Jessie I assumed was a 'weekend toker,' so she was probably already feeling the effects of the strong weed seconds after she exhaled. Her eyelids were already starting to lower and she was happy. them."

"So, what did 'they' say about me?" I asked her. "Eric and all."

"Eric? He didn't say anything really. Just said he

knew you and you'd definitely hook up with me and you weren't ugly!"

We had to sort of yell over the music. "Oh did he, now?" I said with a raised eyebrow. "Some smooth talker."

"Yeah, he did," she laughed. "But I know a couple of... acquaintances that you know, too."

The 'acquaintances' she spoke of probably didn't keep it secret that I was in fact easy to get with in spite of my demure appearance—if you could ever find me. But aside from the recent months in which I'd become especially hermitic, all any girl who really wanted me had to do was physically impose themselves upon me, and I'd give little resistance sometimes even to the not-so-pretty chicks. They have rude words for people of that nature that generally apply to females.

She put her hand on my knee and slowly crept it further upwards. I felt a sudden movement in my pants to where her hand crept. "So, you in college?" I said.

After noticing the emerging bulge in my pants, she squeezed my leg hard and pulled her hand away, apparently satisfied. It was sort of embarrassing, but I was lonely in that sense. Between her hand and the image of the hostage's legs that I couldn't help but recall for some reason, it left me teased and wanting. "Yeah, I am. You?"

"Hardly. I mean, I'm going this fall."

"Oh, are you? I'll probably be seeing ya then. That okay?" "Sure, I guess. I mean, you seem very nice and all!"

She laughed. She wore a tight t-shirt and had an athletic body. She was as tall as me, and had some good muscle tone and curves on her big bones. She had straight, shoulder-length brunette hair, and her rounded heart-shaped face with some freckles only enhanced her overall cuteness.

She whispered into my ear, and I did not catch it as I

was gazing forward at nothing and not expecting her to do that. My brain had started to seep back into the 'dream mode' again.

"What?" I said while acting surprised and innocent. I'd almost killed my forty by then, but I was far from drunk.

"I said..." she put her arm around my neck and her fingers tickled my neck below my ear. "Do you want to go someplace a little more private, and you know...talk?"

"Oh, talk! Sure," I told her nicely. "But we should chill out first for a bit. I do know of such a private place, but it's still early. Chill like that gentleman there."

I pointed to Tom, who was in his own little world making smoke rings. He said, "Huh?"

My new acquaintance and I waved to him.

He quickly looked away and a few seconds later he shook his head and smiled to himself.

"See?" I said to Jessie. "Now, let's have a few more drinks and we'll 'socialize' some more." I made a quote sign with my fingers. I gave her what she wanted: a good, strong, French kiss. I ran my hand through her hair. "Just like a half-hour or so, promise. Oh, and don't drink too many drinks because I heard alcohol lowers your inhibitions."

"Good," she said. "That's exactly what we want, square bear."

We got up and made our way to the gallons of wine and refrigerator full of beer after I'd briefly recapped the previous year's World Series last out in my head to soothe my libido. You just can't walk around like that, you know? Most people had moved from the kitchen to the backyard. We were truly a diverse crowd of young people of every race and income-class, as people were just naturally drawn to my friend Tito's charismatic persona. Jessie and I poured each other some nice sized cups of white wine and ice, and she gave me a playful smile and pat on the arse before we went our separate ways.

Outside a few moments later, a stoner-hippy-kid I knew asked me a question. "Hey bro, you got any of that good weed for sale? Smelled it!"

"Yeah. How much y'all got...need?"

***

I TALKED TO NO ONE in particular after dealing with the stoner dudes. I just chimed in on a few conversations and went back to the loud spot by Tom in the living room.

"So what's that chick like? You seem to know everyone," I said to him after turning down the stereo a few decibels. We were the only ones paying attention to the music anyway.

"Let me think," he said. "She's rich or something. Well, kinda rich. She plays volleyball too, or something."

"Awesome. Is she any good?"

"How the hell am I supposed to know if she's good? I'm guessing she is if she's playing in college. Anyway, why is she with you?"

"No idea."

"Must be slumming it."

"Fuck you, dude! Too true, though."

We both laughed unnecessarily loud and I took a swig. We never said anything important after that aside from comments about the music, which we'd changed to an older Led Zeppelin CD.

I started nodding in rhythm with the music, just getting lost in the sounds and thought I'd finally forgotten the world when I felt the urge to cry again. The music drifted away from me. I took my last long drink and did not even feel it go down my throat. Inner-demons pulled me earthward. *You pray like a baby '...just this once,' and then indulge in drunken sin— laughable. Hah, hah! Go...away! Okay, breathe steady. Do not close your eyes, they'll assail you more then. Lost. Slam more beer. It's cold like your blood. Maybe*

*some weed. No, maybe later. Take a swig. What is that,
your meds? This isn't you any more, it's just a
doppelganger of what used to be you possessed. What
the hell is a 'doppelganger?' Get that music louder. And
the mother's picture of her dead son falls from the wall.
What the fuck, stop bothering me! This is your eternal
salvation and it ends tonight.... Go get a gun again,
might as well end it before they come....*

Incoherent madness to all but a few. Something
urged me down quite suddenly, a beautiful young raven
haired woman with small, blue- lens sunglasses on the
other side of the room. She stood fixated on me by the
doorway.

I liked what I saw, and nodded to her in recognition
and politeness, as we were the only three people in the
room. I wanted to ask her to chill next to me just because
she looked cool, had calmed me down somehow, and
most of the other people were outside. But maybe it was
not a good idea as Jessie would probably take offense.
She raised her eyebrows, mouthed the words 'later,' and
even over the music I swear I heard her distinctly. It
sounded like she'd whispered into my ear. She
disappeared as unobtrusively as she came in, and left me
to believe that maybe she was just a figment of my
imagination. She wasn't.

"What was that about?" said Tom. "I never saw her
before. She was hot in her hippy-like way, though."

"Real hot. She wasn't a hippy, though; Gothic or
something. 'Goth,' hah hah! I just like that word because
it makes no sense."

"Nah, just because she had naturally black hair and a
black sweatshirt or whatever, don't mean she's 'Gothic,'"
he took a long drink. "Ah-h-h. See, she was a hippy
because she had those weird shades. Maybe grunge or
scrounge or whatever like you with those clothes."

"I dress very nice sometimes, and besides, these are
Cedric's extra clothes. Anyway, she's just a cool looking

gal. Everyone's a hippy to you, Tom. That's because you're always stoned all the time and think everyone else is too."

"Whoa," he mock contemplated my statement. "You mean, they're not all stoned? Why would they not be? It must be rough."

"No, Tom, you and I are the last people in the world to smoke weed. All the hippies have died except us."

"So we're hippies?" said Tom as Jessie made her way back into the room. Tom didn't notice her. He raised his fist and looked into the sky and yelled, "N-o-o! I'm a hippy!"

"Oh, are you?" Jessie said startling him.

Tom was unperturbed about the awkward situation he found himself in. "Whoa, scared me. We're labeling everyone. You're probably a jock. We're...we're just burnout loser hippies. 'Dropped out' and 'tuned in.'"

He busted out laughing kinda hard. Perma-laugh, where it's hard to even catch your breath you laugh so much. It's contagious, and sometimes you even forget what you were laughing at in the first place.

I looked at him, and shrugged to Jessie like I had no idea what was going on. Tom thought that this action was invariably hilarious as well, and I nearly joined him in his laughter. I suppressed my own growing perma-smile as I felt the effects of a strong buzz starting to creep up on me again. I stood up, and motioned for Jessie to come with me to one of the back rooms.

We went to a guest room that I had no doubt passed out in a few times before. I switched on a tall, neon green bubble lamp, turned off the main light, and locked the door.

I sat next to Jessie on the bed. "So, what did you wanna talk about?"

 She leaned forward and kissed me. I went with the flow and kissed her back as we both laid-back and wrapped our arms around each other. "This is the good part of the conversation," I said in a stupid voice.

It all happened very fast and very lustily. Once we got off most of our clothes, it seemed we had to be touching each other with the maximum amount of flesh and mouth contact at all times. It was fun and sloppy as the wetness of our mouths mingled with the alcohol, cannabis, and her perfume smell for a primo taste.

When I started slowly pulling down her matching bra and frilled underwear with my teeth, it seemed like I was taking very pretty wrapping paper off a gift. She seriously must have planned on getting laid that night.

After Jessie put on my condom properly and skillfully with her mouth, we started the actual 'doing it' process. Can you believe they actually teach some high school kids to put condoms on like that? It was almost as if the school system had encouraged me and Cassie to participate in the behavior we were indulging in right then. I guess the condom made it all better, now didn't it?

We were both consenting adults, however, and I could tell Cassie was no stranger to doing it, or at least knew what she liked, because she was very active and vocal. She wanted to try every which way it seemed before it was finished.

We lay naked for a few minutes after we'd both relieved our creative juices, relaxing and still kissing and licking each other all over.

I got aroused again before long. To be so young and full of cum... "You're big! I wish we had another condom," she said. "Yeah. That was fun."

We both wanted to do it again, and I know our minds wanted to conveniently forget about the condom problem, or lack of one. I dug around in a top drawer. *Nothing. Blast.* I started begrudgingly putting on my clothes. She copied my action and said, "You won't tell everyone, right? Keep it on the low?"

"You ashamed of me? Kidding. I won't, don't worry. I

guess we both just needed that. Good exercise!"

Before we left the room, we gave each other one last groping and tongue wrestling kiss. Then we rejoined the party as if nothing had happened. No one even noticed our momentary disappearance, as someone was yelling at me for an opinion about basketball in the conversation he was in.

So the party raged on, although Tito made sure everyone remained reasonable and started moving people inside of the house as the numbers started to dwindle. My spot on the one couch was taken, so I had to sit by Tom on his couch.

"Seat's taken. Kidding. So...you and that girl do anything?"

"Not really," I lied and yawned. "I got her phone number, and we kissed a little."

That was that and I cannot tell you if he believed me or not. It was a trick I learned: not to blab about girls I'd been with. I could get with the girl later on if she knew I'd keep my mouth shut about it. The old adage a gentleman never tells had for the most part worked out very well for me as that reputation had gone through the grapevine and landed me a quickie date with Jessie.

Jessie had left with her friends and I did feel slightly used. A 'pretty boy toy' was one chick's prior description of me. What was I to do at my enviable age though, complain?

I felt an inner hollowness as I thought about everything else. My life was somehow incomplete, and I knew that was why I did what I did: the robberies, smoking weed, hallucinogenic drugs, drinking, and the other anarchic behavior. Being young was part of the excuse, but I may have needed some serious psychological help. I was committing sociopathic acts, but as of then I felt remorseful. So I guess I wasn't completely malevolent.

I went outside to contemplate the night and had the

longing to look over my own life seeing as I'd just ended one myself.

Life was not hard growing up. It was too typical if anything. The only circumstances that would call heavy attention in a psychiatrist's notes—besides me being me—would be that both my parents had died in a car wreck when I was a baby, and my best friend had died the previous year. I was less than a year old with no brothers or sisters when the wreck claimed my parents. I was the sole survivor. I was in the back seat uninjured. The wreckage trapped me in and they had to use the Jaws of Life to saw through the door and part of the roof of the car to get me out—or so I'd been told.

My grandparents raised me on my father's side; I was half- American Indian Northern Cheyenne and German descent. In the region I grew up in with Indian reservations in every direction, being half-white and half-Indian was not uncommon.

But what was it with the Germans and Cheyenne? I suppose it was just a matter of where German immigrants settled in America. However, I heard even in Germany they had places you could go to learn to live like a supposed traditional Cheyenne or American Indian. I'm dead serious. Live in a teepee, et cetera, over in Germany of all places. As if!

Anyway, I'd never been to the south to visit my mother's side of the family, although they'd invited me to visit more than a few times. I was seriously thinking of going there to visit that summer before college started just to do something different. They contacted me a few times a year through Christmas cards and such, and occasionally an aunt or uncle would sometimes make a strained effort to visit me. I was always fascinated see my own mother's bloodline through them and appreciated it, but basically I was alone with my grandparents as my father was their only child. Hopefully that somewhat clears up my Native Americanized family tree.

Anyway, how could I be angry over the death of my parents when I couldn't remember them? It's kind of hard to miss something you never knew, you know? My grandparents were both strong Christians and were probably more resentful at the loss of their only son and daughter-in-law than I was, so I felt their pain before I felt mine. I guess I learned an indispensable life lesson when I was a baby sitting in the back of that mangled car wreck whether I knew it or not: death happens.

I went to church all of my life until about midway through high school, and then I became the wrong crowd in a way. I was not influenced by others, as I was probably the main one doing the bad influencing. I'd made good grades and kept my grandparents happy, but they had no idea what I was up to otherwise, or maybe they just turned a blind eye to it.

As a student I liked learning and could tell the teachers enjoyed me, though I was not what you'd call a teacher's pet. I couldn't pinpoint the reasons that would lead me to make near suicidal decisions. You feel so invincible and make impetuous decisions around that high school and early twenties age. I foolishly thought in the back of my mind that I'd lived long enough like so many young soldiers who died and along with those who wanted to see what was on the other side—or at least come close to the edge. My existence became an even bigger jumbled blur after I moved out of my grandparent's house when I was seventeen.

They were actually happy and proud that I was such an independent person, as they could finally fully retire and not worry about me as much. They deserved to enjoy their golden years and go on cruises and vacations or whatever, that's part of the reason I moved out at a young age in the first place. I didn't want to be a burden if I didn't have to be one just to wait for the move-out-when-you're-18 rule.

Life was grand and I lived a Bohemian-type lifestyle

for the better part of a year with my best friend and then roommate Andrew. Abidan and Andrew, or A.D. and Drew, who both needed AA. Actually, he was down for a good time but was not as bad as me when it came to indulgences. I do have to say that he had a good head on his shoulders that set a strong precedent for me to follow although he was only a year older. He'd died unexpectedly in a helicopter crash while working as a forest firefighter for the Forestry Service late the previous summer. No words can describe how I felt about my loss, to be cliché. I fell deep into a depression that I tried to eventually hide. I was determined I wouldn't let his death be an excuse to give up and stop living my own life, as that's what he would've wanted. He loved life and died honorably. A man's death. I wouldn't taint his memory with constant defeatism and feeling sorry for my own self while I still had full perfect health and breath. You can question God's will, but eventually you must accept what is instead of what's not there and move on—no matter how hard it is.

I got myself into college and must've become overly content as I quit my crappy job and started selling marijuana as my main income aside from selling custom paintings, drawings, tattoo designs—anything that people wanted, especially if it was extremely racy. After doing well for a few months, I started regressing back into a depression and just sort of holed-up most of the time, read books all day, wrote, and drank myself to sleep at night while reading some more. It was not exactly me being in the spotlight of life, but like an addict's fix it made me temporarily happy and let me escape. Turns out it helped to make me more depressed in the long run.

I visited my grandparents less frequently as time progressed after my friend died. My grandfather had worked as a museum curator before retiring, and I helped out there a lot and enjoyed being there. I was always glad to see them and all, but aside from eating dinner with them once a week or so, I never really talked to them that much as of then aside from phone calls to check-in. They were doing fine on one of their extended vacations in Europe, and were thinking of moving to Alaska of all places for a couple of years when they learned I'd be going to college. But I wouldn't hinder their life any further, even though they would have gladly helped me in any way I needed. They were not overly rich or anything, but we did live in a decent neighborhood. They were thrifty and had saved a lot of money, and I was appreciative of the fortunate circumstances I grew up with. I was not some poor ghetto boy who needed to go out and commit homicidal robberies to make ends meet, that is the point I'm trying to convey here.

So I sat there and sipped a beer by myself, thinking of all these things when Ray came out. "Found you," he said. "We were wondering where you went."

"Yeah, you must have looked real hard. I was sitting on the front porch the whole time."

We both chuckled and he said, "What's wrong? Thinking about dude?" He could read me, and was referring to Andrew.

"Nothing. Everything. Weird night is all. Thinking about him a little, but I don't think that'll ever go away. Mostly the other shit I did, though."

"I guess," he said. "Remember, it's all your choice and you have to live with those choices. None to blame but you."

I poured out a little drink on the sidewalk, and finished the half-can of beer in a single gulp and said, "For 'Drew. But you're right. You're really right, and now I gotta live with this cloud over my head."

"Don't be so hard on yourself, bro," he said and patted my back. "You ain't a bad person. Off in the head a little, but you ain't evil. You're good-hearted. You actually tear up reading a book, or over shit you can't control happening on the other side of the world! You're not heartless. I know you. Or I know enough of you to where I'd trust you with my life. Any of us would. The guy you...whatever...he was a bad type anyway, the type that's why my mom's dead. Don't worry yourself over that asshole."

"Don't make it right."

"No, it don't, but it does in the law! Cops will probably throw a party over this dude. I bet after their initial, 'Let's get the murderer!' front, they'll gladly file the case under unsolved, and never look at it again unless they want a good laugh."

"Right on. I mean, not 'right on,' but you know what I mean!" "So..." Ray said. He grew up in almost the worst of circumstances with a father doing life in prison and a drug addict mother who'd died of an overdose, yet he beat the supposed odds and became one of the most responsible and trusting people I ever met. I really respected his opinions. "What else you got going on in your oddball head?"

"Mostly life in general. I mean, something is missing, it's like an itch in my brain—a void. I think I like art, reading, and writing because it seems to fill that void. I unhealthily drown life with it I think, to be honest. You think I could do that for a living?"

"Hell yeah, you can," he said. "You don't drown life with art. Art is life. Just keep at it and you'll only improve, my friend. I'm no expert, but I think you already are, so that's a dumb question. Go to that college and tear it up." He laughed. "I know what you're missing! It's so obvious now."

"Oh? And what, pray tell, might that missing link be?" "You need a woman!"

"I had one tonight, or I thought I did."

"No, no, no. You need a steady girl to keep you in line. That's what you need. Hate to tell any dude that, but in your case it's true. Get yourself a good woman, and you won't have to walk so alone."

I was going to say the only halfway steady girl I'd ever been with was the dominant type, but that would've been redundant. He knew who she was. She was very fun and had pricked my mental state of sexual and carnal desires well. Perhaps I should've stayed with her, as minus this night, I hadn't even tried to get a girl in the past few months. Like a jerk, I left her crying and shattered her poor heart like an antique mirror falling on rained soaked cement with seven years bad luck. I'd heard she tried to kill herself and wound up in a psychiatric center for a bit. I felt bad for leaving her, but I was just too afraid of getting too close and platonic with her. I thought I needed time alone, and I did. I wanted to say something about her, but the words escaped me.

"Could be," I said instead.

"No, it's true dude. I'd feel sorry for her putting up with you!" "Okay," I said. "You talk about me, but how come you don't have a girlfriend then?"

"What do you think I'm trying to do with that girl inside right now?"

"I see. Let's sko den inside then. You guys already out of that good stuff I gave you?"

"Hell yeah, we are! That's why we finally cared about finding you!"

"Funny. But, hey man..."

"What's up?"

"Just...thank you, bro."

If only it were that easy: finding a chick and living happily ever after.

Chapter 3—To the Stars

AFTER A COUPLE MORE BEERS I told everyone goodbye and left. I didn't want to get completely plastered and pass out, I just wanted to go home and read whatever like I habitually did until dawn unless I felt like drawing. A couple of people offered me rides but I declined, not wanting to risk them getting a DUI as everyone was faded, and for once I had the money for a cab. Mostly, I needed the brief walk. I'd started dialing on a payphone for a cab when a newer dark Ford Taurus pulled up to me. It was the raven haired girl that Tom and I saw from the party. "Hey!" she stuck her head out the window. "You need a ride, dude?"

"Sure," I said without hesitation just because it was her. I ran to the car and got in. "Noticed you earlier!"

"Me too," she said and pulled out fast, hitting about fifty miles an hour cruising the residential roads. "Better put on your seatbelt!"

She slowed down abruptly, and a few seconds later a police car turned and came towards us. It drove on by, and she sped up again. "I wanted too, but it's nothing you should worry about. I'm just in a hurry is all."

"Don't you wanna know where I live?"

"We're going to my place out in the country a bit. You'll be fond of it," she said. The secluded country sounded like a good idea if we could actually make it there without wrecking. "Here," she said, reaching into her pocket and pulling out a small plastic baggy. "Eat this."

It was a large, blueish-colored mushroom cap. I

started taking bites off it, force- swallowing chunks. "I see," I said. "You want someone to trip with tonight! Tom was right about you."

She nodded her head. "Yup. I suppose he was."

I took a long look at her and noticed how strikingly perfect her facial features were. She was prettier than any model in an exotic way one couldn't commercialize in this newer, generically fake era. She also had the height to be a model without the anorexic clone look. Her high cheekbones were not sharp, but delicate and smooth as they merged to her slender jaw line to give her an almost too perfect face. I could tell her hair, which fell nearly to her waist, was naturally black, just as I could tell by her deep-set almond eyes and full lips she was part Native American as I was. Her skin was a peculiar florescent tan golden color that was otherwise close to mine. I noticed her eye color was particularly striking behind the blue lens glasses she still wore. They were a very gold, hazel color that I could actually see well in the dark.

We had reached a road that lead out of town by then when I realized that I didn't even know her name.

"Deedra," she said suddenly. "That's my name. Not Sussudio." "I was just about to ask you that. They call me A.D. My name is 'Abidan, the son of Gideoni,' though. Not really. I mean, Gideoni's not my dad's real name."

What am I thinking? Idiot.

It was part of a Bible verse were my name had come from, but I was too nervous because off her driving to explain that to her. She nodded her head as we cruised around the 90 mile per hour mark. I said, "Where we going, Indianapolis?"

She covered her mouth and laughed. "We're almost there. Only a wee bit more. We have to go to bed momentarily. Don't want to have to tie you down for the day!"

"That's all right," I said. "Wouldn't be the first time. Besides, I'm drained."

I didn't want to get lewd just yet in a conversation with a stranger.

"You can see the stars pretty well out here," she said after slowing down and turning on a dirt road. She drove at a reasonable pace then. "You like the stars?"

"Oh yeah. I know a few of the constellations and such. No astronomer, just appreciate 'em. Nature's most humbling marvels, they are. Hmm. We used to come out and hang on these back roads, just gazing at them and such. We weren't even abusing mind-altering chemicals or whatever this one night though, and me and this one dude and his girlfriend saw some UFO's flying around. They looked like those laser pointers moving around they were so fast. They'd always end up in a rough 'v' formation—those red orbs flying around. They were scary and fascinating at the same time. Of course, we had no camera to record the event."

"And no one would believe you because you were on drugs, or so they postulated!"

"Yes, postulated! I mean, we weren't on drugs, but that's what they always assume, so whatever. We knew everyone was going to say 'drugs' as soon as we saw them and started discussing it. Just knew it!"

"I believe you," Deedra said in a voice I noticed had the subtlest hint of a southern drawl. She also sounded somewhat proper British if only because of her word selection. I couldn't quite pinpoint where she might be from. It was nice to have a name to go with her pretty face anyway. "I saw something similar to that before. It only lasted a minute though."

"Really," I said. "Sure it wasn't one of the effects of this all- natural food product you just gave me? Kidding! Yeah, these red orbs or whatever were there like for at least 20 minutes before we left. They were still there when we left, actually. Pretty scary, honestly."

She turned again, we stopped, and an electric gate pulled itself open.

"You know," she said as we passed the gate, "most of the constellation names and stuff we all know are what the Greeks organized—or combined from Greece, Egypt, and Babylon—because Alexander made the world do so. He Greek geeked everything, but that was all for the best I think, as far as the old world goes. People used to always study the stars, as they had no nightly images of the television that we have. But constellations and such, the names and zodiac stuff have been around at least since Babylonian times. Back then for most cultures, astrology and astronomy were one in the same basically."

"Wow," I said. "I always wondered if there was an actual Christmas star. I heard that the actual Christmas was the celebration of the Celts and other pagans' Winter Solstice holiday."

"Yeah, sort of in a way. I think they might have gotten the Christmas star idea—if you do the math—from the Halley's Comet in 12 B.C. Or it could be from a prophesy found in the Old Testament book of Numbers, and it was just what it was, an actual star that guided the Wise Men. We weren't there, so how can we pretentiously discredit them? You saw orbs flying around, after all. So the Christmas date isn't so weird because it's always been around. I don't think people can ever really know the exact day of Christ's birth. The Romans made Christianity the state religion eventually, so they need a date to celebrate Jesus' birth. They themselves already had a weeklong celebration around December 25th for every other pagan God in the Empire, why not combine them all and make it work for them so they don't lose their party time?"

"Yup," I said. "Typical Roman fashion, but good diplomacy too.

I mean, combining all those to make everyone happy. Anyway, my name comes from the Book of Numbers, that's so weird you'd mention that. I'm impressed."

"Yeah, it is very weird. Anyway, the solstice stuff, a lot people knew it aside from pagans. But the Babylonians get credit for 'inventing' astrology, but why?"

"Because they could write in cuneiform or whatever."

"Exactly. Akkadians around Northern Babylon to be precise. I mean, people wrote down their observations in their head or even drawings. They knew what time of the year it was. They knew by all different things unless they lacked common sense. December twenty-fifth, or twenty-first nowadays, that's like the day people in the Northern Latitudes would especially notice the skyline rose a bit or something after the shorter days."

"Fascinating."

"Yes, indeed," Deedra said in a mock British gentleman tone. "We will have time to finish this later I pray tell dearly, this interlocution. But for now we must hurry, hurry!"

"Are we not in quite the hasty mood? I dare say. So, to be like nosey, where are you from?"

"Everywhere. I'm nomadic. But I came from the Seattle area most recently."

"Oh. Thanks."

We pulled up to yet another gate with a ten foot high or so iron fence with electric wiring on top. Another steel gate opened after Deedra punched in a code and we pulled in.

Inside of the fence I saw a massive and bulky-looking log cabin style house that must have been two stories. It was very grand, but I wondered if all of the protective measures with the electric fence and all were absolutely necessary in the first place since we were so far out in the country.

"You know that electric fence thing on top is not on," Deedra said. "It's there for show, mostly. Like a dummy lock. I should turn it on though."

"Maybe," I said sarcastically. "Good for Mountain lion protection."

47

We pulled into the garage and Deedra practically drug me out of the car and into her house. I stopped to stare at a painting of a white gate with the shiniest, most realistic looking gold-colored fence for a moment before she urged me on. The gate had something foreign inscribed on it.

"You do that? What's it say?" I asked amazed. I wanted to know how she got such a mixture of brilliant paint. It really looked like it was perhaps actual gold.

"A friend did. I gave her the idea and gold paint though. It's real gold in the paint. It's Hebrew and says, 'Shamiyim.' It saddens me. Let's go."

We made it to an upper level bathroom and she motioned me to go in there.

"Yes, it's a bathroom. A very good looking bathroom," I sarcastically said partly as a result of her forcing me to hurry.

She laughed. "I'm sincerely sorry to be so pushy," she lost some of her intensity. "But could you use the bathroom very well, please? Shower, piss, do whatever. Would you mind throwing that mushroom up, please? I know I just gave it to you, but could ya do it? I'll give you something better. Shit, shower, shave."

"And serve on Sundays. Sounds like a real hoot."

I probably already smelled like sex, and she probably wasn't impressed with it so I figured I'd better go with the flow. Throw up the mushroom? That was an odd request, but it was not like people had not thrown up after eating mushrooms before. I didn't need to use the bathroom except to piss, but I would get in the shower to get Cassie's smell off me to be polite, and shave my face again. It was Deedra's call. *It might get hardcore kinky up in here. Sinner.*

I vibrantly came out of the bathroom a few minutes later, and Deedra seemed especially pleased as she licked her lips. "Let's go downstairs," she grabbed my hand and it felt so cool and silky I checked to see if she had a glove on. There was no glove. "We have to do something trippadelic."

"Trippadelic?" I said. "Like satanic sacrifice trippadelic? You just make that word up?"

"Yes, and maybe."

"Well," I took a deep breath. "Can't help ya there. I'm Christian as of tonight. Again. Born again."

Objects were swirling around and I felt my stomach rise above my head. The big mushroom was starting to take hold all right, despite the fact that I threw it up as asked and had to brush my teeth thoroughly afterwards.

"Satanic sacrifice," Deedra said. "We need a sacrifice!"

"Man," I said as we descended into a large den area in the basement. I suddenly felt the room shrink, and then become bigger. "Don't be saying things like that now. I've had a really unconventional night as it is."

"I'm sorry, babe. I don't mean to frighten you. I want to make this as smooth as possible, and I do hope it works."

"Me too." I was rubbing my eyes and noticed a lot of bookcases and a huge stereo system. "You read all these?"

"A lot of them." "Can I look at 'em?"

"Later," she was putting on some music. The Doors song "Soul Kitchen" played. "Have a seat, relax."

She turned around, doing some sort of weird gypsy looking dance, and came towards me seductively. She slid off her pants, revealing black, silk bikini panties. They were superbly choice. Her eyes, which nearly seemed to glow, were somehow even more enticing than the shapely curves of her legs and buttocks. Maybe it was the lighting, maybe it was the drugs. Who knows.

Deedra sat me down, then slid next to me on the couch and licked my neck. *Everything suddenly so cold.* I had goose bumps. She undressed me, and then took off her sweatshirt to reveal a tank-top shirt that showed off her ample but not overly huge breasts. I had a good view as she leaned towards me with no bra. Her arms looked well defined, though not excessively muscular, and she had great abs from what I could tell. I was spacing out on her body anyway.

"Kiss me," she said and laid on her back. "Feel what I am. Love what I am."

"As you wish," I said and lustily started on her neck. I tried going for her mouth but she moved it towards her breast area. *So good...so good.*

"Me on top," she said before I could slide her panties off and fully indulge myself in her taste.

I laid back and she sat astride me. "You love me?"

What? Already? I thought ignorantly. Then I recalled the first time I saw her. "Of course I love you. It was love at first site. I've often longed for an alluring intelligent girl like you. Somehow you know that as well."

"Yes, I do," she smiled wide and I saw her teeth. Her fangs.

Are those real, or am I tripping?

"No, you're not," she said.

Did I just say what I was thinking out loud, or did she hear what I was thinking?

"Yes, I did." She seemed amused. So was I. "Check this out!" She cradled my face and turned my head to the side and moved her mouth to my neck. "You'll love this," she whispered.

There was a sharp pain, then a humming sound in my head and a reverberating feeling from my neck to my brain. My brain was trying to tell me something. *So relaxed, so faded.* Then it occurred to me: this Deedra chick was trying to kill me somehow! I tried to heave her off, but she tightened her legs around my body. Her arms cradled my head and encased me.

No death; not like this, by her! Not content to die, my free arm struck her backside. My arm felt heavy, but I was going to pull her head off like a Barbie doll by grabbing her hair if I could. I pulled hard, but she whirled her head and I lost most of my grip while she still cradled me like she was an immovable marble statue. I supposed there were worse ways of dying than having a beautiful female wrapped around you, but...

I said a prayer in my head. *Please God, please get this bloody demon vampire whatever the fuck off me. Please, take her to hell with me at least. Please take her and leave me here. Please take me to you then...*

Deedra pulled her head up with a nefarious bloodstained grin and licked her lips. It was way too surreal, and I didn't know whether to laugh nervously or yell. "I think you'll like me," she said.

I felt like I was going to faint forever. *Like hell*, I thought, and took a swing at her that caught her in the cheek fairly well considering I could barely lift my arms due to the lack of blood flow.

"Yes," she said and laughed it off while she pulled a little more blood out of me. "I think we'll be fine. I think you'll be fine. I think we'll be oh so consummate and oh so perfect!"

She slid her hand to her calf and pulled out a dagger-looking knife that was sharp on both edges. She tilted her head and put the knife to her artery. I cringed, and so did she as she stuck it in and blood emanated from the wound.

She said, "You want it all back?"

Before I could answer that I really did want it back, she leaned towards me and the blood was in my mouth. I drank without hesitation as if it were natural. I drank and drank until I felt my stomach get full, and the blood went back to the rest of my body. My arms felt lighter, my fingertips and toes no longer felt numb. It was ice water in the Gobi Desert.

Deedra lifted her head with a blanched look of bewilderment on her face as she held her neck. I sat up, completely forgetting that I hated her, and then my entire body dry heaved and jolted with an unseen possessing force.

"Man...I got the worst gut ache ever! 'Shrooms or something. It hurts, it hurts!"

I defecated out of both my mouth and rear something fouler than typical fluids.

I heard her laughing somewhere. Such compassion. "'Shrooms, huh?"

"Frick you, dude! Not kidding!"

I had no comprehension of where she was. I felt like everything was underwater in some whirlpool, and I was trapped in the center going under deeper. I felt naked, sitting in a gulag solitary cell. Everything seemed so distant, so hopeless. Terrible shudders of pain shot through my chest and up to my brain.

I wanted blackness, and it started to come when Deedra picked me up. We moved to a bookcase and walked through it. *We walked through a bookcase? I'm so fucking scared. Don't cry, eyes. God, it hurts!* My body descended into a cool darkness, and I lay on a cot of some sort and curled into a fetal position. *I'm coming home, back to the ground of Earth.*

They say the universe is constantly expanding, maybe it's because people are always dying. Let me become a star at least, was my last thought before the world as I knew it went away.

And so that was my untimely death.

Chapter 4—Value Menu

I WOKE UP surprisingly clear-headed with Deedra standing and staring over me. I was incredibly hungry, or thirsty. I was naked, but cleaned. But my stomach hurt and I felt drained—maybe dehydrated. "What's up?" I nodded to Deedra. She wore a plain black t-shirt with blue jeans that had holes in them. She nodded. "Listen, I'm sorry I tripped out last night—"

"You never," she said a-matter-of-fact like. "It really did happen, and I'm sincerely sorry."

What the hell did happen? Oh yeah! The murder, scary fangs, drinking blood—usual Friday night stuff. Drinking blood? That was new, or was it? I couldn't rightly recollect of a time I 'went down' on a chick when she was on...*that's not the issue!* "Listen," I got up from the bed and started putting on my folded clothes. Were we sleeping in a vault? Do not think about it. Act brave. "You're a vampire chick, right? So why ain't I dead by now?"

"Oh, but you are," she said touching my hand, and then clasping it. "This is your reincarnation."

So maybe I was dead. A ghost perhaps? I looked at my own skin which normally had a natural tan color, and noticed we both had the same ashen golden glow. Wait a sec, my skin looked like her skin? Maybe it was the lighting, which consisted of a lone bulb hanging from the ceiling, but I knew that was wishful cogitation. I touched my canine teeth hard with my tongue, and tasted my own blood.

I knew what I was then: a vampire, of all God

forsaken things, like her. I logically waited to wake up like when you realize that you are dreaming in your sleep, but that moment passed, and all was still as it was. I shrugged—there was no sense in flipping out just yet—and walked to what appeared to be the vault door, half anxious and half apprehensive for what was to come. Deedra undid a few steel lever- locks and put both of her hands on a handle. I asked if she needed help opening "the cell." She shook her head no, and thrust the heavy looking door wide-open with a mighty irritating noise and heave. I made out a very dark, steep, dirt stairway leading upwards. "Sorry about that screech! Should've warned you that it definitely needs some grease. Follow me," she said. "You must be famished."

"Sure," I naively said. "What do ya got?"

"We'll find someone right away tonight. You're lucky, since it appears we'll have guest over for dinner if I hurry!"

She got a kick out of that. I thought it was only somewhat funny, that vampiric humor of hers, but I didn't fully grasp what she was talking about at the time. I followed her up the stairs, which led to another vault door thirty or so feet up that ended up being the back of one of the bookshelves. All at once, the early morning nightmarish memories started to surge back as I recalled moving through the same bookcase. I still kept expecting to wake up at any time as I entered her basement. The couch didn't seem to have any bloody, or otherwise, mess on it. In hindsight I recalled there was plastic on the couch cushions. She must have taken the liberty of disposing of it already, as well as cleaning me up with a 'bird bath' of sorts. I'd definitely have to take another shower to finish the job.

I watched her close the long sliding bookshelf door. It reminded me so much of those secret passageways in the castles of the Middle Ages. She flicked on a light. "Come upstairs and wait," she told me. "I'll go get us a meal.

Look around for a while, browse the books. You'll have fun."

She quickly left and I sat in a comfortable armchair, suspicious and paranoid of Deedra popping out and eating me or something. I heard a car moving away from the house. The paintings I glanced at made me swear I was still feeling the 'shroom effects. A beautiful painting of some fully made-up geisha lady doing a dance shifted in the frame. I glanced away and stared at the floor. I should've gone with Deedra. Oh well, I knew she would be back in a few minutes, or so I hoped. If not, at least I had a cool pad to chill in. I must admit though, I was anxious, perhaps I'd even go so far as to say panicked, without her, and I was generally very calm and collected even if I had to fool myself into believing it. Deedra did scare me half (all the way?) to death that morning, but I longed for her because she had the answers to the growing number of preposterous questions quickly formulating in my befuddled brain.

After the briefest of showers—I was too overwhelmed by the water droplet sensations to want to stay in there any longer than I had too—I tried to put my situation in perspective, since this chick had said nothing to me so far to make my situation feel less odd. *Who were the dinner guests? Did I really sleep all day?* Of course, it was already a few minutes past dusk, and it was getting darker by the second. Perhaps it was still early morning. *No. I'm way too awake and it feels warm.*

This vampire chick I was with, how the hell did I ever get involved with her? I heard of bad influences before, but gimme a major fucking break...

And me, finally. Was I really going to 'feed' on humans, or at least organisms with blood in them for that matter? Every kid knew that's what vampires did. Relax. I wished that Deedra would hurry.

I turned the porch light off, walked outside, and thought if I was dead, then that must've been Heaven. As

I studiously observed the scenery with my new and improved nocturnal vision, a thought crossed my mind: so this is how a feline must see at night. Everything appeared in an extraordinary, cartoonish, and surreal night color that looked sort of 3D. I saw the sloping prairie hills around me as if there was a full moon shining, providing me with its pale but efficient light, yet the moon was only a little more than half. The words bluish and purplish came to mind upon first glancing at the skyline and terrain. How I'd strived to capture those blue and purplish hues in the grass, hills, trees, mixed with dashes of silver gray lighting in my own paintings many a time before. The stars were even more plentiful and brighter than I'd ever seen them before. The air, the untainted, sunless cool air, was enough to make me want to become it—whatever the hell that meant. I breathed deeply a few times with my body feeling as fresh as that cool, country air. If I never saw the Sun again, who cared? As long as I felt like I did at that moment. *But the hunger...* Plus, I hadn't eaten in well over twenty-four hours aside from the mushroom I'd thrown up.

I waited patiently on a hammock on the cabin's front deck, trying to fade every extraneous thought away so I could fully analyze the scope of my plight. Despite my best efforts, it didn't work. A distant pair of lights neared after the most impatient ten minutes or so of my life. She was coming back! I was the child waiting for his mother to come back from the grocery store with cheap nickel and dime candy at the bottom of the grocery bag.

After the vehicle pulled in, I noticed two female passengers with Deedra. They looked like young hitchhikers judging by the backpacks they carried with them. One pack was an old-school Army issued green one, and the other was a newer looking mountain pack. The girls were engaged in their own personal conversation that I paid no heed to as they followed Deedra up the porch. Deedra pointed behind her with her thumb at the girls. "Guests," she said. "This is A.D., gals. A.D., this is Emily, and this is Tierra. From Oregon."

"Hi," I said with a nod.

"Hello," they both spoke simultaneously and shook my hand.

Then just Tierra spoke. "Just you two live here?"

"Uh, yeah," I said. I did? I guessed so. I love the way they smelled even if they were somewhat greasy and dirty. "Uh, come in."

Sugar and spice...

"Some trucker dude like hit on us when he gave us a ride hitchhiking. He was so gross and awkwardly hinting to pay us to at least kiss each other. Hah! Like, in general he was a nice guy, but no way dude!" said Tierra. "I suppose he had to try."

Emily whispered to the other girl while flirtatiously looking at me. They laughed and walked in. Deedra called out to them, "There's a bathroom upstairs to shower in one of y'all can use. There's another bathroom in the bedroom past the kitchen. It's to the left."

"Okay. Thanks."

They each went to clean themselves up or whatever. I wondered what Deedra was up to, though I had a good hunch as to what she intended for them. "Why are they here? Where'd ya find 'em anyway? Not that I have a problem. It is your house."

"Oh, calm yourself," she said. "Picked 'em up a few miles down the road. They were by that truck stop, actually. No one knows they're here. They said they were hitchhiking to Chicago, so I said I couldn't give them a ride, but I'd let them wash up here and eat if they wanted and stay for a night. I better fix them something to eat anyway. Oh, and I also told them you were my twin brother just in case."

What's the point in telling them we were twins?

She went into the kitchen and opened up the freezer. I sat down and curiously studied her. *Fascinating. Did she actually have food in there?* She grabbed some frozen fries and threw them on the counter.

Then she went over to the cupboard and opened it. Only four cans of soup and spices were in there. She grabbed two cans of the chicken kind, and then pulled out a pot and a cake pan for the fries and started cooking right away.

I was in no mood for canned chicken soup or fries. I knew what I wanted, and I was startled at my own stolid manner that it'd be blood. The sight of the girls and smell of them aroused me, and the thought of drinking one of them did not overwhelm me. On the contrary, it only fired my inquisitiveness. Would I have the courage to do what Deedra did to me the night before, sink my teeth in one's neck and drink? *Intense.*

I thought of when I drank the vampire blood the night before. If the sensation of the human blood was anything like Deedra's blood (apart from the excruciating pain afterwards), well—Lord, forgive me— give it to me! After all, I was already a murderer, right? Sadly, killing was something that I knew I could do.

"Deedra?" I said as I approached her. She turned around and acknowledged me after flipping the fries. "We get to have these two tonight, right? So, what I want to ask is, how or when should I do it? How do you...proceed?"

"Hmm," she sighed. "You are so sexy. I haven't cooked in forever. Well, I like to be creative, I guess. Don't scare 'em to death like I did you, and be patient tonight. That's the best way. Let them eat, or whatever. Then when the time comes, do it. It'll be natural anyway. Try to seduce them, yeah. Go with the flow, and your thirst will give you the courage easily. The rest is either being a dick and slovenly about it, or being smooth. You pick. But these girls, no one will know about. How lucky you are to have them on your first night. This is as easy as it gets."

"Okay," I said. "I'll probably just sweet talk one of them. Ask her if she wants to make out after I give her some cheesy lines. Which one you want?"

"You probably will! Doesn't matter, but you'll find out that Emily will be easier for you. I'm gonna get Tierra alone. That's why I said we were brother and sister—privacy!"

"Yeah, the Emily chick seemed to like me."

"You know, she actually said, 'I hope he's not gay.' She said, 'I hope he's not a fag, dude.' Those were her actual words!"

"Charming. I didn't know people from Oregon were allowed to be un-pc."

"Anyway, wait a bit like I said, then take Emily up to the room upstairs and use your good looks and lack of charm and social skills. You'll have no problem with this. That I'm sure of."

"I get what you're getting at. I'm jumping ahead now, but what do we do with the bodies?"

"You'll find out soon. Don't worry about it." She grabbed me by both shoulders and shook me slightly. "Relax! You're getting too anxious. That's good though, I guess. That's why I chose you. I knew you'd be perfect."

"I know," I said. I really did not.

I opened up her refrigerator door and nosily peered in. Two wine bottles, one white and one red, was all there was. I also saw a bottle of vodka on the counter. "This for them?" I said holding the red one.

"Yeah," she said. "Try it."

I grabbed a wineglass from a cupboard and filled it with red wine. I smelled the wine, it smelled fine, and dipped my tongue into it. "Ugh! You like this?"

"What, it's not your preferred 'wino brand?' Ha hah! Funny. Not really. I don't drink anything except blood. I just like the smell of the wine. It seems to keep me warm. Hot chocolate and coffee, too. The vodka is here just because."

"Cool," is all I said, feeling annoyed at my own insistent pestering, so I sat at the table in silence, just looking at the fancy wineglass. Would I ever need water or liquid again? I hypothesized 'no,' unless I counted blood. Sick. I also knew that I wouldn't eat again. The simple pleasures I took for granted like eating soup and being an alcoholic would no longer be mine to enjoy. I asked Deedra about nourishment to be sure of my conclusion, though I felt stupid just for asking.

"Do you ever need to eat or drink at all?"

"No," she said in straightforward manner. "I haven't eaten in a long time. I tried it once, but my body rejects the food right away. Probably be the same with you."

"Oh."

I had the sudden urge to run into the hills screaming like a madman, I was so dumfounded by the events that were unfolding. I was seriously lost, but desperately trying to go with the flow. What was the flow? They needed a handbook for these types of incidents. I studied my fingers like a newborn, and it looked like I had a fresh coat of clear nail polish on my fingernails. Every simple gesture seemed impossibly absurd, but I had to see how it all ended even though I'd long thrown out the possibility of it all being a dream. I sensed way too much for that.

"I can take a small taste though," Deedra continued. Can she still hear my thoughts? It didn't seem so, or maybe she wasn't trying to hear them. "It's meaningless to do so, but I can. I think the extra liquid floats around until it eventually dissolves. Any more liquid than a small drink and you'll probably puke."

"Cool."

I don't know why I kept saying everything was 'cool.' It beat saying I was 'dumbfounded' out loud, I guess. I knew I had to ask one more question before leaving her alone for the time being. She didn't seem to mind. "What about smoking? I need something to chill me."

"What about it? You mean like smoking a fag, me love?" she joked. "Try it. It really won't hurt you, I suppose. It's not that exciting though. Marijuana, you meant that. That is...sort of like the drink you just had! No, not that bad. You can smoke, I guess. I do it once in a great while, as it's just pointless motions."

"Is it worth it then?"

"No, you can get cancer! Well, once you drink someone's blood that'll be all the mood altering you'll ever need. You'll see."

I knew she was right just by the I way I imagined I suddenly knew what an aching heroin fiend on edge felt like going through a cruel phase of withdrawals. I grabbed a pen and started doodling in the notebook I noticed earlier in the den to take some of the edge off. I noticed right away how much control I had of the pen. Deedra's fierce grin complete with fangs and the view of her chest from what I remembered from the previous night's escapades surfaced upon the blank paper. How disturbingly hot. Nice rack, too.

The food was prepared and set on the table. There was enough china for two people. French fries and chicken soup. What a strange meal it was, until you compared it to my last meal of nothing and blood. In a few minutes, Emily came out all fresh and clean with different and newer clothes on. How pretty her brunette hair and gray eyes looked, especially with the green pants and similar black striped sweater. "I grabbed these clothes in the closet you told me about," she said to Deedra. "These ones all right?"

Deedra was sitting at the table with nothing in front of her, apparently nodding to imaginary music. "Sure," she said. "Would you like some fine French wine or vodka with your meal?" "Uh, please," Emily said.

Deedra grabbed two wine glasses and two cups. "Both?" she asked.

"If it wouldn't be a problem. Gee, thanks," she

laughed nervously.

Tierra walked in with a black dress that showed off her thick and curvy body. She turned in a full circle and then said to Deedra, "I thought I'd try this on tonight. Ya sure you won't get mad if we keep some clothes?"

"Yeah, I'm sure. Whatever fits," said Deedra. "There's a surplus."

"So I noticed," said Tierra. "By the way, nice house!"

"Thank you," said Deedra, entranced by Tierra's new look. "You do look lovely in that dress. I'm glad you chose it. Sit down. Eat, drink, if you will."

Deedra laughed at her own words, and I put away the notebook and smiled at Emily. I wanted to know these two souls. "So, which area of Oregon you come from?"

"Portland," they answered at the same time.

Emily with her quieter voice spoke. "We're going to Chicago." "Really," I reflexively took another taste of wine and nearly dry

heaved. It did have a decent smell, but right then I just wanted to spit it. Embarrassed as Deedra snickered at me, I put the wine away from me for good. "Why Chicago? Sounds like a big boring city. No offense."

"My brother lives there," said Tierra as she dug in to her food. She obviously enjoyed the soup, and I wished I was getting nourishment, too. I unconsciously started leaning toward her so I could better smell her. Damn my hunger! I sat back. "He gave us enough money to make it by bus, but we figured we would hitchhike a ways just to do it; party on the way, camp out, whatever, ya know? An adventure."

"Adventures kick ass!" Deedra said. I looked at her funny.

We let them enjoy their food, only interrupting them for a few questions here and there. Other than that, they told us the basic information about themselves on their own with little prompting.

Tierra was twenty-two and Emily was twenty. They'd

been the best of friends for about five years and had pretty much lived wherever was convenient. Deedra kept their wine and vodka glasses full like a waitress keeps a coffee mug filled. Towards the end of the meal, Emily asked if they could smoke in the house after she exchanged glances with Tierra.

"Even bud?" Tierra asked with her eyebrows raised.

"Go ahead," Deedra replied. "But may I suggest that you might find it more pleasant on the back deck right here. It's very nice out there, and the weather's nice."

"Yeah, let's do that," Emily seemed braver by then, which was likely the result of the alcohol she'd downed.

"Very pleasant," I dumbly concurred, recalling what it was like before.

Deedra led us just outside the sliding glass door in the kitchen to a spectacular southeastern Montana view of a small forest and some hills. The tall iron fence still made its prison-like presence known, although the back gate was wide-open. Emily pulled out a quarter ounce of green stuff from her pocket. Tierra handed her a small glass pipe. I was fascinated by the swirl designs it had although I'd seen the same kind of pipe many times before. "From Humboldt," Emily said while showing us a pretty looking bud. "It's real good."

I was interested in how the weed would affect me, or whatever Deedra had been talking about earlier, of just being high for a few moments or whatever and nothing else. That would be experimenting with drugs, I figured. The experimenting with drugs thought stuck in my head. After we smoked I had to let my feelings out. I sat down and addressed the group of pretty young ladies while they smoked cigarettes.

"I always wondered why people, especially older ones, say they, 'Once experimented with drugs when they were young,'" I said. "It was always 'in college,' too, man. I mean, what did they do, sit in a laboratory with notebooks and computers and all types of science shit and get high like Tim Leary and his LSD? 'The results are conclusive in my experiment, Project Smoking Reefer, it's positive!' Or, 'I was smoking crack in a lab shack, but when I read the results I wrote while feeling the effects all it said was, 'This is intense. Stratosphere, baby!' over and over about ten times. Or maybe they tried meth once and typed out the results on a typewriter, but it's like a fifteen page printout conclusion though about curtain designs and why the mailman and the 75-year-old man walking his poodle are possible DEA agents and a drug dog. It's why he keeps drifting to this area day after day at 6 in morning! He's an advance SWAT team.' And, 'What to look for when one is deciphering drywall particles from imaginary pieces of meth off of the carpet.'"

"Fucking tweakers and those damn five layers of curtains!" Tierra said.

Emily said, "I've seen them picking stuff off the ground too, and once I scraped the ceiling and they knew I scraped it, but they couldn't help but pick through it, dude!"

"Funny," I said. "Tweakers are persistent if anything. But those curtains, it just makes it even more obvious when they're 'high beaming'—just being able to see their wide-open eyes and nothing else. Curtains all shifting, then you see just a pair of eyes following you, and they think they're all sneaky!"

We all enjoyed a good-hearted laugh. I knew what Deedra meant about 'being high for a moment' with weed, although it was more like no effect. I was just high on life with the sweet girls, and I loved them.

"So I'm a CNA nurse sometimes and there's this really old guy like, 90," Tierra said. "He says to me, 'The doctor said I should quit smoking, otherwise I'll die. You think I should quit?'

"I was like, 'Man, are you fucking serious? You're like a hundred, dude. You'll probably die the day you quit just because you quit!'"

"Oh, I know!" Deedra said. "They have these outrageously inflated statistics of people who've supposedly died of smoking—and it does happen of course—but in reality most of them died because they were just old. Granted, people around fifty do die prematurely as a result of smoking, but you shouldn't include people who are like 91 as they do."

After a few more minutes of group discussion, I began chatting to Emily more, and drew her to my side. How could I hurt such an innocent and pretty young thing? Do not dwell upon it.

The issue of selling drugs came to the surface again, since that's essentially what the two girls did for extra money.

"I like to sell weed better than other shit like crystal or coke or any other fiend-type drugs," Emily said. "I mean, it's less money and people say what they will, but potheads are generally generous people! Some are just peaceful good citizens, and yet they're frowned upon."

"But in Oregon you guys have more lax laws there in regards to weed, right?" I said.

"True dat. Potheads will try to get you back however they can if you hook them up," Tierra said.

"Yeah," Emily nodded. "Whereas you like hook a fiend up with other drugs, and they expect you to like do them that favor every damn time! So you got to almost sort of rip 'em off just to like keep 'em happy."

"That's right," Tierra added. "They're like always short on cash, and want credit, too. The best and most trustworthy person for credit: a dope fiend."

"Yeah," Emily said. "Then they always bring something for credit that is useless too, like a book of stamps. 'Okay, I got like seventeen dollars and a pack of stamps with five of them in there.'

"'Pack of stamps?' I say.

"Them: 'Yes! Now hear me out. I figure you gotta

hook me up with twenty-five dollars' worth, since...well...I figure this is worth the extra five dollars in gas and hassle I'm saving you in having to run clear to the post office to get the stamps!'"

I laughed heartily, and finally asked Emily the fatal question as a result of my aching body and our cheerful mood. "Um, tired yet? I am. Do you want me to show you where to sleep upstairs?"

She nodded eagerly, got up, and said something to Tierra who was engaged in her own conversation with Deedra. Tierra did most of the talking though. Tierra just nodded her head happily to Emily and said she'd be all right. Deedra winked when she glanced at me. So she was right. Tierra kissed Emily quickly on the lips and whispered, "Have fun."

I was not meant to hear it, but I did. Of course I could have easily lip read it if I had wanted too, but the fact that I could hear it impressed me. So did Emily.

She grabbed my hand, and we kissed gently with the tips of our tongues brushing ever so slightly.

In an upstairs bedroom we began to make-out like I had the night before with Cassie. Not long after we'd both stripped almost completely, I was feeling her petite body all over. I knew my skin felt cold and unnatural. Emily especially knew my skin felt cold and unnatural. She only seemed to enjoy it the more I touched her, kissed her, and vice versa. I hadn't been laid the entire year, and suddenly I had three girls in two nights if you counted Deedra.

"This is the part you always wake up," I said when I pulled my boxers down.

"What?"

"Like when you're dreaming and—" "Oh. I get that too!"

Anyway, I started doing her unprotected. I seriously doubted I would get any disease or get her pregnant. I mean, how could I get a deadly disease, or get someone pregnant, when I was already supposedly dead? After a few minutes of doing it and feeling the beautiful human that lay beneath me, I, the monster, whispered gently into her ear, "I'm a vampire." I tried to not cause a panic. "I just thought I'd tell you."

She opened her eyes wide and took a good look at my face. Her pleasure-feeling face returned. "I know."

"But, you don't believe in vampires," I said.

She continued her enjoyment and said, "I do now." "Me too!"

I guess we believed each other then. I am quite sure she was serious. Didn't she know vampires generally killed people from what I'd conjured, and that 'people' meant her? I figured she did know, but I wouldn't risk scaring her to death before I got to do what it was that I was having a hard time controlling: not my hormones, but biting her and slaking my hungry thirst. I don't think I'd ever felt so hungry in all of my life.

I kissed around her neck and held both her hands above her. She moved so that I could see her neck more easily, and it obviously tempted me insanely as I smelled the blood underneath. *Rip it open!* I kept my calm, however, and pierced my sharp 'virgin' fangs into her artery gently. She squealed in delight. *So far, so easy.* I quaffed a huge amount of blood within a few seconds and told myself to slow down. My mouth and lungs seemed a vacuum of death. *Holy flip, that was cool!* Emily squeezed my hands and said, "Harder."

I didn't know what "harder" she meant, so I sucked and did the other lustful act with more dedication and gusto. Really. I thought I might break her little body.

I stopped sucking and doing it altogether for a moment, realizing how lightheaded and overwhelmed I was with pleasure. Was it really that good? Yes. I mean, this was the ultimate high, rush, trip, and orgasm all at the same time. Only it was better. The taste of her, the beauty of her, and especially the quenching of the hunger, these things were enough to make me want to commit the ultimate sin over and over.

Emily laid there in her stupor with little comprehension of what was happening to her, yet seemed to love it. "Again," she said barely audible. "Please."

"As you wish," I said, sucking her off slowly.

Wait! I stopped myself. Make her like me, what Deedra did to me! It was too late though. She was dead. What good did her unassuming sense of humor and delicate beauty do for her now? I had killed someone's daughter and could only feel pure ecstasy and euphoria in my blood drunkenness. I still managed to say, "Lord, forgive me," while unintentionally grinning. She forever went away.

Does the creator forgive demons that do what I'd just done?

Chapter 5—Karma

I LOOKED AT THE SMALL PRETTY GIRL who was laid in peace on the bed. I tried to feel remorse, but with the new blood that flowed through me revitalizing me, feeling penitent was hard to do. How could I feel sad with such a throbbing pleasure keeping my feelings at bay? It was the ultimate 'fix.' Like the glutton I was prone to be, I still wanted more of the carnal bliss I was experiencing. That reminded me of the other girl.

I walked slowly to the stairwell and looked at the scene on the couch. Deedra was brushing her hand through Tierra's hair, her hand creeping up her inner thigh. Interesting. But they're finally getting to it? Hmm. I watched the action unfold.

"You are a beautiful person," Deedra said to her, sounding oh so seductive. "Can I do something to you?"

"Yes," said Tierra, staring at Deedra starry eyed. "Anything you want."

So Tierra was a lesbian---or bisexual. That figured into why Deedra told me Emily would be easier. Or maybe Deedra was just that hot to turn someone. Deedra sat on Tierra's lap, and slightly startled her when she began to undo the top of her dress. She rubbed her shoulders a short while, kissed her thoroughly, and I barely saw her mouth go to her neck when she struck like a rattlesnake. I sat down on the top stair with my hands on my chin, watching them with great elation. Who would have ever thought that the age-old myth of vampires was not a foolish superstitious myth, but real? It was as real as the sight of Deedra draining the girl in front of me. Tierra didn't fight back a bit. Maybe she knew it would be to no avail anyway, or maybe she didn't know what was even happening to her. It all happened so fast.

Deedra pulled her head up and Tierra's head flopped back. "Yes!" Deedra yelled with orgasmic sounding pleasure. She noticed me. "Come here, lover. Lovah. Hah! Let me enjoy the pleasure with you."

"Okay," I nodded once, and walked to her purposefully slow.

She ran to me almost in a blur of impatience and twirled me around, half-scaring me. "Don't you love this?"

"I do love it," I said. I did not lie.

Watching her frolic and dance around the room reminded me of a young child on Christmas. She ran her hand through the corpse's hair in admiration as she intently studied her face before fully closing her eyes. I sat next to her. "This is the happiest day of my life!" she said.

"I know the blood was good, but I'm sure you've had happier days before."

"Oh, the blood is always good." She came closer, grabbing my hands. "But it's been awhile since I've had someone to share this with, you see? So it's not just the blood. I love it, but I love it with you even more. So how'd it go?"

"Very smooth." I gave her the okay sign with my fingers. "It was no trouble at all."

"See, I told you not to worry," she said. She nodded at Tierra. "You can do this more, can't you?"

"If it feels like this, yeah, easily, unfortunately," I said. "I'm an addict already. What do we do with them?"

She seemed to ignore my question as she grabbed Tierra's face with both hands and actually kissed her hard on the lips. "I love you, I love you, I so-o-o fucking love you!" she told her, and then her stiff body fell over.

Then she looked back at me. "We bury them, of course. We can go back in the hills a bit. It's such a lovely night."

"It is," I said. "And the stuff they packed with them?"

"Hmm," she pondered. "Check it out, then bury it with them. I doubt they have anything you need though. Besides, you have all you need from them already in you."

She walked over and kissed me full on the lips. She had just kissed a dead girl before that! Then it didn't seem so strange after I remembered again that I was sort of dead, too.

We found the backpacks in each of the bathrooms. In Emily's bag I found only a few dirty shirts, a couple pair of pants, shorts, under garments, a toothbrush, some combs, brushes, make-up, an ounce or so of weed, and another fine pipe for smoking. Sixty-four dollars and some change were in her pants' pockets. It also looked like she'd laid out a few pair of clothes for herself to keep judging by the way that they were neatly stacked in front of the closet. I put on Emily's limp body a lovely looking vest suite she'd inadvertently chosen for her funeral. Did Deedra ever wear any of these fancier clothes? I stuffed Emily's own old clothes in her backpack.

I asked Deedra what she discovered in Tierra's bag. "Nothing much," she said looking at some photographs. "These pictures and clothes, some novelties, one hundred and forty dollars, too. You find anything?"

"Nothing spectacular," I said. "Well a few bucks and some more grass, that's about it aside from the essentials. I put it by my stuff. Say, I have a bit of it now. We should have matched the girls and...oh, never mind."

We both wore their packs and carried the girls over our shoulders, grabbed a shovel conveniently located on the back porch, and headed out the back door.

Emily was small, but when Deedra told me to hurry, I really noticed the weightlessness of her as we sped through the trees at a dangerously fast pace. I knew I could have easily traveled faster, but I just liked 'gliding' and being able to check out the scenery while I did it.

After half a dozen or so miles of steep hills and small forest areas, Deedra stopped in a small coulee. "This is the spot," she said.

I looked at the area. Not a sign of civilization was in sight, not even the faint glow of the city lights on the horizon. Deedra quickly went to work with the shovel and with eye blurring movements she had a good five foot deep, four foot wide, trench dug. It would easily accommodate both the bodies and serve as a final resting place.

"Want to put them in?" she asked.

"Why not?" I said, picking up Tierra from the ground. "You did the dirty work."

After I laid the friends side by side facing each other, I took one last thoughtful look at them. Poor things, they didn't know that their lives would end by some fluke of nature. I dropped a handful of dirt on them and I actually felt like crying for the first time. Deedra saw my sorrow.

"Don't fret," she said putting her arm around my shoulders. "They all die, you know. You just have to think of it as it was their time to go. There's a time for everyone. Their time was now, in order that we could survive."

"I know," I said even though I barely agreed. "But don't you think it's messed up, the way they died? Us, you know, sucking their blood?" I cracked a smile it sounded so obscure.

"There are worse ways to die," she said before throwing a handful of dirt on them. "There are worse ways of living, too. Maybe they wanted it."

"Maybe, but I doubt it. They loved living. They look so benign and peaceful, like they should be waking up in the morning or something and going to church."

I threw the backpacks by their feet and started

burying them. Deedra threw a small gold crucifix on them that must have belonged to Tierra, and said a small prayer. "And though I walk through the valley of death..."

***

WE NONCHALANTLY DRIFTED towards the house. I was thinking about the irony of the night: who goes and intentionally murders people, and then has a heartfelt funeral for them? I guess I mourned for them out of respect for their lives because no one else would ever know what became of them. They might end up on missing posters, but no one would ever see them again. They didn't deserve to die so young. Their fate just so happened to have them hitchhiking on a road that wasn't even a main road going towards Chicago and crossing paths with us. "If not them, someone else would have died by me tonight, I guess," I unconvincingly reasoned to myself out loud.

I noticed that our skin looked almost normal again and not so ghostly and ashen. It must've been the fresh blood rushing through us.

I thought about that near unbearable longing for blood that I'd had when I awoke, and knew I'd have to get used to killing, otherwise suffer that incredible hunger and thirst. I asked Deedra if she was that hungry every time she woke up. She gave me an answer that somewhat comforted me.

"After I turned, I was always hungry during the first nights. I think it's because your body needs fresh matter and science and DNA stuff to help with the change," she said. "Then after the first few days, I noticed I could go a day or two without blood. I'd still lust for it a ton though, and your skin gets a little pallid."

"So I noticed. You look better now that we've fed."

"Thanks. But then after my first couple weeks, I knew I didn't need any blood for a few days before my body would be in pain. But I never tested it more than five or so days. A week was my tops, but I was depressed.

So I guess it's best to fill up whenever you can. Right now though, it'd be pure torture for you to go a week without it. You'd probably literally shrivel up."

"I don't doubt it. Just waking up killed me." "You were killed."

Walking through the desolate hills, I went through the thoughts of the hour. In scientific terms and explanations, vampires did not exist. There was no evidence to support them, so I was written off as a generic creature of fallacious folklore that graced cheap novels and cheesy films and that children often dressed up as with capes and plastic fangs. *Hiss!* these unscary monsters were fond of saying. As far as being a holiday accessory that temporarily boosted the economy through bad teeth, I guessed it was better than being one of those crazy looking gorilla masks.

There was one scientific explanation I could come up with for myself: I was a step ahead of man on the food chain, and it was still survival of the fittest. I would do what I had to do in order to exist in my own selfish peace, so in essence 'survival' meant destruction of the weak, just like most of God's other creatures. Hence, that's why I possessed the powers I had. But was I even one of God's creatures anymore?

My philosophical viewing of myself was kept simple: karma made me a vampire, and I could not change that fact. Even if I did want to change it, well, too fucking bad. All I could ask of myself was that be the best person, I meant vampire (how I inexplicably loathed that dumb 'v' word suddenly) I could possibly be. Now that would make me a scary monster.

We both sat down on top of a hill and looked up at the moving sky. I wondered if God chose this fate for me. They say He's omnipotent and all knowing, so maybe He knew I'd end up a vampire. Then I figured He'd probably want nothing to do with me in my changed state. That was disheartening. I did know of one person who knew why I might've been chosen for my new line of existence. "Why did you choose me, Deedra?" I asked. "Why turn scrubby old me into a metaphysical whatever super being like you?"

She looked me up and down and shrugged. "I don't know to a point, actually. I was going to just kill you, but then I talked to you once for a bit, and couldn't. I mean, look at you..."

"I don't have a mirror."

She liked my purposely lame sarcasm. "See?"

"I still don't have one."

"Moving on, I followed you when I knew you were up to no good after I drove by your friend Cedric's house. I was thinking of killing you."

"So you were the CIA spook! I knew I wasn't like them tweekers. Go on, please."

"Hmm, you're strange, me thinks. But as I followed you, I became fascinated by your determination to do something so uncommon for normal people. I've seen robbers before, but I never cared to watch them do their vulgar thing. I actually went all the way up to the next block to watch you shoot that man. Then I followed you to where you parked, and I must've fallen in love after you never killed the lady. You should've killed her, actually. She would've answered to someone about dude's death, and that would've gotten back to the authorities eventually, not that they would've ever known you from her vague description. I mean, I would've killed her if I were you, but never mind. She's no longer a problem for you."

I was aghast. "You never—" "I did."

"What did you do with her?"

"I never drank her. I wanted to keep myself pure for you, or that was my slapdash consideration for the time being. I hadn't made up my mind yet on what to do with you, maybe keep you prisoner until I did decide, and I'm only half-joking. Heh heh. But anyway, I sliced her throat and threw her in a garbage bin a few miles away from your direction since I knew you'd probably go to Cedric's. I'm sure they don't have anything to go on except for a random homicide robbery motive."

"That's fucked," I shook my head.

"What's really 'fucked' was watching all that pretty blood going to waste. I think I came in my panties when I saw it, dude!"

I was appalled by the thought of that pretty young lady getting her smooth throat slashed, and pictured the crime scene photos of her in a garbage bin. "So why did you follow me after that?"

"I was enamored with you. You were the one. I liked your nearly no guilt trip after you killed that man."

"Any cold-blooded fool could've done that, but nonetheless always a perfect quality to look for when choosing a mate," I said dryly.

"Hah! Let me explain, although you know some of this stuff. I never saw your face or anything, but you had these crazy thoughts going through your head after leaving the lady and I was like, 'Who is this kid?' You already know what you were thinking, but you just killed someone, you're fleeing the scene, and you're contemplating about all these ridiculous things like history books you needed to buy, poems, some crazy short comedy story you wrote that took place in a grocery store, and...wondering if America should've exploited diversified communist countries instead of treating them all merely as evil Soviet puppet extensions which actually made them unified and more powerful—all to keep yourself cool."

"Sounds like me, but I don't rightly recollect all of that," I said.

"So obviously, I just had to see your face and study you further. You were just too weird and too much of a trip to pass up. I knew you were not a murderer, but you could do it without a second thought. It was not out of hate, or wanting to kill, it was what a trained soldier would do in battle out of survival and instinct and without hesitation. As a vampire, that's a very important trait to have that, and I knew you'd understand the necessities of being like me without eventually letting it give you dementia-like symptoms, lest you give yourself or me away. It's a delicate mental balance, and there is no distinct psychological or scientific formula. You wanna know another main reason I chose you?"

"And what would that be?"

"You're beautiful."

I'd never been called beautiful before. Beautiful was for scenery, flowers, and women like Deedra whose bodies alone were works of art. I was a young male scrub, not beautiful. Handsome, maybe. I could live with that.

"I'm beautiful?" I asked.

"Yes you are," she said and touched my face. "I never got a real good look at you until you first saw me and I was like—excuse the annoying term—*damn*! So I did actually 'like you for your mind first,' as they say, but I wanted someone that was not only smart enough and deserving enough for these abilities, but also someone who'd bring aesthetic pleasure to the mix, too."

"Deserving—is that good or bad?"

"Both. To me, you were an interesting person, not a common uneducated hoodlum with little to no prospects. You may have been a perfect servant of God in any other life or circumstances, but in this one you were going nowhere, though you had every chance. Sorry, as of the moment anyway. Your intelligence, whether you know it or not, is extremely high, and I can use actual, honest to goodness vocabulary around you. You just had the perfect mix of arrogant evil, and feelings—or maybe lack of them in certain areas—to succeed in this so-called vampire world. Whoop-dee-do. You have a curiosity and acceptance of that which is sepulchral in life—C'est la vie! Such is life. Besides that, I can hardly think of another person who should look the way you do forever, just to reiterate myself."

"You use weird words," I said. "Well, looks certainly never got me rich! I've just been a decent looking loser so far."

"Credit yourself you're young, dude. Anyway, looks are a very deceptive power in themselves, and they are very necessary in my opinion. But I know you're not like those pricks who know they're hot, and then act like it gives them a God-given right to be a prick."

"I know. I don't even like people taking second glances at me because of it—my looks. I keep thinking I have toilet paper stuck to my heel, or my fly is open. Hah hah! But yeah, I guess I was fortunate to be born not ugly, as it were. There's nothing I can do about it unless I wanted to complain about it and wait for me due sympathy. As if!"

"Hah! Anyway, your natural proclivity to be reclusive is actually a big plus, too. You have the right blend of everything to be one of us in my singular opinion. The trivial troubles of the world are no longer yours. I see you don't have a problem with this, right?"

"Well, I don't know really. I mean, it's only been a little bit." "I understand."

"But right now I have no problem with it at all. Anyway, I just think it's all a big trip or something. I know it's happening, everything that we're doing and stuff, but I feel like I'm not really doing it. Like I'm watching myself in a movie."

"Well, you'll get more used to it the more blood you get. You may even feel better than a human. Actually, I won't lie. You'll feel downright superior than them if you let yourself get carried away. But do not do that, please! I beg of you, hold on to your humanity, your humbleness, as much as you can. That's why I liked you so much in the first place. I don't have to tell you how important your natural self is."

"Yeah," I said. "Can you flatter me with one more example of why you chose me? I like this."

"I could name a lot to 'flatter' you, if I must, but it was mostly the simple things you did last night. The way you really looked at the paintings instead of just glancing at them; your laid-back voice; your calm demeanor at the house party; the way you looked at me, and our small conversation about the stars. You seemed so much deeper than most, yet so nonchalant and cared less about the generic drivel drama around you. I couldn't kill you after I got to know you. Normally, when someone does the stuff you did last night, I drink him or her up. Don't get me wrong, I wanted to drink you just because of the fact I actually liked you—and I did, technically—but I knew I could not see you cease to exist. That would've been a mistake for me.

"And also...all right! You got me. Cat's out the bag. You made me hornier than I've ever been before! Is that what you wanted to hear?"

"It would've sufficed instead of all the previous mentioned.

Horny pussy in heat out the bag."

"Hah ha! Fuck you!" she said lightheartedly. "Smart-ass."

I got up slowly and stretched out. I chuckled when I realized that my muscles did not need stretching. I was just going through the motions of it. Deedra shook her head at me, smiling. "Tired?"

"Not really," I said. "Do I get tired now?"

"You will," she also stood up. "Especially near dawn. Stay up till the latest moment you can. Then let your eyes just fall. Don't worry about sleeping now, though. We do have the rest of the night to enjoy."

Yes, we did. I walked towards the house, and Deedra walked alongside of me and stared at me in fascination for most of the stroll. I sensed she was extremely proud of her devilishly handsome creation.

79

I didn't speak much during the rest of the walk as I occupied myself with drinking in every simple thing around me once again. A thicket of cedar trees shook with a swift, prolonged breeze, and I stopped and closed my eyes. It was the most soothing sound I'd ever heard. *Did the trees have any feelings? Listen, and they'll talk to you.* Such a strange and transcendental thought. I imagined the plants had souls, and everything was connected. All matter from galaxies, to dirt, to animals, to the smell of the sage and cedar, to me, was the extension of God's fingers. Countless rays of star light hit the dirt from distances impossible to even comprehend, yet there they were, shining in all of their glory like proof of angels.

The house came into view while we walked atop a hill a quarter of a mile away. Deedra was gone and standing at the back door waving to me in a few seconds. I waved back and decided I'd run too. I did run for a few seconds, but I wanted to enjoy the scenery while the sensation was still brand new to me. That was already exciting enough for me as it was my first night as a newborn 'fledgling.'

When I reached the back doorway I felt the urge to drink blood again. That soon... I knew I could fend off the hunger easily, since I had just had a good meal. I also knew I was already addicted to blood like a junkie to a crack pipe, or a moth to a flame. I could not lie to myself about that. Right now, I wanted music.

I grabbed a CD from my backpack in the closet. Whoa, some weed. I'd nearly forgotten about it. What the hell was I going to do with it? I could smoke it, but I just didn't have the urge to do so. I'd give it to my friends. I knew I'd better talk them since they were worried.

I called my house. Eric picked it up, sounding very tired. "Hello?"

"Yeah, this is A.D.," I said. "Was up? Who's all there?"

Eric went in half for the rent at our house. He also

owned a nice car he'd let me borrow whenever I truly needed it. "Aw, was up man? Where ya been?"

He told me Cedric and Ray were at Cedric's house. He had some stoner chick visiting earlier to smoke a bowl, but nothing else had gone on. I told him about the methamphetamine stash with cautious code words, and that he should go pick it up and go to Cedric's house with it. Grumpy sounding, he asked, "Right now?"

"Yeah, you better," I said. I wanted to be gone with it as quickly as possible. "It won't be safe for too long. Tell him to walk over there. It's not too far, just so you don't look suspicious pulling up and shit."

"Fu-u-uck. And what do I get out of this immense favor I'm doing for you?"

"Um, an ounce of bud or so. Tell Cedric to sell the shit for cheap and get me whatever amount of money by tomorrow night. He knows who'll want it. I'll give him some buds, too."

"Damn, I was just kidding! We don't need that much, even though that's nice. You're just gonna give away all your weed?"

"Well, I don't need it anymore really. I'm just gonna keep some of it. I still got a lot though. Even some new shit."

"You gonna quit using?"

"Sort of. For now. I got some...never mind." I had almost said blood. I laughed. "No, it's just that I don't need it that much. I gotta sober up for a bit. I'll probably be around tomorrow. Around night."

"All right. Where are ya anyway?"

"At some mansion log house. It's not a mansion, but it's in the country and it's fucking nice. It belongs to a girl. You'll meet her. She was at the party. Not that one you hooked me up with, but thanks for that anyway, by the way! This one I got now, whoo wee, she's cool."

"You going out with her?"

"You could say that. I don't think I can stay at our

house anymore though."

"Why? Paranoid?"

"Never. I'll see you tomorrow night. Get rid of that shit, or tell Cedric to. Cool?"

"Yeah, yeah, yeah, I'll tell 'em. See ya."

We hung up. Would my ties ever be the same with my friends? I knew I'd still be acquainted, but also knew it'd be hard as hell to hide the fact that I was now such as being a vampire. I'd at least visit them anyways. Deedra came into the room right about then.

"Your friend?" she asked. "The half-black dude?"

"Yeah, Eric. Getting the rest of some business settled. He prefers 'colored.' Kidding. But he does say that to joke and confuse people!"

"About your friends," she said taking a deep breath. "You'll miss them."

"Why?"

"What I mean is, we gotta leave this town soon. We'll wear out our welcome here shortly. It's a good town, but we gotta go to a bigger city. It's science."

I knew what she was getting at. I knew we couldn't keep killing without sooner or later drawing a lot of heat so we'd have to be especially selective. "Which city do you have in mind?" I said open- minded.

"Seattle," she said. "I know some places there. It's safe. We can roam freely without worry. Do you know why we must leave your friends?"

"I do. This town ain't big enough for the two of us to keep killing in. Plus, my friends will know something is up eventually if they hang out with me."

"You're exactly right. I've lived here awhile too, draining old people in nursing homes, but I want you to experience the freedom of being in the city to kill. That'll help you learn."

"How thoughtful."

"But we gotta go in like two days. I got some plans."

"You're right. I want to leave from here and go to

Seattle or even Denver for a bit, but I never thought this would be the reason. I'll have to tell my friends, 'Hey, I gotta move because I might end up serial killing too many people here."

"By all means, tell them," she said. Maybe it was a little guilt in her voice I sensed. "But tell them soon. What about your house and rent share?"

"How did you know about..." Then I thought about her mind reading. "Never mind. I'll give Eric money for rent for a couple months, and he can live there with whomever after that. I'll go to them tomorrow though and check 'em out. Tell 'em I'll stay in touch so they don't think I went off the deep end."

I played a CD Deedra had laying on a coffee table, and it sounded as if I hadn't heard it before, and soon I was lost in the melodies of The Smashing Pumpkins. Every sound and instrument was so distinct. Deedra explained to me how she was tired of 'nursing home hunting' for blood while I looked at the paintings in the room, and they inspired me to do my own art. I asked Deedra for some art paper and a pencil. I began drawing the room, but soon I wanted to draw either Deedra or myself. How did I look now?

I walked into the bathroom and expected to be shocked at the sight of myself. I wasn't. Although slightly paler, my face looked very clean, smooth, and devoid of pores. My hair was black, slightly long on top with shorter sides and was a style that was timeless and popular in the 1920's and 30's. It looked clean and shiny.

My eyes pleasantly startled me when I first looked into them closely. They looked like they had gold sparkles in them. They looked...pretty. That was the word. They were glowing-gold and pretty like Deedra's. Before, my deep-set eyes had been a brown-hazel color, and now they were bright and glittery hazel. I knew the way my eyes looked most likely had something to do with the reason why I could see so well in the dark.

I remembered my face in the mirror before I cautiously looked at my fangs. I took a deep breath. So there they were—the allegorical part that distinguished me a monster from a man. They were not as large as wolf canines, but they were at least a quarter-inch longer than they had been and they were definitely noticeable. The canines were actual canines. I would call them fangs, since that was a more appropriate term considering their use. I did not disdain them, but admired their diamond-like sharpness a bit and then I went into the den to do my drawing.

Deedra had told Emily and Tierra that we were twins, and I guess I would've believed it if I were them. From an artist's and writer's point of view, her description could've been used for me if you changed the sex and other trivial details like hair length, body dimensions, and other obvious feminine/masculinity things. Not to be narcissistic, but if I was a homosexual, I would've done me.

I planned my impromptu self-portrait: with or without the fangs? Without, or I'd at least close my mouth and give a slight smile. I finished the drawing and liked it. Prior to my transformation, I'd obviously been an exceptionally skilled and practiced artist, but I finished that drawing faster than any other I'd done. I put the picture away and went to speak with Deedra who was reading in the basement when I interrupted her. It was a road map of the northwest she had. "Why can I see myself in the mirror?"

"Because a mirror reflects images, duh!"

"But I'm not supposed to have a reflection, right?"

"What do you mean?" She laughed as my silly point struck her. "Oh, that's just inane! You're talking about myths?"

"It would appear so," I said. "And what would happen if someone shanked you in the heart with a wooden stake?"

She shook her head. "I'd probably pull it out and do the same to them, if I did not throw them as far as I could first, and then drink them for healing power."

"When you gonna turn into a bat? Or is that only when you open the belfry in your pants?"

"What...ever!"

She was on me in a flash and wrestled me down. "I'll show you belfry," she said as she dry humped my face. She was perhaps truly stronger than me, although I wasn't fully trying to defend myself for select reasons. We enjoyed our childish adult play for a bit, then she sat up and explained most myths about vampires and killing them were far-fetched and for the movies; like us not liking garlic, crucifixes, and silver bullets killing us. I thought that silver bullets were for werewolves, but I never interrupted her.

This she did know: that vampire powers varied and were unpredictable. That sunlight hurt everything in our bodies and could kill you as we were combustible. "Ever hear of human combustion?" she said. Theoretically, that may have happened to a few vampires before. So if I set myself on fire, it probably wouldn't be a good idea. Also, we could not turn into bats. Darn. Other supernatural creatures might exist, although she herself had never come across anything out of the ordinary like zombies or werewolves or what have you.

"You mean there are no fairies or trolls or unicorns?" I asked after she explained these things to me. "Or Sasquatch and Yeti?"

"You're a fairy troll Sasquatch! I mean, yeah, I suppose," she was thinking deep then. "I personally don't feel in my head that there is such a thing as a werewolf, as that sounds silly."

"Wait, let me interrupt. Okay, some Native Americans are said to have possessed powers to shape shift into animals like deer or whatever, including wolves. We'll discuss that later. So really, it sounds more reasonable than us if you look at it in that context. However, plains Indians would disguise themselves as wolves and creep up on buffalo or spy on people dressed like that. Anyway, continue."

"I suppose. But bigfoots, or whatever you want to call them, I believe they exist. Sort of. We exist, so why not them? They seem more likely to exist than any other so-called mythical creatures; maybe some kind of Neanderthal or Ice Age leftover. It would be unfair to shut them out of reality. I mean, there are a lot of stories about them that back their existence both in Asia and North America. They've found numerous tracks that ain't linked to any other creature. Someone once told me a story of a band of sasquatches tearing up everything in a logging camp way out in some dense forest in Northern California back in the day. It sounded like a believable motive at least, since they probably just wanted to protect their habitat. But besides that, sasquatches are probably afraid of humans in the first place. Do you think that all those forest and mountains have been explored from Northern California to Western Canada? I don't think so. That land is just too dense to positively rule out the existence of a creature that just too many people have claimed to see. They could be extinct by now, though. As for the Yeti, I don't know much about. All I know is that people over in Asia believe they exist, and who is anybody to dispute them? Those Himalayas are not exactly a small mountain range for them to live in seclusion."

"You know, that reminds me," I said. "I heard they supposedly caught a small Sasquatch before. That's a funny word, Sasquatch. Sasquatch! He was a young male, weighed about one-fifty I think."

"Really? Who did this?"

"Some railroad guys or something in the 1880's. Serious! They even named him Jacko, and took him on display in all the railroad towns in Northern California. I sort of don't believe this though. Maybe they might have old newspaper accounts of him or something. I originally read that in an old cowboy magazine from the 1960's I found at a garage sale."

"Interesting nerd talk. I wonder if they ever got a picture or something of Jacko. I might want to find out more about him if it's not tabloid stuff of the past. Yeah, those regular newspapers back then were about half-fictional just to sell better. Jacko? Hmm. Maybe Joan knows about that."

"But, do you believe in ghosts?" I changed the weird topic. "I know they're around."

"I do too," she agreed firmly. "I don't think of ghosts or spirits as particularly supernatural, but almost like a scientific extension of electrical humanness. Like our brains and consciousness are wired by electrical impulses, and sometimes that can be harnessed. They just are and always will be around. What do you make of them?"

"Spirits are scary," I said. "I don't want to mess with them. They can possess people in the right areas with bad vibes—especially demons. Take old prison areas for example. Ghosts, I don't think I fear much. They're harmless, but I do know they will make their presence known if they're powerful enough. But other than that, ghosts are beings that want to keep living, but their spirit cannot accept death whatsoever. Or even if someone's family member or whoever won't accept the person's departure, it's not good for their soul. People need to let dead people be dead. Otherwise, I think that clinging to your loved one's soul will not allow it to R.I.P. and make it hard for that person to leave and cross to the other side. As you can see, I've thought about this subject a lot!"

"Excellent points!"

"What do you think of witches? Have you ever heard of one or seen one before?"

"Yeah," she nodded. "I've come across quite a few actually. They seem to have inhuman powers to control spirits that even they're not fully aware of. Some like to call themselves psychics, or wiccans. That is the more politically correct modern term for them these days I guess, wiccans. Hah!"

"Heh heh. Why is 'wiccan' funny?"

"It just is with the stereotype of them and all. Some non-wannabes can use their powers with skill, but they don't have any real uses for them, and so they don't really try or even realize their power. I think that they are cursed with power, sort of like us, but they don't know how to or care to take advantage of it."

"Probably," I said. Then I rationalized. "But logically, we have a specific use for our powers, which is to give us an advantage to hunt God's most cunning creature: man."

I saw her face drift into thought. "God," she said plainly. "And what of him?"

"He doesn't care about me anymore," she said. The sadness in Deedra's eyes told that it bothered her, and she truly felt abandoned by Him. "I'm sorry I did this to you, making you like me and everything. You don't have to forgive me. I...basically killed your potential because I was greedy and needed someone."

I came close to her and hugged her gently. She struggled to keep her tears in. "I keep sinning," she said. "I think I'll be judged for it someday. I want to keep living, yet I have to keep being so...awful. If my soul dies, I fear facing judgment."

"Why's that?"

She relaxed a little, then faced me, speaking with her eyes closed. "Obvious? Simply put, 'Thou shalt not kill.' Please don't hate me."

"Maybe later. I think I might be in love now though. Anyway, God doesn't like murder, but he won't ever abandon you. I remember reading something like that." I walked over to a bookshelf and picked up a Bible. I randomly turned to the book of Joshua and scanned it. "Ah yes, here is something. He's talking to the Hebrews. He compares how he was there for Moses. Blah, blah, and, 'I am with you; I will not fail or forsake you.' See? That means something like, you're his child and always will be. He won't forget you. But of course we're not to live in sin, so it's not that simple...but you know."

I closed the Bible. She seemed happier and spoke. "Thanks. I think he's referring to Hebrews, not me! But yeah, I know it says stuff like that all through the Bible. It's comforting that you seem to believe it so strongly, and it gives me some hope, too, I guess."

"I can be skeptical. I noticed your eyes got really red when you were sad."

"Yeah, the tears are blood. I hate to cry, because the tears scare me, make me feel inhuman. I just need someone to talk to, I guess."

I didn't want to dwell on my judgment day, but I knew that my soul's destination would probably bother me some day as well. Who knows how long it must've plagued Deedra.

"Deedra," I wanted to change her mood more. "Let's go upstairs to that one room, the one I haven't been in yet."

"The one with the blue light bulb?"

"I guess. But like I said, I wouldn't know since I haven't been in there yet. The...your 'belfry!'"

She laughed. "Let's 'sko den.'"

Chapter 6—Just A Kiss

I FOLLOWED DEEDRA CLOSELY and wanted to love her lustily. Then, I recalled the sex with Emily and decided straight sex wasn't as great as it used to be. First of all, I couldn't cum as far as I knew, which was needless to say annoying, but at least I didn't have to worry about prematurely ejaculating if I wanted to look on the bright side of things. At least I could still functionally do it and feel the pleasure, but it was no longer my biggest priority with a girl. Well, with Emily it wasn't. What about Deedra though? I knew we liked touching each other, and I'd always greatly appreciated the mental aspects of sex. Plus, Deedra was like an 11 in hotness. I could taste and put my mouth on any part of her body forever.

The blue light room, as Deedra called it, was like a miniature living room. We sat on the couch and stared at each other for a bit. I spoke up and said, "You really 26?"

"Yeah, but I'm 19 like you forever, really," she answered.

I thought about the minor age difference between us, and wondered if she perhaps felt a lot more mature than me. Probably. "Why did you pick someone my age and why not...older or something?"

Her eyes sharpened like it was a good question, but she had a well thought out answer. "I don't want someone like you to get old. Maybe I'm selfish, but I wanted someone that at least looks my age to hang out with. Besides, you're already mentally beyond most college graduates."

"I just read...a lot. I think I've read and re-read until I

memorized several college curriculum books from things interesting to me from psychology to history to poetry."

"But you're like brilliant; I'm not just stroking your ego. Anyway, I...I want someone to be with interminably, hopefully. It wouldn't be like marriage though. We might at times love each other to that extent, but we don't have to be tied down and die together—if we ever do die. I mean, you can fall in love with other girls and I'll be happy and shit. Woe to them. I don't want other guys in the love sense. I want you. I want you and me to be good friends, and to be happy."

"Coolest proposal if I ever heard one," I said. "So you want someone to grow old with, except for the aging process part? Weird shit, dude."

"I know, sounds strange. But you think you can keep in touch with me if we ever part? We can stay together as long as you want, but I don't want to in invade your space or life. As if I haven't already! Can you?"

"Yeah, I can," I said. "It won't be a problem. All you're asking is that we be really cool friends or something. We're both congenial people, so why not?"

It was true what I had said. Had we not been what we were and just met on the street, we most likely would have assimilated into each other's lives. She obviously cared a lot about me, so I would feel for her also. In spite of what she'd done to me, I'd forgive her. A year later I may not like being a vampire, but for then it was okay. It's not like I could change it and many others would be envious of my fountain of youth, so I'd have to live with it until I ceased to exist, apparently.

Satisfied with my answer, she ran her hand through her long hair before moving closer to me. "Thank you a ton," she said before kissing my lips with a relieved smile. "I was always afraid that this would never happen, not finding someone so I wouldn't be so lonely. It's like I lost a heavy load that's been on my shoulders for years."

"I know."

"No, you don't. Sorry, maybe you do. But...this is what I've been worried about for a lot of years now, even when I was alive. Not having someone to talk to, not having anyone to listen to. Shit like that. It frightened me to death, or scared me anyway, to go on forever like I was. I'd end up the bluh-y fookin' mad slag who lost the plot talkin' to me-self whilst pushing a shopping trolley, innit? You, I could probably tell anything and you'd probably never judge me. You have strong sense of loyalty and honor about you."

The way she said the 'mad slag' sentence in her mock British accent made me chuckle. She was random like that. I considered what else she'd said. "Right, you mad slag. 'You only have your honor when you die,' they always say. I forget who *they* is, but they seem to always know. But you have some friends, don't you?"

"Yeah...but not really," she said, and moved yet closer so that the sides of our bodies were adjoined. "But you forget the obvious reason and difference between us and them. Your friends and mine are not like us. We're like...not only introverts, but detached of understanding by the populace, and I think that's why I've never talked to anyone ever in my life as much as I've to you."

She grabbed my wrist—as if I would actually push her away— and started licking and kissing my neck lovingly. After a few seconds of gentle kissing, I felt a small piercing of my skin. *Remember these things!*

"What are you doing?" I nervously asked while blood throbbed steadily from me into her mouth. Excuse me if I felt neurotic, as it was still unusual and I still did not fully trust her with my life as she'd taken it once already.

She lifted her face to mine quickly, bloodstained smile and all.

"Just a taste," she said. "Just a kiss."

Her mouth went back to the holes in my neck.

Some taste, I thought after a few long seconds of waiting. My body grew weaker, and she finally brought up her mouth when I felt my head spin. I was surprised blood did not squirt like a sprinkler from my neck. Instead I felt it as a slow trickle.

"Don't worry," she assured me. "It'll heal real fast. Don't wipe it!" She licked the trickle off with her tongue. She sounded very hyper and anxious. "Your turn! Just a quick taste, don't drain me."

She tilted hear head as if to show off the pulsing artery below her ear; that irresistible throbbing lifeline that we all possess. "My turn," I said casually.

I laughed, looking at the big mirror across the room at the scene that was us. *Cute couple.*

Positioning myself so that no blood would leak out the side of my mouth, I proceeded to give Deedra a 'hickey.'

As I bit into her delicious skin, the euphoric feeling of Emily's blood almost returned. By the smell of it, I knew the drink from Deedra would be different than from Emily's blood. Just the fact that it was her neck I drew it from made the experience seem lusty.

It was.

For a long ten or so seconds, I was in ecstasy from her stronger blood mixed with a little of mine, and of course a little of Tierra's and Emily's. She moaned as I took my fangs from her neck, and I kissed off the leaking blood. I wanted to drain her completely, but I forced myself to stop. She took some back.

We looked at each other a few moments as we basked in the daze that came from our quick blood drinks. I spoke first. "Is it a sin to feel this good?"

"Only on Earth."

We both cracked-up. Everything might've been funny at that time. Our vampiric blood was not better than the human blood, but I knew we loved it more than any kind of buzz or sex. We did the latter of the two anyway while we were still high.

Chapter 7—A Daymare

WE LEFT the 'blue light bulb room' after relaxing and lying unclothed for a good while. I knew it'd soon be morning as I puffed on a funny cigarette just to stare at the smoke. Deedra and I talked about all kinds of stuff while we chilled in her basement. I remember babbling on about all types of warfare from the Spartans to Vietnam. She talked about different religious creeds, particularly the associated afterlife beliefs of each. In short, we changed the subject a lot, and they were all studious as well as picayune topics. We just loved listening to each other's voice.

"Want to sleep in a coffin?" Deedra asked excitedly as she sat up. "I have one, you know. Actually I have two."

"You serious?"

"Jah, I am. You can try it if you want. I don't because I get claustrophobic in them. Not really, I lie. But they're in the vault thing-y if you want to try it."

"I guess I don't want to if I don't have too, then. We go in the vault soon?"

"Yes," she sounded weary, "Too soon. Let's go down and I'll show you the coffins. You should try it once. Cocoon like. You might like it."

I decided to give the coffin sleeping a chance as we walked to the bookshelf. What would it hurt?

I closed the bookshelf door behind us and walked down the dark steps. I shuddered as the chilly, thin, underground air settled in my lungs. "How well do we sleep? Do we wake up at all during the day?"

She shrugged. "I don't know. I usually wake up right

after sunset feeling fully refreshed. I've only woken up once during a nightmare I had. Sorry, daymare!"

That was the first time I had ever heard the word "daymare," and I wanted to know what it was all about. "What was your...'daymare' aboot?"

"Aboot, eh?"

"You wanna tell it?"

"Not really, but sure." She closed the vault and locked it. The single light bulb hanging from the ceiling lit the small room. She pointed to two coffins on end in the corner. "See the coffins?" I nodded and she pulled one down and sat on it. I was lying on the small bed, lounging, eager to hear her story. She was a beautiful speaker.

"Okay," she said as she brought the memory back and took a deep breath. "Here it goes. I was in daylight. Foof! Is all I heard as I looked at the Sun. I felt my body catch fire and dissipate to the bones as I heard myself scream. The scenery was delightfully clear with mountains and a blue sky with puffy clouds. I'm not sure I recall seeing those specific mountains in my life, but I certainly remembered blue sky and the sun from when I was alive. I only caught a glimpse of this scenery before my withered, burning, bony, hands went to my eyes, because they too started burning. Oh god, the whole pain in that dream seemed too real for it to be a dream." She pretend shivered. "I felt it was actually happening.

"Then after a long second I was out of my misery and in a room surrounded by nothingness. It was white for as far as I could see, except for the millions and millions of people in random scattered lines about around me. The only visible thing in front of us was a seemingly infinitely long wall with a huge golden gate."

"Like the one in the painting that said Shamiyim?"

"Yes, exactly like the one in the painting. It's actually in Hebrew, but I knew it said Heaven, which is weird since I know nothing of how to read Hebrew. Well, I kind of knew where I was, so maybe it wasn't so weird. Anyway, I heard voices start to murmur as the presence of something great neared. I felt a strong radiance, and without looking I knew it was on the side of me. When I finally did get the courage to look at what everyone else was interested in, I saw the most spectacular being ever!

"I knew he was Jesus, Allah, Yahweh, the Creator, or whatever you want to call God. This being, or Jesus the Son in particular, wore a white robe that covered his pure white body. Oh, how clean and pure he looked. His eyes were not eyes at all, but flames of the coolest orange fire. The fire did not look fierce, but beautiful. His sinewy hair was the most dazzling white. The more I looked at him, the brighter he got.

"Then I noticed the golden scepter he held. What purpose did it hold? I thought. I viewed everyone else. We all looked basically the same, but how different we were as souls. We all held wood pallets of hay before us. This was our one common link overall: the hay.

"Out of the blue—or white, I should say—God stops in front of an angry looking man. The man held out his pallet, and God touched it with his scepter tip, and the hay incinerated in puff of smoke. Poof! There was nothing but ashes left. Right after the ashes fell and hit the ground, a couple of angels appear and the guy is roughly pulled away. The poor guy is cursing God as he's taken the opposite way from the gate. 'Why was I ever born if you fucking knew this would happen to me? Why did this happen to me? I hate you all!' he kept yelling.

"I didn't know what to think after I saw him being pulled away so swiftly and easily. All I knew was that I was scared. In no particular order he walks over to an old woman and she smiles. The old woman held her head down humbly, and looked to be praying. He puts out his scepter and poof! a bunch of lustrous emeralds, diamonds, and gold pieces fall from the burned pallet. Then God the Son spoke in a voice that sounded like a brook, or a stream. It sounded pellucid, like the purest and coldest glacier stream water anyway if you can fathom that, and it was gentle. 'I accept you, my child. Thank you for your servitude and faith. Your place is waiting behind the gates.'

"A smiling angel appeared next to her to take her hand, and led her to the gates. She jumped and screamed, 'Hallelujah! Praise his name!'

"The gate opened and a thousand joyous sounds come from within. It was people signing, instruments I had never heard before, angels singing! The sound overwhelmed and engulfed everyone who heard it for those quick seconds. Most people shuffled restlessly with smiles, and others looked to be paranoid.

"Then he looked toward me and I was scared. He walked right at me and my knees shook. I remembered what I was, and thought at any moment he would bring out his angels to cast the lowly demon away, or maybe just as easily destroy me himself.

"But he stopped to the man next to me. I knew this man was a preacher or priest of some sort. I don't know how, I just knew it. He reluctantly held out his bundle and again, poof! I expected to see the emeralds, diamonds, and gold again. I wanted so much for this man to have that drop in front of him, but there was nothing but soot and ashes. The man put his head down and said he was sorry.

"Angels took him and led him away. The man didn't even fight. He just kept shaking his head, and saying he was sorry as he broke out in tears. I stopped staring at him and turned around.

"He was right in front of me! He looked at me with no expression, and immediately I had to turn away. I could not look directly at his face even with all my sheer will, although I wanted to. He was just too radiant. I felt his presence throb heavily into my body. It gave me butterflies and happiness.

"I knew the happiness was not for me though. I subserviently fell on my knees, put my head to the ground, and began praying and chanting, 'Accept me like the lady. Please God, accept me! I want to know you! I want the joyousness. Forgive me for all the things I've done. Please God, please!' I pleaded.

"I looked at my bundle as he reached out his scepter. Anything but the ashes, is all I could think. I saw a blinding bright flame ignite the pallet, and heard a crack of the fire vanquishing it. Please God, please!

"And then I saw smoke, and woke up screaming. It must've been in the middle of the day. I cried myself back to sleep after a few minutes. I woke up later at sunset and my head felt like it was spinning."

"What did you do that night?" I asked.

"I put the dream in the back part of my mind as far as it could go, and then I went and drank two victims right away. I wanted the dream to disappear, so I defied what it probably stood for by killing right away, as it did bother me so much. That's what usually clears my head of any guilt."

"I felt that way too when I killed Emily," I chipped in. "I felt no guilt, but only euphoria. I was like disheartened when I buried her, but at the moment I killed her, I think it was the happiest I ever felt. Messed up."

She walked over and massaged my shoulder. I was in deep thought about her dream. It sounded too prophetic. "The first is always fun. Go to sleep," she said. "Don't worry about the dream. After all, it was only a dream. It'll be nothing to you later. You'll see."

I climbed in the coffin, immediately I relaxed. I said, "This is so Dracula. You're sleeping on the bed?"

She nodded no, motioned to the other coffin, kissed me on the lips softly, and closed the lid. The darkness seemed a peaceful, comforting quilt. I was afraid of what she told me. Not the dream, but that death would mean nothing to me later; the guilt and shame, and whatever I felt about taking human life. Sleep in your coffin, monster. My eyes shut themselves as one last wretched thought flitted through my brain: God works in mysterious ways, but I think we're mistakes.

Chapter 8—All-American Immolation

I SLAMMED OPEN THE LID OF THE COFFIN.

"Careful," Deedra said, also waking up. "You might break it."

Surprised at the sight of her, I only stared dumbly as she put her hair in a ponytail. Being a vampire was going to take some getting used to. A few moments later we were in Deedra's living room watching television. Typical human behavior. I thought about Deedra's dream and what it might've meant as she flipped through the channels.

"Haven't you ever felt, you know, guilty about killing someone and taking their whole future?"

"Once."

"That many times, huh?"

She gave me a sarcastic, annoyed smile. "I don't want to feel bad about being me and shit. I enjoy and love drinking blood enough to where it's practically the only physical thing in this world that's cool or makes sense. It's just, like natural, you know? Why ruin the fun and pleasure of it? If I don't want to feel bad about something, then I really don't have to, do I?"

"I suppose." "You know it."

"Yeah, if you can convince your conscience of it. But about that one time you felt guilty, what was that about?"

She shook her head with a smile. "I think it's funny now, but back then I worried about rotting in hell for it." She paused momentarily. "I think it made me realize what my existence really meant—in the eyes of mortals at least."

For some reason when she said 'mortals' instead of people, it made me feel like a Greek God. I was a real-life myth at least, the Greek lamia that was the supposed cause of Sudden Infant Death Syndrome as Deedra had told me about the night before. Knowing what I knew then, perhaps it was not altogether a myth.

She got up casually to light an incense and inhaled some of the perfumed smoke. She blew it out and continued.

"Anyway, this is like a major flashback. I never gave a fuck about who my victims were at first, as long as they were easy. I still don't! I rationalize everything in the big picture, like the way the world goes 'round type stuff. I know that everyone dies anyway, so why let them suffer out their meaningless lives, you know? That's how I used to believe; sorta nihilistic. But not everyone has a meaningless life, as hard to believe as that notion is. Just because my life sucked when I was living does not mean everyone else's life sucks also."

"And your life still sucks, blood, technically speaking," I added with a raised eyebrow. It sounded lame to me as soon as it came out.

"Hah! That was terrible. No rim shot drum roll for you! But if the person's life was not like bad, I usually still didn't care because I probably was jealous deep down. That's where this girl I took a few years ago comes in.

"She was at this football game in Dallas. It was a high school game, and she was a cheerleader and that miss popular type: blonde hair, great body, honor student, and all that which makes her the stereotypical all-American chick. I followed her and her groupies after the game to a party, hoping I'd get one of her friends or her even. Don't tell me, I know it's deplorable to be following teenage children like that."

"You followed me, so I don't think it's deplorable. Just sorta flattering in a way."

"True, but at least you're college-aged. But she was so confident from what I saw of her. She had the 'I love living' sparkle in her eyes definitely. For some reason that night, those blue eyes sparkling like a beautiful lake made me want to take her blood even more. I wanted the feeling that was in her to be mine! It was not jealously at all coming from me, it was just the pure idolatry of wanting what she had in her blood pumping through me. Nothing wrong with wanting, right?"

"Not really," I said. "Only if it's us! Wait, I don't even know what that one means."

"Okay? So I'm going to some after the game victory party and I knew I'd have someone that night. This was a big party and there were a lot of faded people there. As you know, I presume, it's pretty easy to get someone alone and disposed of in a situation like that. Especially if there is a bunch of young horny drunk kids that want a piece of anything to brag about. So naturally I forget about the girl and blend in with the people for awhile. It was a huge school, so no one really notices they never saw me before. Plus, there were people who never went to the same school before, drop outs, and etcetera. It was too easy for me to worry about miss popular.

"I already had my pick of at least a few guys an hour into the party, so I'd relax and wait for them. Man, I'm heartless. Teen kids! I coulda sipped from these two girls that liked me also, but never mind that," she giggled. "After pretending to take a sip of a mixed drink this kid handed me, I decided to zero in on my girlfriend across the room. See what she was up too. But damn, I was thinking maybe that kid was trying to drug me. Maybe not, my 'spider senses' weren't tingling."

I'd obviously noticed that she could easily read people's minds telepathically or some shit, but she'd not read my mind since I'd become a vampire, I guessed. I decided I would ask her about that particular ability shortly.

"Well, the girl was talking about leaving the party, so I thought I'd lost her. I figured she'd leave with a couple of people in a car. Oh well. I knew she had led me to the party, so I felt obliged to her for that and thankful. But then I heard her tell her friend, or friends, that she was walking home. Lucky me. Her boyfriend, a dude that she really did not care for, was already too faded to drive, so she obviously did not want a ride from him. Her friend offered to walk her home, but she made up a lie and said she just had to get up in the morning or some bullshit to baby-sit. 'Don't let me ruin your fun,' she told everyone. She also said it was good exercise to walk a couple miles. It was a safe neighborhood, et cetera.

"As my good fortune would have it, she left a minute later totally disgusted by her drunken boyfriend. I left the party—which was getting insane by then—to follow my all-American girl victim.

"At first I walked in the opposite direction of her, so no one would link me to her. Everyone loved staring at this girl, so I was cautious. Two blocks down, this older guy offered me a ride, and I almost took him. I should've taken him, but I had already chosen my victim. I was not giving her up for a loser when I had the perfect chance to get the perfect person. I told the guy, 'Thanks, but no thanks.' Lucky pervert.

"Then I ran up through the nearest alley to where she was and read her thoughts. She wanted to go to the park and think to herself awhile. I let her pass the suburban alleyway instead of taking her then. I'm surprised I didn't take her because the alley was somewhat hidden and perfect. Just dump her in the trash, stab her, take her money for motive, and dash. I guess I was curious to why she wanted to go there, to the park. She didn't actually think it, but she was holding a lot of bad feelings in her. The euphoric aura she had around others started to fade, and became lonely." Deedra looked at the ceiling for a moment. "I mean, why would she be sad?"

"I don't know."

"She wanted to die, sort of. Suicide. She almost did it, too." "Really?" I turned down the television. Deedra's story was far more interesting than the blather on TV. "How did she almost do it?"

"Well, when she got to the park she sat there on a merry-go-round for a few and did nothing. She wasn't even thinking anything either, she just kinda spaced for a bit. Then she started crying with her face in her hands. There were so many things at once buzzing in her brain it was hard to decipher and pull one clear message out of her head.

"I won't go into detail, but she needed a break from everybody. Everyone, or at least she thought, had always put a lot of pressure on her to succeed. She tried as hard as she could to impress everyone, but she still felt it was not enough, that she wasn't good enough to live up to everyone's expectations of her.

"I read thoughts like, and mind you, this was a perfect girl: 'Divorced idiot parents, y'all embarrassed me anyway. Dad screwing those dumb whores like that. They're mad because my grades ain't perfect, and I'll never get into that Ivy League school like my sister did. I miss my sister. She's all the family I had that listened, and now he's gone forever. Fuck them. I'll do what I want for once!'

"Then she pulled out a gun, which I guess she used for protection, from her purse. This wasn't going to be a 'cry for help' suicide attempt. It was the real deal."

I interrupted, "Off topic, but did you know the rural areas always have the highest suicide rates? Must be loneliness and easy access to guns. So basically, she got tired of everyone else's standards, and was missing her deceased brother? I know the feeling of missing someone. Was she drunk and just thinking stupid?"

She shook her head. "The spoiled kid didn't think those things exactly, that's just a summary, but she wasn't drunk, only irrational because of pent-up feelings from having to be so fake in front of everyone all the time, and she even blamed herself for creating that image. She felt strongly enough about everything going on that she wanted her life to end, and only she knew for certain why. This wasn't the first time she'd contemplated suicide, but she was just ready that time.

"I stood a bit closer to her then, by a tree that was maybe ten yards away. She stood staring at the gun for a minute and I knew she wanted her life over with. I could tell because she thought it, and also she flipped the gun's safety off and held it to her forehead with the finger on the trigger. I mean, one twitch and she would've died, dude. I stared in fascination at this ordeal and wondered if I should intervene. Should I drink her before she killed herself, or should I give her counsel?

"I was almost too late. She moved the gun from her forehead to her temple and said, 'Fuck this!' out loud. In a split-sec I appeared in front of her. She saw me and instantly thought I was an angel sent by her deceased brother. She put the gun down, and I almost started crying when she did!"

"Intense," I said.

"Definitely," she agreed. "She cried with no shame and with no regard to whom I was, so I had to comfort her with a hug. I let her cry a minute to forgive herself before I took her."

"Did she still want to die?"

"Nope. She thought that I had come to save her. A guardian angel or something, me! She was crying about the fact that she was actually going to shoot herself. One of her last thoughts was, 'How could I have been so selfish to everyone that loves me? Why make my parents bury two kids?' She knew people did truly appreciate her, and her preconceived expectations were mostly imaginary, as she was just pissed about her parents' divorce and her reputation being tarnished among other things during the trying time of her life that was high school."

"Is this why you felt guilty, Miss Angel of Death?"

"No, it's not. Well, sort of. I mean, here she thought she had a second chance at life, and I robbed it from her. Her blood tasted like it wanted to live when I drank it. I guess that's why I wanted to fiend on her in the first place though. Damn, it was good. Make me cum with that... Oh! But here she was on the front page and shit for a few days and I ignore it and don't give a shit, right?"

I nodded.

"I forget about her almost completely after a month, and much later I'm finding new victims in new places. Then I just so happen to be flipping through some channels and see the girl's picture on TV!"

"Whoa, dude!"

"After they showed her picture, her pretty face glued me to the screen. Her parents came on then, and they'd even gotten back together since the trauma. They realized they needed each other, and that no parent should have to see their kids die. I watched them talk about how much they cared about her and that they just wanted her back. They had a big reward for information. Anyway, they didn't have much hope that she was alive, that I could read in their faces, but they at least wanted the 'cowardly criminal'—as her dad said it—brought to justice. When her mom started talking again, and then crying, I joined her. Both their upstanding son and daughter had died before they did. I almost called the number at the end of the show to say I knew where her remains were to give them some closure, but I never did."

"Gotta be rough."

"But damn, I felt horrible! I was thinking about all the lives I affected by taking her. Why didn't I take someone else that night? Why didn't I take that one guy in the car, or at least someone who deserved to die?"

"Like us."

"Precisely," she said. I could see the emotion of the girl's mother on TV began to creep up on her. She pushed it away. "For a while after that, I only drank from criminals; the bad apples I guess that no one would be fascinated by if they ended up dead or missing. That's what the guilt trip made me do, try to play God or be Don Quixote, I guess. But now I know that I'm definitely not any kind of god, so I'll get whoever when I need it."

"You still like to get criminals, don't you?"

"No, only you," she teased. "The thing with criminals is that everyone expects them to die, so it's never a big deal when it happens."

"Indeed. Ya have any particular type of criminal you pick on?" "Pretty ones like you maybe."

"Flattered. You'll make me blush."

"Mostly dealers and shit, since they always die violently or go to prison anyway. Crack-heads, addicts, transients, and derelicts are all always easy, but the blood in some of them seems like it's already dead sometimes! But I'll always try to take out the perverts. I can't stand them."

"You mean ones like me that stare at you?"

"All the time. No, I mean the molesters and fucked up pederasts trynna ruin some kid or person's life."

"Sick bastards."

"No one can help them. Usually when I read their minds, it's like, they won't stop doing whatever until they're dead anyway, and even they know it." She lowered her eyebrows. "I'll usually go out of my way for those types of people. Make it look like a mugging or something gone bad or even a car wreck. You got to be careful, still."

"Right," I said. "You get any shit from the dealers? Dumb question. What's the most stuff or cash flow you got from someone before?"

"Let's see, I don't really recall off hand. It accumulates, though. I suppose if I were ambitious

I'd...I'd have a lot of money. But I'm sort of set already and have various accounts all over."

"I'm just saying, you ever purposely try to get a real rich dealer to get money?"

I was intrigued by some of the prospects.

"I got people with money," she said. "If we wanted to do it for money alone along with some blood incentive, it'd be easy enough, I suppose. Just go to the south border."

"I am so over that, though! I'm seriously going legit. I made a promise to someone."

She shook her head, smiled, gave me a peck on the lips, and left the room as I tripped on the story she had told me. Would I ever feel as guilty as when she saw the girl's mother on the television? Most likely. I'd cried over the death of a drug runner.

She returned with round-rimmed mirrored sunglasses covering her scintillating eyes. A long, hooded, sweatshirt covered her well- defined body much to my dismay. It was her simple idea of a disguise or something. "So, ya ready or what?" she asked.

"For what?"

"For this," she answered, and grinned with her mouth wide to show off her fangs. She licked her lips and made a slurping noise.

I feared her for those types of reasons, she was a classic bad guy, but I needed blood. I didn't really need blood in a hunger sense, but I swear I was having withdrawals from not having any.

"I'm ready," I said as I lazily copied her fang and tongue joke. "Shall we take the car?" she asked.

"No, let's walk tonight. We have enough time."

I walked to the front door and opened it. "After you, Ma Cherie, or Madame, whichever you prefer."

"'Madame.' And Merci!"

Chapter 9—Mind Blowing

AFTER LETTING DEEDRA OPEN the iron fence gate, we commenced walking briskly down the gravel country road which led at least three miles before reaching a paved road. The paved road would go another 10 or so miles before it reached the town. We took a shortcut after a mile, however, and went straight over the hilly terrain.

It was such a beautiful evening, as most days (nights) for me were. All the stars in the countryside flashed with more grandeur than they did in the small city. In town you could hardly see the majority of them through the glow of artificial lights.

We stopped on top of a hill to watch the sky. The countless number of stars on that clear but brisk night gave me as many questions. I asked for some more answers. "Deedra?"

"Hmm?"

"How come you can read minds?"

"Whoa!" she was surprised. "You can't do that?"

Was I supposed to know that already then? "Not since I was seven," I gave my wise-ass answer.

"That road we were just on...you can barely drive it in the winter, but we're hardly here in the winter as is. This is like a summer vacation home to hide away. Anyway, I'll show you how to do it if you want. Actually, I'll make you learn since it's vital. Trust me, it should be easy with your new heightened extra sensory perception skills, and it'll be helpful, since you don't already know," she teased. "And then you can practice it on someone."

"You?"

"No, you can't read my thoughts because I made you, or killed you. Strange. I don't know why I can't read your thoughts anymore, but that's the way it was with my maker and so on. Others like us can read your thoughts easily if you don't want to cloak them."

I'd oddly never even considered actual others like us before. Fascinating. "Who is your maker anyway? You mentioned a 'Joan' earlier."

"Yeah. She lives all over, but she likes it around Seattle." She rolled her eyes and laughed. "She can fly!"

"How?"

"With great skill, I guess. I don't know. Now listen," she began sternly to her pupil. "With the middle of your forehead, imagine there's a whole bunch of small lights coming from your third eye. Not your anus, but your forehead. Hah!"

"What? How revolting, you."

"Couldn't resist. Anyway, sort of like, your forehead's a daisy and the lights surrounding it are petals. Imagine tie-dye sunbeams."

I complied.

"Do you feel any unknown senses yet?"

I smiled. "Yes. Like, whoa, man-n-n! Far out!"

"Good. Now imagine the whole light illuminating around us with your thought and a mortal could read your mind."

Deedra is hot. I want to eat out her from behind again.

"Why would I want that?"

"You don't, but that's how you should transmit your thoughts if no one is listening to you! But I'm kidding, even though it's true. That's how other people's thought processes will travel to you if you can pick them up. They usually don't know this, skeptical people and all, but every thought around them travels from the center of their forehead and brain like a small, invisible, electrical energy to whoever is around them and wants to read it, or attempts to. It's very slight but it's there via science and matter. Because brain power is run by electricity, and matter/energy like that must go somewhere. You ever notice how when someone comes into a room, and without even looking at them you can sense anger or positive energies? That's what I'm talking about. This is just background info I want you to know.

"The real trick is to focus on someone else's 'third eye' and boom! Get a clear reading quickly and the rest will follow. It will become easier to read minds with practice, as with most things. Surface thoughts will come easy. That's like if someone is standing in front of a vendor trying to think of what to get. 'Shall I get Skittles or M&M's?' That will come fast. At least for me it did without even trying, and it drove me crazy. Now I can read thoughts in people's heads they don't even like to think about. Thoughts only known to them. That's how I can almost get a full life reading on people, their gestalt and take on the world. Questions?"

"Yeah, dude," I answered. "What if I don't want someone reading my mind?"

"I'm sorry," she said. "That's very easy, actually. Just don't open your mind like I told you to do just now. The flower petal shit. Just bring all the light back into the center of your forehead and close it down. I was just explaining earlier that's how thoughts travel. The flower stuff. Anybody could cloak their thoughts if they wanted too or at least scramble things up, but they usually leave their mind open without even knowing it, obviously. Now just imagine your flower being turned to blackness. Why do I keep saying flower? Or just do exactly what cloak means, which is put an imaginary black tarp around your body so nothing seeps out. It works, oddly, because you consciously shut it down or something. But really how often are you gonna have to do that?"

"Flower power girl, you sure I'll be able to do this?" It sounded simple yet complicated to actually do it. "You make it sound like anybody could read minds."

"Well, a lot of regular people could with practice," she said. "But let's just say it would be positively hard to learn these tricks without our powers and the right teachings or something. But then again, I guess more people than I think could read minds if they only tried it a few times. ESP is not a new phenomenon. It just has not been studied a ton in a textbook like way. I mean, it's not like every college offers classes for it."

"Wow," is all I said. I sat in silence for a minute. Was that my Libra constellation? I bet Deedra knew.

"You hear that?" she had her palms to her temple.

"Uh, no," I had no idea what she was talking about. I tried to hear something out of the ordinary. Nothing. "What is it?"

"Car."

"Oh."

The highway, or rural road to be precise, was still a few miles from where we lay. I still did not hear a damn thing.

"There's a lady at the wheel. She's very tired from having to drive for the last two hours. That is the only thing she is thinking about except food. In fact, she is going to order a medium pizza for herself on her cell phone in a couple of minutes here. She lives by herself, so she'll indulge and eat the whole thing tonight, but of course. With a bottle of white wine."

"Deedra, who the hell cares?" I acted agitated with overblown hand and face gestures. "Besides, you didn't even tell me what kind of pizza it was! What kind of Jedi whatever mind reader or witch are ya?"

"Be quiet!" she said. "She has not decided yet, and if you must know, it will either be a supreme pizza or taco. Something especially filling. Otherwise, she would have dialed. See how that used to drive me crazy? Now let's go get our dinner."

"Damn, girl! You are a strange one, me thinks."

I thought it would freaky to know such inane details about someone. I wonder how much she picked at my brain before... It didn't matter, I would tell her anything as our fates were intertwined now, and I had a feeling she'd probably do the same.

We both got up. "We better run," I said.

Now, if I had a vampiric power that was at least almost equal or greater to Deedra's, it'd have to be running. I can run like the wind blows.

Let me describe this absurd experience: I would take off at my normal sprinting speed, which was not that slow by any means. Then I'd prepare for 'warp-speed,' and shoom! I was gone. I could've easily taken off at my vampire pace if I wanted, but the human in me like to run at a normal pace before I got ready for 'lift off.'

I felt like the comic book guy with the yellow lightning bolt and red suit, The Flash. Perhaps I was not quite that fast since I could not out race a Daytona 500 car like him. It was hard to tell exactly how fast I was. Probably almost fast enough to cruise a highway, as my feet were barely touching the ground. If they did touch solidly with every step, I do not think my shoes would last. Come to think of it, they might've caught fire or something with all the friction. Anyway, I just sort of floated forward while my feet propelled and guided me forward.

The control I had while running that fast amazed me the most. Everything out of my peripheral vision was a complete blur, yet somehow I saw straight ahead with ease so I didn't slam into anything. I was the wind incarnate.

When we reached the town I was breathing hard, but not as hard as 10 miles should've had me breathing. Deedra was hunched over, panting. "Oh God, that was hard. Let's not do that again, please."

"Yeah, but it was fun!"

"Sure, for you it was. I guess you have to test your

strength, though. Learn about your limitations and all that jazz."

We moved swiftly through the first houses we reached as to get to the center of the town to find our meal. Deedra keyed in on people who came near us, no doubt scanning their minds. I tried to read a late- night jogger lady's mind passing us by with a large yellow lab dog, but I didn't care to fully concentrate. I just wanted to do something fun then, not kill people. Well, watch a movie or something, be normal. I also wanted to change my clothes, as I was sick of them.

Deedra was on the prowl. We came near a park that the jogging lady must have just come from. Deedra pointed. "There!" she said.

I saw a human form by some thick bushes that lined the edge of the park like a hedge of sorts. Someone was passed out there. We bolted towards him, then crouched low as we neared. Deedra studied him crazily, her eyes darting like a cat watching string, then grabbed his wrist and urged me to do the same unless I wanted to drink through the puke on his neck and chin. The guy's face was severely pockmarked, he smelt like a dead animal, and he'd pissed and perhaps even shat on himself. I wouldn't have been so sure he wasn't already dead if not for the loud snoring. He had a couple empty pints of cheap vodka next to him, and a bottle of half-drunk cheap wine that was likely the 'chaser.'

"What's on this dudes mind?" I asked Deedra as a joke and laughed crazily.

"He's dead, or he is going to die soon, and we can't let him go to waste. Now grab his wrist."

"Go to waste? Too late for that! Smell that? Augh!"

I followed her lead and bit down on the guy's wrist. Immediately I started feeling a drunken sense of what the wino guy might have felt earlier that night. I thought I would join him and pass out before Deedra tapped me and signaled me to stop. "All done!" she said.

I stood up and prayed a quick prayer for the one whom no one would probably care about. He was still somebody's son, uncle, or brother. He died because of us, but he was already dead long before that. He was like a zombie. I remembered seeing him before, a sad sight to witness. He'd given up on life. I think we just put him out of his misery, as he was one of those drunks who drinks themselves to death out of sorrow or just plain addiction.

We left the wino in deathly repose next to his bottles. With her own blood, Deedra did a very handy weird trick of healing over the wounds in his wrist so we could leave him without worry. He then must have died of alcohol poisoning or a heart attack or whatever the authorities assumed first. It's not like he was running for office. A coroner might be baffled if he checked his blood and found so little of it, however.

"Let's go practice that mind stuff," I said dazed and merry as we casually strolled from the park.

"Where?"

"That movie theater a few blocks from here," I answered. "The late show people."

As we walked, Deedra again went over the directions and gave tips on how to explore other people's minds.

We immediately saw someone in the back of the theater smoking a cigarette butt he'd picked up off the ground. He flicked it. I judged him to be around thirteen. "Try him."

I did what I thought was not possible almost instantly. His surface thought hit me smack in my forehead. I wish those idiots would hurry! He was referring to his friends in the bathroom.

I looked at Deedra and laughed. I could not help it. "We better hurry!"

"Ex-zellent. What else?"

I hardly even had to try the second time. The thought already passed through me. "Ya got a cigarette?" I said referring to the boy's thoughts. "That was...his last one.

He'll ask me when we approach. The boy anyway."

We came within ten feet of the dude and he asked us a question. "Hey bro, got a cigarette?"

Déjà vu.

Now that was trippy—the mind reading or telepathy, whatever you want to call it. I blinked hard and shook my head, perhaps to make sure I was still awake. He probably asked everyone that anyway, but still.

"I got a smoke," Deedra said cheerfully to the fellow. She did? Sure enough, she walked over and handed the boy a cigarette looking object. "Here."

The boy's eyes got big. "Is this..." he did not want to say weed.

"Special blend? Of course," Deedra answered for him. "The good stuff."

"Whoa," the boy was amazed. As we left to the front, he yelled out, "Thanks man! People! Lady! Whatever!"

'Whatever' might've been rude, but it was right. We turned the corner, and I came to my senses. I should say that I was not so shaken by my sixth sense. "You gave that kid a joint? Why? I didn't even know you had one."

She nodded. "Of course I did. It's better than those cancer causing sticks he's addicted to already."

"He's addicted? I mean, you know, know this?"

"Yeah. Well, he wants to quit, actually."

"Quit so soon?" I found that funny. "And you think the joint will help him? You're so good with children."

"Well, I'm not so sure it will help him quit at all. I'm not a psychic yet or fortuneteller, but he'll always remember us."

We headed to my place and I was anxious and nervous at the same time. I'd be the only one at my place, but I was going to call them from there and tell them I'd see them the next day to get the dope money or whatever. I was just going to change and grab what I needed, which was not much when I thought about it. What the hell does a vampire need when he leaves town? A set of capes and tuxedos? Was everything a joke to me in my new changed state? I was having fun and that was fortunate, I guess. Maybe Deedra had found the most perfect person to be one of her kind. Deedra, I was going to have to figure her out. She was a weird wild one. Leaving town with her seemed like a good plan for a weekend, but I'd already fallen deep into the proverbial rabbit hole—or her black widow's web—and this was the real deal, I was a real being, and I was not some little fat kid drinking red Kool-aid on Halloween pretending to be a vampire. I was actually killing people. I had a feeling that, although Deedra was perhaps slightly deranged just from living her lifestyle, she'd be a very good teacher. But who the hell would make her what she was, and why? We were heading further into the great Northwest, so I wouldn't worry about it until the time came. But she'd said her maker could fly? Wonder when I get to learn that trick...

One thing we had to our advantage was that no one believed in vampires. They'd become so diluted and commercialized by popular culture. I hated pop culture to where I had never even watched MTV or listened to a top 40 radio station in years, but on this occasion that was a perfect guise—not that there were vampires on MTV from what I'd heard.

"How old is the one that made you, Deedra?" I asked her as I opened the door to my place after grabbing the hidden key.

"She's like 400 or something."

"You serious?"

"Yeah!" she said as she followed me to my bedroom. She flopped down on my mattress on the floor bed as soon as I turned on the lights. "You don't believe me?"

"Sure, I do," I started digging through my papers. Poetry, short stories, art work, I'd keep some of it. The rest of my stuff was nothing I couldn't really live without. I closed the door and started changing into some fresh clothes. "But I don't believe in myself anymore, either."

"Nice," she was looking at me, shirtless. "You work out?"

"Sort of," I said, also knowing that I never had the body of a supposed hunk. I had the slim, broad shouldered, athletically toned body of someone who did a lot of calisthenics, but I wasn't really buff. "I've been running from the cops a lot lately. You ever see the commercial about the track star turned junkie who is running from the cop and gets grabbed from behind? Well, I'm sort of like that, except I was the one who got away."

"Funny," she said. "What you grabbing?"

"Nothing. I just needed to change. I think I'll just tell dudes to put it all in storage except some notebooks."

"Where's the roommate?"

"At work 'til like one. Well, I guess that's all. I just needed to change. I can get clothes later and they can keep all the profit from that meth junk because I'm ghetto rich. Let's go!"

"Well, I kind of wanted to have fun, ya know. Fool around. You made me horny! Do you wanna?"

"Yeah, but we should do it later." I was in a hurry to leave that room forever. "We got to get out of here and do something."

I saw a look of hurt in her eyes and immediately felt stupid and sorry.

"I just wanted to hang out here a bit," she said and started getting up. "But we'll go if you want to."

"Chill," I said and pushed her back down and took a seat next to her. "I'm sorry if I came out sounding like a dick. But, may I ask, why ya wanna chill here?"

She smiled, and I was glad I'd avoided a mood swing from her as who knew what she could get like once provoked. And I thought I was intimidated by a woman's behavior before... "Well, this room is your room," she said. "And I just want to hang out in a real person's room a bit...feel like a real person. I want to get your vibe, soak it up a bit."

"Hmm," I said and looked around at the room with new eyes. There were a few pictures of sexy ladies on the wall which were in fact very well drawn by yours truly, and a couple posters for decoration. The room to me otherwise was just a mattress on the floor, a stereo, and a nice desk. It was small, but it felt comfortable. One of the pictures I noticed bore a striking resemblance to Deedra if she had fewer clothes on. "I see what you mean. My room rules."

Deedra knew we were staying so she was content. "Let's read one of your poems!"

"Nah, my poetry is just random stuff, not actual poetry."

"Well, of course no poetry is supposedly any good unless it doesn't even make sense—including to the person who wrote it! Then it's called 'deep' poetry, and you're an idiot if you don't at least fake like it's good and nod your head while looking intrigued by the complex nature of it's supposed meaning."

"Well, that describes my poetry perfectly. It's like those big, ugly corporate sculptures that people make, just plain old vile things, and people are afraid to diss it because then others will think they 'don't appreciate art.' Yeah, I really appreciate it because it's a few hunks of metal welded together, and it's supposed to be 'modern?' 'Modern' is a word for goofy looking, I guess. Rembrandt, Michelangelo, or ancient Greeks would be lousy by today's standards, as they are way too skilled!"

"Well, let me read one of your poems. No, you read one to me!" "You can read them all. I don't want to read one."

"Read just one. It's called, a reading, you know?"

"Fine, I will then! Gosh!" I mockingly said as I and grabbed my notebook. I must have had about seventy or so poems, and I picked the shortest one I had. "This one is called 'Off My Chest,' okay? 'I write... Apprehension turns to droplets of teary ink...rolling off a ballpoint... Feelings too deep to say conjured...I strive to put them into written words... Like art, my hand heard.'"

I tossed the notebook at Deedra.

"Wow," she said and started reading the very poem I just read her. "That is what poetry is, just a song from someone's heart. A song. How long you been writing?"

Deedra had been perhaps the only person I had ever read a poem to aside from my dead best friend. Eric had read through them on his own, however. "Forever. I mean, I liked writing stories even when I was a kid. Poems just come out when they do without warning. I spend my days doodling, writing a few lyrics, mostly reading, being a bum basically. That's why I had to get in to school, because then you can be lazy call it studying!"

"Hmm. But how can a basic reclusive geek be turned on by doing what you did—those robberies? I mean, then you finally come out of your den and all you do is wreak havoc on society, rape women, pillage, and drink beer. You're like a Viking. Well, that's what you were doing when I saw you!"

"'Reclusive geek?' Hey, I represent that. I didn't rape, either. That's not nice! More like the opposite. Anyway, I did hang out at the library a lot—as if that makes me sound less geeky—and I went fishing a few times so far, and went skiing about every week in the winter when I had enough cash. I got out, it's just that I hardly socialized as of late. But I've been thinking about life and death way too much, and wanted to be on the edge far out from conventional life to tell it, 'Fuck you.' But only for a bit. I can't explain."

"Hmm," she was flipping through my poetry book, and referred to a line in it. "Where does it come from?"

Being on my own bed, at home, with someone that was actually interested in understanding me, I gave perhaps the most correct and honest answer.

"Loneliness, as of late," I said. The word 'loneliness'

sounded like a stone hitting the bottom of a well and the echo came back up to me. "At the same time I'm thinking how could that be? I have friends and people I can talk to. I feel so ungrateful, especially when the loneliness is mostly brought upon me by me."

I caught a glance of Deedra's face and a teary glint in her eye suggested she knew what I was feeling. "You ain't ungrateful" she said. "Sometimes it just happens without us ever even knowing it. Your head can't fool your heart. I used to watch couples and close friends from afar and wanted what made them tick. I wanted to experience those little things."

"Aw, yes! I want to tell you something, Deedra. I want to be honest."

I was finally feeling poetic, and a deep accumulation of life, thoughts, art, and all that I ever wanted in love spoke to me at once. I was in love for the first time, and comprehended it as I knew it. I flipped through my notebook to find a poem in there that was then complete.

"Paintings we so admire," I looked at the scribbled words as a guide, but also let my soul speak. "Little drops and dashes...of paint upon canvas...add up...to make the whole painting beautiful. The painting...our time. Even if burned, it existed...you can never take that away.

"Hauntingly teasing...when not beside us. Enjoying a good novel or film...alone. Wishing they were there to enjoy little sparks...of time...not described...but only felt.

"Simple things that made you smile. Our hearts' deepest desires...blending in swirling faith of hopeful colors. Sometimes nothing shared...but our presence to be content. Conversations irrelevant...to everyone but us...were best. Total surrender...to what is. Knowledge if all else failed...it wouldn't matter. We'd still find each other...on the other side.

"I make a prayer...I may enjoy this painting with you."

There was a momentary silence, and Deedra leaned

forward and softly gave me the most meaningful kiss I'd ever felt.

"It's a work in progress," I said, slightly embarrassed even though it had impressed Deedra.

I heard Eric coming in the house and we moved a spot away from each other like guilty high school kids who were making out on a couch and whose parents showed up unexpectedly. I flicked a black light on and Deedra whispered it was good idea. About a minute later after a television came on and I heard beer bottles clanging into the refrigerator. Eric knocked on the door.

"Come in."

"Oh," he said. "I didn't know you had a guest."

I formally introduced them. Eric said he was sorry for the interruption and would let us be. I said, "Nonsense! Have a seat! I'll leave the rent money on the TV later."

"I long for human camaraderie," Deedra said.

Eric nodded, and went to grab another two beers for himself so he wouldn't have to get up again five minutes later. I said we didn't need any. I thought Deedra sounded odd saying what she'd said to Eric.

Eric came back and said, "I was going to tell you Cedric already gave me that other money from 'zee' other merchandise. It's way more than you owe, but I'll figure it out."

"That's alright. Keep it. The rest can be for interest or whatever.

Cover next month. You've covered me already before."

"Thanks, bro!" He took a swig. "Good shit. You sure? It's like...triple what you owe!"

"Yeah, have some drinks on me."

I explained to him in short that I'd be leaving town for Seattle supposedly, which was in fact his birth town.

We made small talk for a moment before getting into issues which were sort of a continuance of me and Deedra's everlasting conversations. Eric was smart and followed along well. I didn't even attempt to read his mind. It was his business. But he did tell us how nice of a couple we made. "Just an observation," he'd said.

We all imagined what hell would be like if there was one. I thought it would not be fire, but total blackness. Total burning hot blackness like the center of the Earth, and total anonymity among others, with no singularity or uniqueness at all but you'd have a fully aware conscious. You could also be a drifting, anonymous, haunting demon-like ghost configuration struggling to be heard or noticed by anyone on earth with a billion other souls suffering the same fate. Those were a couple imaginings I had. Deedra went on about what Dante said, and thought those levels would be fitting. The worse the deeds, the worse the punishment. Eric was agnostic, but he wondered if there was a hell, could just anyone, like the worst of the worst, ever get out of the Catholic Doctrine of the 'purgatory state' if The Almighty were really all forgiving? As far as most Christian branches went, when you died that's where you stood for eternity.

It was nearly one-thirty a.m., and I told Deedra we'd better get back for no reason other than I wanted to walk around. Eric offered to give us a ride, but it was late for him and I could tell he was burned out from work. We said we'd be fine, and I told him I'd stop by the next day to say bye before we left if anyone wanted to see me. I made it clear I did not want a huge party or anything, as I had to get on the road. I was emotional thinking about it, but I knew a drastic change was good for my life.

We slipped out the door, and I turned and took a good look at my little dwelling. Maybe I would miss it.

Chapter 10—Moonlight Drive

I'M ALREADY GUILTY, so I might as well tell you.

We left my place feeling as upbeat as the conversation we'd had. Well, it was morbid but we'd had fun. The night would be over in about four hours, and I queried Deedra on how we'd get home since I'd foolishly refused Eric's ride. Perhaps we'd get a cab to take us at least to the edge of town, and maybe front him a hefty tip if he'd take us even further. Or we could just hurry up and walk and run, but I was tired from running earlier.

"Let's go get a drink," Deedra said. "You serious?"

"Why not?"

I was in no mood to argue, and had nothing else to do anyway. Although Deedra and I had never had argument per se, we did debate things as I loved a good intelligent discussion.

"Where?" I said. "The bar."

There were a lot of bars, so we walked briskly towards the nearest one. I naively figured maybe we'd just hang out there for a moment. I didn't want to drink any more people than necessary out of basic regard for humanity.

When we got to there, Deedra just stood in front, peering through window on the door. It was nearing two in the a.m., which was closing time. She led me to the next alley, and we stood along the wall.

"What are we doing?" I said.

"This lady in there."

"What about her?"

"She's drunk. She won't let the dad have the kids so she can get the child support money. She knows he's a good dad. She's crying in her beer almost every night as if it's his fault they broke up. She shouldn't have left him, but of course it's 'all his fault.' It's always is the other person's fault, ya know? I don't see quite how it's his fault, but she sure has convinced herself of that. She barely even lets him see his kids. He has to practically pay her extra even for that privilege. Real conniving, this one. She has no shame."

"So, she has kids?"

"That's right."

"And you want to...you know?"

"Shh," she peered around the corner. "She's leaving now."

A lady dressed in sort of 'cowgirl' clothes with a brown bag of liquor walked towards a plain four door Honda across the street. She started it.

"It's a one way, so she's got to go up a block before she turns and goes onto that street over there," Deedra said as pointed to the other end of the alley.

At this point I felt I should say something, that we should not go after the lady. We'd already drank someone that night anyway. I asked slightly irritated, "Why do we have to kill her on a 'Doctor Laura' whim?"

Deedra grabbed my hand to walk with me on the sidewalk. "We don't have to kill her, actually. We can drink just some of her. But that would not make much sense seeing as there are two of us."

She kissed me good and hard, and a police car drove past us up the block not more than a couple hundred feet from us. "Must we at all kill some little kids' mom?" I pleaded more than asked.

I looked behind us in time to see the lady do a right on red turn. The town was full of one way streets and she'd be on the going left of us in a couple of seconds.

"Yes, it's best to fill up whenever possible. Don't be a wuss. The kids will probably be better off eventually. We're leaving tomorrow anyway. I gotta hurry."

She pulled out the dagger that was attached to a sheath on her calf, and made her way to the street where the barfly was headed. She stopped to yell impatiently, "Let's go!"

I wanted no part in it, but she was literally bloodthirsty. I mean, I could have used a drink of blood as it's an addictive substance, but it never occurred to me to only drink a little blood out of a person. I didn't feel right about killing some kids' mom on such a simple impulse, as if it were just a beer after work, or nicotine at break time.

The car was going about the speed limit in a 25 mile per hour zone. Deedra stood at the corner like it would actually stop for her like a bus. Of course the car never stopped, but Deedra was soon running next to it and in what was one of the craziest things that I ever witnessed, she opened the door, and hopped into the back seat.

The car came to a screeching halt, and I ran over to the car. "Get in!" Deedra yelled impatiently at me. My criminal instincts kicked in and I hopped in the passenger seat. She told the driver, "Get going, Angie!"

Deedra had her knife to the lady's throat and I got a good look at her for the first time. She looked to be in her late 30's or early 40's, wore big glasses, had brunette hair, and was not exactly petite. She was not obese either, but was slightly hefty. She kept saying, "Please, don't rape me!" almost as a chant.

The car was swerving erratically so I said, "I better drive before we get pulled over. She's too drunk and scared. Pull over in that alley."

She did, and in doing so hit part of a curb. Deedra's knife dug a little into her neck. This set off a panic.

"Oh my god, please don't hurt me, don't rape me, please!" she said as I pulled the emergency brake, and we stopped roughly. I grabbed the keys so the car stopped running altogether.

"Get out," Deedra said.

With few options left the lady yelled out, "Rape!" at the top of her lungs and honked the horn.

The car horn blasting startled me along with the screaming outburst. Deedra yelled, "Shut the eff up!"

She pulled the woman by the hair and neck to the backseat, choking her. I was amazed how the lady made it between the two front car seats so quickly considering her size. She was still struggling when she was pulled fully out of the car and tried yelling again, but Deedra covered her mouth. I didn't know what Deedra's plan was, so I just snickered to myself, amused by the bigger drunk woman fighting away violently. She was tough! The woman bit down on Deedra's hand, actually forcing her to pull it away. "Rape!" the woman yelled again and tried running.

Deedra caught her easily, turned her around, and promptly slapped her hard across the face with an open hand. The woman sprawled onto the ground. I knew she must've been seeing stars, and I was surprised she was still conscious. "I'm a girl, Angie," Deedra said as she rubbed her bit hand. "How the hell am I supposed to rape you, stupid cunt?" She repeatedly kicked the woman, who had gotten up on her hands and knees. I felt sorry for her. "I dare you to yell 'rape' one more time! Now you know how your daughters feel when you beat them."

She picked the lady up roughly and started viciously drinking from her. The lady's struggle diminished as her life drained. Deedra stopped, closed her eyes, and smacked her lips. "That's almost worth the hassle," she said and signaled for me to drink. "Well worth the hassle."

I started drinking, a bit leery of my conscience, especially at the fresh reminder she had kids, but that went away soon enough in a fresh drunkenness of blood. A car drove by on the street. I paused. "Don't worry," Deedra said. Angie mumbled something unintelligible.

"Bar people who won't even notice. You gotta attune your senses more."

I finished her as Deedra opened the trunk.

I was of course to throw what was left of the dead weight of Angie into it, and did. "You know, Deedra," I said. "You can't just go around killing people on a whim."

"Are you complaining?"

"No, it's just that it's not...civilized." I hopped in the car to start it. "I'm not judging you or anything, it's just common sense."

Deedra had an uncaring look on her face, and readjusted her ponytail. "I suppose. Look, we gotta get rid of this car anyway. Know any places in the boondocks?"

"Uh, yeah, actually." I pulled away. "The river sounds all right. I mean, just abandon it a dozen miles below the one bridge. We'll have a walk though."

"Walking...blah. Oh well. Should we drive the car in the water?" "I don't know. Well, no. It's just not cool, messing up the wildlife and all. Maybe we can throw the girl in though. Fish food." "Yeah!"

She sounded a bit overly excited about the prospect of throwing someone into the river. I imagined the whole murder act was also sort of an addiction to her, which seemed logical after probably having done it for years. As for me, the one murder I had committed prior to my resurrected life had strengthened my resolve to avoid those kinds of situations if possible.

We drove in silence for a few minutes. I tried turning on the radio, but it was broken. Oh well, I had something far more interesting to listen to. Someone. "Deedra, tell me about our kind. How many of us are there?"

Deedra seemed happy to talk to break the slight tension we had after I sort of lectured her on how not killing people on a whim. The prior minutes of silence had seemed a bit uncomfortable to me at least. There was just too much intensity with the dead body and all.

"Not a whole lot, obviously," she said. "I guess there were select times when there were a lot of us, but no more. The eldest of our kind won't have it that way. They don't even like themselves. They're like self-hating queers. Let's say that if we started trying to make a lot of vampires, or got sloppy and drew even the slightest suspicion, we'd probably ended up getting hunted down by an older one and rightfully so."

"What about the one that made you?"

"Hmm, Joan. I bet if I started making a bunch of vampires, she'd kill them and maybe even me if she feared I lost it! She loves me, though. But it's not easy to make us. I know someone that has tried twice and failed both times, though he said he did what he was supposed to. It's selective, this blood. It has a mind of its own. It's not a science. It is the supernatural, you must realize."

"There's got to be some science involved somehow. Some sort of demonic DNA molecule at least! Anyway, this dude, this vampire who tried making others, what's he like?"

"He's very handsome, of course. Blond. He's like around a hundred. Someone made him in WWI. His 'maker,' or whomever, was destroyed when an artillery barrage blew up the hole that they stayed in, then he got exposed to the sun. He's a German, a 'real Kraut' if you can believe that. He stayed for a short time afterwards, feasting on wounded countrymen and Frenchmen in the hospitals and fields. But he got the hell out of Europe after the war feast and never went back until, the next war I guess. We flourish during anarchy. But yeah, he came back here in a casket that was supposedly reserved for some American officer. He has all kinds of stories if you can pester them out of him. But he took care of me when I met him in New York. Well, not totally, but I stayed with him there. Unbeknownst to me at the time, he'd crossed paths with Joan before, and considered himself lucky that she let him live."

"So, what do other vampires do, go around killing others of our kind?" I said. "What's this dude's name anyway, the WWI person?"

"His name is Ulrich, actually. Yeah, I know, tough name. Real fucking metal. But he goes by like Jacen, with a 'c,' now. Who knows what other aliases he has though. Other vampires, yeah, they'll try to fucking kill you, dude. They're assholes and a violent breed. I mean, there is no point in a lot of these scrubs' existence. Some are just plain vile barbarians with no class. Just being one of us gets to them over time as I mentioned. Not so long ago some really old vampires banded together or something and wiped out as many as they could all throughout the world. I'm glad they did, too. So the scrubs that survived, they live in constant fear and paranoia. Not me though."

"Why not you?"

"Well, to be pretentious, because I know Joan, for one. She's survived a few of these 'cleansings' of our kind dealt out by God only knows who. I'm sure it's undoubtedly vicious with the hacking up of unfortunates, then burning them, and them fighting back and so forth. It's not some cheesy vampire hunter who puts stakes in their heart cleanly! I can use her blood and my link to her as a protection. She has much respect from what I gather. You mess with me, you mess with her. She's tiny, but she can lay waste to probably anyone. She owns the whole northwest as far as 'vampire territory' goes. That's why we head there tomorrow."

"Great. Think she'll kill me?"

"Of course not! I already told you that you're too perfect to kill. She'll understand my choice. She knows I've been searching for you anyway these past few years. She'll be happy for me. This I must say: she's going to greatly appreciate my choice on account of the physicality, that's for sure!"

"Why the 'physicality,' besides the obvious? Yeah, I guess I'm hot, blah, blah, but it's not like I flaunt it."

"Oh, she likes 'our type'—our ethnicity. It's fairly distinctive and new. I forgot how she described us, 'Old World blood infused with the New World,' or something. She thinks we Euro slash original Americans are the most beautiful people in the world. I can see what she's saying, as why do you think there are so many Brazilian models? But she found me especially appealing because of my part-Sioux blood and Caucasian mix. And you, you're almost androgynously pretty, in a good way! I'm only like 1/4 Lakota Sioux though, but I do have most of my mom's American Indian features—she was a half-breed."

"I figured you were Native! I couldn't pinpoint the tribe though. I was gonna ask you in a minute too or last night, but just never got to it because my brain is everywhere. You notice that's like the first thing Natives every ask as an icebreaker is, 'What tribe are you from?' But I see what she's saying because if you think about it, there are still few as unique as us North American 'breeds' in the world numerically speaking, although the number has increased in modern times. Brazilians are pretty people, too though. It's like a supermodel haven there. What's the rest of your origin?"

"Mostly Swedish and German, I think, jah!"

Slowly but surely, information about my new brethren and sistren came to me pieces at a time. I did not want to immediately press Deedra into telling me all she knew, whom she knew, or what her life was like, because I knew she'd tell me in due time. She wanted too. We had always for the most part discussed informal things thus far. Although we were forced to become as close to anyone as possible aside from maybe those who were married, we still were in the process of feeling each other out as far as the most intimate details of our life went. Learning what I could about our kind was essential stuff, however.

I turned on a country road and a particular John

Denver song came in my head. I sang some of the chorus. Deedra advised me to turn off the lights and I obliged. I drove through a curve-filled, black road without the help of headlights. I think she wanted me to know I could do that if the need arose.

We discussed our makeshift plan as we studied the area. We'd have to get closer to the river, so that meant driving the car over some rough spots and straight through bushes. We found a suitable spot to abandon the vehicle, and we'd dump the body in the river as originally planned. The only unusual part of the plan (besides all of it) would be that we'd have to cross the river by swimming in order to be headed to the homestead. I would've strongly opposed the idea of swimming at night in a deep, fast flowing part of the river, but in my current state I was curious. Deedra didn't seem too enthused about swimming, but it was her kill.

After we grabbed Angela by her arms and legs, we both heaved her into the middle of the river on count of three. We wiped down the car, and drove it into the spot we had found for it.

I pitied whoever would find Angela's body. A 'floater' was a terrible state to find someone in. Hopefully they'd find her sooner than

later, but in the near overflowing gushing pace of the Yellowstone River at that time of year, that was doubtful especially since they wouldn't know she was in there in the first place for a while. She'd go for a few miles and perhaps even days in this a rural area without being seen unless a recreational boat happened to pass by at the exact right moment. I heard that sometimes bodies found in the river that weren't be found right away often sunk, then came up days later once they'd bloated. I prayed once again for Jesus to forgive us before we heaved Angie into the water.

"You always pray for your kills. Surely, you're one of a

kind." "Oh, I'm sure there've been religious nut job vampires before.

Consider it 'saying Grace.' Taking Communion blood too, for eternal life! No, that's kinda blasphemy."

We crossed the fast flowing muddy river with ease. Although I was slightly panicked at first when the current pulled me under, I got over it and swam both above and underwater until I sensed I was in shallower water and could stand. I saw Deedra on the bank already wringing her hair and sweatshirt out, cursing.

"Good night for a swim, eh Deedra?"

"Fu-u-uck. I guess. Now we have to walk back sopping wet.

Plus, we gotta hurry. Curse these short summer nights."

We crossed through a thicket of cottonwood trees and finally made it to more open, but hillier sagebrush, yucca, and cactus filled land.

Not far from Deedra's, we stopped and caught our breath. "We're about a half mile from the place," she said breathing while hunched over. "There's some deer over there. You wanna drink one?"

"Not really. At least not now anyways," I said. That was an odd question. "Just curious, is it good?"

"Me neither, and no. It's not that good, but potable. I just wanted you to know we could drink one. But that would ruin what we have. It's against that in the Bible too you know, drinking animals."

"I suppose it would be. Drinking humans is probably included, too."

"Yes. Leviticus chapter 7 and verses 27 and 28 read: 'Moreover you shall not eat any blood in any of your dwellings, whether of bird or beast.' And the next verse; 'Whoever eats any blood, that person shall be cut off from his people.'"

I seriously thought about that. I said, "You know your scriptures. I guess that means we're cut off then."

"That we are cut off. I remember things that catch my ear, or may affect me later on. But..." she took a deep breath, "what can we do besides cease existing?"

I had no answer for that. She kissed me lightly on the lips, and I saw hope in her eyes that was probably long neglected. Us being together was her answer, and she no longer had to cease existing. We held hands and languidly strolled the rest of the way.

Chapter 11—Crazy Content

THE EVENING OF OUR DEPARTURE came with the little extravagance as I'd insisted. It's not that no one would miss me, but I was leaving on a caprice and convinced my friends I was just sort of going on an extended vacation. Nothing some of them hadn't done before. So when I got to my house, Cedric, Ray, Tito, and Eric were there. It was the usual gang aside from our other hardcore friend currently in the military. Ray and Eric had a night off from work; as restaurant workers they always got non-weekend days off.

They were a bit faded and a little more emotional then I wanted them to be. We said our normal inside jokes as I packed up and left. They were my brothers, as I had no other relatives. We'd be all right. It wasn't like when our other good friend along with a couple others we knew left to the Army and Marines the year prior and we partied every day for the whole summer. Actually, Cedric was also going to the Army in a while. My friends felt as I did, that I needed to stay low and out of sight for a bit, especially after they saw the newspapers. Eric was concerned if I was still going to go to college or not. I told him I'd have to unfortunately put that on hold, but I'd have more time to practice my art where I was going.

I am a complete news junkie. I even subscribed to like three news magazines. Not being able to resist, I scanned the newspapers quickly and discovered that the guy I'd murdered was from Mexico, and the girl was from Phoenix, though they had indeed picked up the car in California. The car had been broken into and was stripped of everything of value as well. They had little leads other than they had hauled in some poor bastards for questioning that lived in the vicinity of where the guy got shot. I really hoped they let them go by then, but then again they were technically being held on separate drug possession and paraphernalia charges. Wrong place and wrong time for them I guess, but everyone eventually gets caught one way or another when dealing with that vice. A retirement home for the big timers is usually a federal prison cell. Hardly anyone ever seems to 'get in and get out.'

I had only one duffle bag with a few of my favorite clothing articles, and a regular backpack with notebooks. I was packing light, but I'd go shopping when I got to Seattle.

We juiced the car up and hit the road following the upstream road route of the Yellowstone River, jamming Tom Petty's, "Running Down a Dream" and then Tracy Chapman's "Fast Car." We also listened to some of Deedra's chick music including No Doubt, Sheryl Crow, and The Cranberries.

I'd driven up that road numerous times before with my best friend. Although I realized his death was continually eating me up on the inside, neither me nor my friends seriously discussed what his death meant to us aside from our 'what a good person he was' and memory talks. I felt I'd cheated Deedra by not telling her this information yet.

It was my private business, but I still never told her why I had slowly started drifting into my gradual depression that had me caring less about life, although I was determined to do just the opposite as Drew would've wanted me to do. It was honorable to mourn someone, but not at the expense of the present and future as I'd been doing. I felt abandoned, and was still angry regardless of what his supposed 'time to go' was.

"I have this friend, Deedra..." I looked out the

window to notice half of a deer that was probably mauled by a semi-truck. "Deer burger! Can you sense if there are deer?"

"Just with my eyes."

"I thought you could read their minds, man. Kidding. The Crazy Mountains are coming up. I'm not trying to change the subject, I'm getting to it. You ever been by the Crazies before?"

"A few times. On my way in and so forth." "What do you know about them?"

"They do look crazy, and handsome, and they are on the other side of the river on the way to Livingston. Sign just said that's about an hour from here. Well, less 'cause I'll be driving fast."

"That's right. Those mountains have the sharpest, most jagged, and landslide filled peaks ever, and they're right down from maybe windiest town in the U.S., Livingston; hence all those windmills that town used to have. They should put some more up, they're cool. They said it was too windy for those windmills! That's why they're gone, I think. Anyway, the Crazies are sacred to the Crow Indians, as they hold great power. Not even the most feared of all mid-18th century northwest Indians, the Blackfeet, went into those mountains to follow the Crow. The last Crow Chief, Chief Plenty Coup, had his great vision there. The wind whips through those mountains, especially way at the top, so it feels like it's trying to push you off, and howls, it's—"

"Crazy."

"I was thinking of the more clichéd 'majestic,' but thank you. Anyway, I had this friend who I'd always go camping with and he was my best bro. Did you catch any of him when you mind probed me before you, uh, killed me?"

"Just a little bit. Not much though. Honest."

"It doesn't matter, as long as you're familiar. Okay, so we like want to go cross-country skiing in this area because there's always a lot of snow. We could have gone to any place but no, we want to go the Crazy Mountains and camp in the dead of winter. What kind of idiotic plan was that?"

"I don't know, but it sounds adventurous."

"Adventurous, but still idiotic. A little background on Andrew though. We all called him Drew. And, uh, we were friends since we were real young, since we were six or something. He was a year older and a grade ahead of me, but that didn't matter. His dad used to take us fishing and hiking all over to a lot of mountain lakes, Montana stuff anyway. When he got his driver's license at fifteen we started doing that same stuff on our own whenever we could. I'm not surprised that his dad let him do those things on his own, as he'd always been very responsible for his age. We always tried going to places that we thought no one would've gone to or thought of going. Just pick out random obscure mountain peaks in the distance and go and hike up them just because it was hard, it felt beautiful, and we could. We'd feel sorry for those who only lived in cities all of their lives and never got to see the world from the vantages we did, or breathed that air. Gosh, I could write a poem right now, but I'll spare you! We have a lot of stories together.

"So we drive in as far as we could without getting stuck towards the base of the mountains early one morning. We have our backpacks, supplies, a tent, and a ton of Sterno. Sterno is that purple gel stuff in a can that burns..."

"I know what it is."

"Good. Anyway, we're breezing and freezing and skiing along, it's sort of nice out, and we had this rifle with us just in case. I guess there are wolverines around there, probably mountain lions, too, But, fuck it just started getting hella cold. I mean like cold cold, 20 below zero cold, but even colder than that once the wind started picking up heavy. We thought we were halfway close to our destination and had the wind to our backs, so that sorta helped, but we seriously thought about turning around until we turned around facing into that same wind. I'm guesstimating our destination must've been at least 15 miles. Geez, we must've been in good shape. We keep going and going at the base of the mountain, and we want to turn around and go home it's so friggin cold, so we stop and discuss it.

"Of course we're both being tough guys, but we do have common sense enough to know that one could easily freeze to death just by merely standing there. What we reasoned though is that we didn't want to go back into the wind however far we just came, as that would probably literally kill us off even though it was mostly downhill. The same dreaded wind was also picking up even more. We decided we had to keep going and get into the selected area and there we'd have suitable wind protection to set up the tent, and then we'd throw some snow on it for insulation. Igloo theory. It was only like a couple miles or so, maybe less, before we could turn into the gorge we wanted to go into. So it was settled.

"I said, 'It's all right, we'll start a fire, plus I got Sterno.' "'How many Sternos?' Drew goes.

"'5 of 'em,' I said. "They're kind of big ones, too."

"He just starts laughing, 'Shit dude! What the hell on Earth possessed you to buy five of those things, much less stuff five of them in your backpack?' He just thought it was the funniest thing ever, me having all those pretty big Sterno cans. Then he goes, 'But that's pretty cool though. I got some, too.'

"I go, 'How many then?' "Him, '6 of 'em!'

"We both started laughing our heads off for some reason. Just the thought of having that much of that stuff between us set us off. There was a sale on them, and I guess we both went to the same store. Maybe it was the cold or something getting to us, and I think that's why we kept laughing. I think that's it. But yeah, we made it and camped out for the night."

Deedra said, "It is funny though. How was the camp out?"

"Oh, it sucked, dude! But no, it could've been worse. We could've died or been frostbitten or whatever. We found some firewood, ripped up some trees and kept a good fire going, ate our beans and hotdogs and junk, then at night burned our Sterno inside the tent while boiling more snow to drink. Plus, our whiskey. I also had some propane thing for the breakfast. I think that stuff saved our life though, or at the very least kept our toes from being frostbitten. We kept yelling, 'Stoi- no!' for no apparent reason. It was just...something to say that never got old when it's so cold that the cold in itself becomes a joke. Plus, we were continually smoking the peace pipe in appreciation of the Great Spirit."

"Right on. How did you handle the weather otherwise?"

"We're Montanans. We're tough. Drew grew up in a house heated by firewood only. But it was like loud and scary in that canyon or gorge we were in. That wind had the weirdest howl. It was like spirits were speaking to us, plus at night it got really trippy. As soon as we'd turn out the flashlight, the weirdest shrieking that sounded humanlike would make us freak out. Real life surround sound horror theater or something. You'd swear you could make out words sometimes when you concentrated, so you tried to kind of ignore it, but you never could because it would interrupt your thoughts and conversation and you'd have to stop and respect it. Then you'd hear those periodic rock-slides and wonder if an avalanche was going to come down on you. I don't think we had any control over that, aside from the reasonable place we camped didn't look like it was under any huge drifts. You never knew though.

"But the thing that made the howling sounds of the wind so creepy was that we both knew of the story of the

'Crazy Lady' who lived in those mountains whom maybe the mountains were named for. Theory goes, she's said to have lived there after straying from a wagon train expedition or whatever, or maybe after her family was killed by Indians in front of her, and she went crazy probably due to those same crazy noises we were hearing. Personally, I think her family tried to settle there and the Indians killed them all off except her. These particular howls we kept hearing sounded like someone was in agony. The area is serene at times on the backside, but the wind hardly lets up from where we can see the mountains along this highway. I read my little Gideon's New Testament Bible that night."

"Maybe the Crazy Lady was haunting you," Deedra said.

"We thought that, too. Or maybe it was her dead family's ghosts. We figured it was maybe spirits, like I said, the Crow Indians know those mountains possess great power. There are paranormal vibes there for certain. The damned stoi-no saved us though! But the trippiest thing was when we thought we heard footsteps. It was not like the animal-quick-steps of four legs, but a steady scrunch, scrunch, scrunch. Now that was trippy. We thought it was a Little Person."

"A 'Little Person?' I've sort of heard of that, but I don't know exactly what that is. You don't mean a dwarf, do you?"

"Little People are a Native American legend. But they are like little dwarf-like people, even smaller, and they like to play tricks and live in select mountains and such. They're strong too, and are said to possess supernatural powers. Most Indians, not the Crow, think they're bad news, and they have an almost demonic reputation. Whether that's deserved or not I don't know. They're supposed to be helpful to Crow Indians though, otherwise you don't want to see one, I guess. Drew was the one who spooked me out about them that night. We heard the footsteps, turned out the lights, then when we heard the footsteps again after a short bit. We knew weren't tripping. He turns the light back on, and they stop. This is when the wind died down briefly.

"Dude whispers, 'Maybe it's a Little Person. My dad saw one last year when he went hunting in the Pryor Mountains.' The Pryors are those mountains just south of the house where we were staying, you know?"

"I know them," Deedra said.

"Yeah. So dude said, 'He came up over a ridge and he saw a Little Person easily knock over a pretty big tree just by pushing it—roots and all! Then he watched him drag it off. My Dad doesn't know how to lie. Then when he went the opposite direction, he felt like he was being followed, and saw the Little Person spying on him from a ridge, so he left a pack of cigarettes just to please him. Then the Little Person left him alone. I guess they like smoke like Hobbits, so go out there and leave him some bud. He probably smelled it and wants smoke, unless you want to invite him in the tent! They're usually quite nice. I don't know if he'll speak English though. Maybe Crow.'

"I was like, 'No way, dude! You scare the shit of me with that story, now want me to go out there and invite him in? You fucking do it! You know some Crow language.'

"He did, and said he left it on the log we were sitting on by our smoldering camp fire. He had the gun out when he did it too, though he wouldn't have shot a Little Person just because they were little and creepy. That's just discriminatory. But it did sound like two feet walking, the noise we heard. It was snowing hard, and in the morning we could find no tracks because of that, but the bud was gone even though Drew said he made sure it was secure and whatnot."

"That's way trippy, dude."

"Yeah, after that night I knew why the Blackfeet never ventured into those mountains."

I laughed and looked again towards the aforementioned mountains. I could see them way better now with their eerie, super jagged, black and blue moonlit silhouette poking holes in the atmosphere and clouds. The car rocked a bit in a strong gust of wind.

"God, I miss him, man. That's who I wanted to tell you about." I shed a nostalgic tear. I knew it was a bloody tear, but I suppressed that fact when I wiped it. I'd silently cried for him every day since his death, and I was truthfully never ashamed of it, but I generally did it alone. "I...don't why I never even mentioned him to you before."

Deedra looked towards me and shook her head. "You didn't even have to tell me, and I feel cool and trusted that you did. It takes time for something like that to heal."

"I had people to talk to, and we'd mention him and all, but you know, it's just 'not the dude thing to talk about.' Anyway, it was a bad feeling I had when he died, and I never cared tried caring about it for a long while. You try to take a hard line philosophical understanding of, 'That's life's certainty: death.' But it still sucks, you know? We'd always have these long, deep philosophical conversations, too. I wasn't afraid to say anything to him. If he hadn't died and it had been somebody else close to us who'd died, I would've been able to spill my guts to him. Put it that way. We were brothers in every sense, and his family took me in as that. After his funeral his parents wanted me to leave to Jackson Hole, Wyoming with them, and dude's little sister, around the Grand Teton Mountain Range. A lot of rich and famous people stay around there. It's really magnificent area. They weren't leaving our town because their son died and they wanted to start over, they were leaving because that's where they had always wanted to live when they retired. I guess they had the chance to sort of retire early, and they had put the down payment on the house already. So they must've been wealthier than they seemed, or just been ultra-penny pinching so they could do just that. They prolly had life insurance for everyone in their family, too.

"I didn't want to go with them. I felt bad telling 'em that. I'd just moved in with Drew to that house we rented together, you know, the same one me and Eric are in, and I felt like they wanted me close to remember their boy that much more. Maybe Jackson Hole would have been best for me, but I'd never lived there, much less knew what I'd do when I got there for work or school or whatever. I just wanted to hole up, but not in Jackson if you get my pun. Some of his posters were still in his room but I gave some of his photos and stuff back to his mom and all. I just couldn't stand seeing the hurt in her eyes every time she looked at me, and it got tough just being around them, as bad as that sounds, even though I wanted to comfort them whenever possible. I also needed some alone time. I needed to mourn in my own way."

Deedra said, "So you just 'holed-up,' as you put it?"

"Yeah. I really did," I said after briefly pondering my days in the months that followed his death. "I even dumped the girl I was with. She was all right, and was rightfully offended I pushed her away so quickly like a jerk. It was by every means my fault we broke-up, but that was under...extenuating circumstances. Who knows if would've lasted anyway. Maybe, maybe not. We were mostly in lust. She was an artist, too."

"I read her in you. I didn't know she was an artist though." "Oh," I said feeling better. "Just asking, but were you ever jealous of Cassie that one night?"

Deedra grinned, shook her head, and then punched me hard on the arm. "Hell yes, I hate you for that, you little slut! And then you're such a womanizer for going with me so soon after."

I laughed.

"Then again," she said, "I realize you hadn't been laid in a long while, and you had other things on your mind.

Crazy kids these days.

Gotta let you 'bust a nut' one last time. But yeah, I'm still jealous of her and Emily too, even though I said I wouldn't be."

"Well, for that I apologize."

"Don't. I try not to be...controlling or whatever, but I am of course only female and somewhat mammalian."

"Right. 'Somewhat mammalian.'"

We passed the Crazy Mountains and came in sight of new mountain ranges. Deedra prodded me to tell her more stories about Drew. It felt good just to talk about him. I started remembering our times together as a time to cherish instead of a time to solely grieve for. It's not that me and my other friends had never done the same thing, but with Deedra it was different. It was almost as if she listened to me in a nurturing way, and I in no way resented it. I needed it. I was her baby that she could never have in a sense, as she'd told me the previous night.

I thought of the poem I'd recited to her, about sharing the beauty of life together like a painting. Deedra knew I was far from perfect, had done terrible things, hurt deep inside, but she wouldn't have it any other way as it was all just an accumulation of what made me.

It started raining an hour later as we drove on new mountains along the Continental Divide. Going up a steep hill, I listened intently to the steadily increasing and replenishing rhythm of drops on the car roof as the scenery around us became less transparent, making me lethargic. I forgot about all of the ordeals behind me, and if there were any ahead. For once in a long while, I was mostly certain about where I wanted to be in life, and whatever that included, I was looking right at her. I laid my head on Deedra's shoulder, and she kissed me on the hair. I closed my eyes and slept.

Moonrise Falling: A Modern Gothic Tale

Chapter 12—Buckshot Elvis

I AWOKE as we entered the college town of Missoula, Montana, and guessed we had about an hour before dawn. It was a natural and essential sense that I'd further developed, knowing the coming of the dawn, but I also knew we had an hour just by the fact that I'd stayed up until then plenty of times before. You could sense it in the air as the stars dimmed away.

Deedra went to a decent hotel, and insisted that I come in with her to pay for the room. She'd do all the talking.

At the reception desk was a bored looking young lady playing solitaire on her computer while also reading. She smiled at us as we approached, looking almost relieved she actually had a customer at that hour. "Hello. What can I do for you?"

"We need a room," Deedra said.

She typed. "Single bed? You two a couple?"

"Yup," Deedra answered. "Just married. We're on our way to our honeymoon, aren't we, dear?"

I barely realized she was talking to me, as I was gawking at a fish tank and all of the colorful fish. Whoa...

"Uh, yeah!...'dear,'" I said. "Well, congratulations, then!"

I paid the cost, and Deedra gave the clerk an extra 50 dollars on the condition that we were not to be disturbed under any circumstances, as we were very tired or something. Then she whispered to the clerk and they both started giggling.

It got me suspicious in a friendly way. I read the

clerk's mind, as she was gazing our way with lusty eyes. 'I would too, lucky girl,' she was thinking.

Deedra grabbed my arse and goosed me, then my hand, and we walked to our room as she twirled the car key chain around on her opposite hand.

"What did you say to her? That clerk." "Oh, nothing, 'Dear-y.'"

"You said something. Tell me, please."

"Yeah, I did. I told her we also didn't want to be disturbed under any circumstance, because I was going to make you my bitch today."

"Shut up, dude," I said. "You did *not* say that. How...just lewd."

"I did!"

"Well then...Whatever, dude!" I mock backhand slapped her. "I guess that is funny though; honeymoon and then what just you said. Sort of. Hah! Damn, you got me."

She had a cool sense of humor.

We went into our room and I hopped over on the bed. "So...you gonna do what you said to that desk person, huh?"

"We could," Deedra nodded her head and grinned. "That was payback for fucking Emily under my roof, you whore."

"Some other time we'll get crazy. No time really now, and besides...I have a headache, honey." I laughed and flipped on the television. "That was good though, at least she won't bother us now, and probably make it real clear to the workers not to bother us."

"She probably wanted to join us, dude. See that sex novel book she had off to the side? A.N....something that started with an 'R.'"

"Nuh uh, never saw it. I think I know what book you're talking about. My ex used to have those. Very sexually graphic books with ideas to enhance your sexual pleasure or pain or one in the same. I highly recommend them to the school board for the curious adolescents in health class. Hah hah!"

"What is it with you artist types and writers?" she said as she made sure the curtains were closed. "A higher percentage of y'all's sexual habits usually seem or want to be so...outlandish and deviant. Why?"

I was flipping through channels trying to find a good movie. Deedra hopped on the bed next to me, slid her hands down the front of my pants, and said, "Well?" in a kidding, overbearing tone.

"I was thinking about it. Are we all like kinky, you mean? I'm not terribly experienced, but way more so in some ways than most my age, but yeah...I like it 'outlandish,' you could say."

"I'm not stereotyping all of you creative types, but they're probably more prone to being kinky," she said. "It's not like a mental disease though, so no need to feel ashamed or anything. I'm just curious as to the 'why.'"

"I do feel ashamed. I feel there must be something terribly wrong with me, and I'm mentally inadequate and morally deficient for not preferring the missionary only position for the sole purpose of procreation only, and only then when you're married and both virgins. Heh. To answer your question, I guess creative minds like to be creative in the sack. We get off as much on the mental stimulation as much as we do the actual fucking. Now there's a lovely poem. Sorry, I mean 'making love.'"

"I'm curious too, I never got to do anything penetrating and physical really 'cept with you, and that one lesbo girl."

"Oh, that is good. Details!"

"You...tease me. But yeah, I'd like to fool around a bit more whenever we get settled in. That okay with you?"

"Hmm, let me think. Beautiful chick wants to get crazy and perhaps kinky with me and um...no. I refuse to do it, for I'm like totally flaming-ly gay, girlfriend. I'm a 'flailor' named Gaylor who loves men in sailor outfits.

Hell yeah, I'll do it! But only if you dress up like an 80's biker with chaps and wear a fake bushy mustache and leather harness. Joking! That look on your face right now!—priceless. Hey, where we sleeping anyway?"

"You're gay acting was too convincing! Under the bed. No, wait! Check that: closet."

"Closet? I was just kidding about being gay, you don't have to literally put me back in," I said. I checked it. "Whoa, it's pretty big. But if we fool around, we gotta get married or it's a sin."

"Really? I mean, think we can get married somewhere?"

"Elvis impersonator in Vegas would do it. You serious? All we need is an I.D., right?"

"Yeah, it'd be cool. But then again, it's best we avoid being on any type of new paper from now on if possible. But, um...throw the top blanket in the closet, and spread it out and such so we have something to lay on. We'll sleep together in that closet."

"Cool."

"Yeah dude, just 'cool.' Just totally and super neat-o couple of cool hepcats!"

We geekily cuddled and petted each other amongst other things until the sun came up before retiring to our overpriced closet sleeping quarters for the day.

Chapter 13—Sunny Elixir

DEEDRA CONTINUALLY DROVE in and around the 100 mph range out of Missoula jamming some country music station and rarely slowed except for when we passed a highway patrol radar checkpoint. I doubted there'd be any good country music stations in Seattle, so I had to get my last country boy fixes in. I offered to drive, but Deedra said it was hard to find where we were going and we had to get there in a hurry. Our route took us deeper into northwest Montana, near Idaho and Canada. The country was a plush carpet of green pine trees providing cover for the stout mountains, numerous creeks and streams, and trout-filled rivers. We were very close to the preternaturally beautiful Glacier Park area, which I liked to call—and wasn't alone in calling—'God's Paintbrush.'

Make no mistake though, the postcard perfect Glacier area was as rough as it was beautiful, and only the hardiest of mountain men had been able to survive it back in the day. Many of them died as a result of Blackfeet Indian attacks. The Blackfeet had despised the American trappers for encroaching, and for the fact that they desecrated and nearly decimated the local beaver population for the in-demand pelts. Beavers were sacred animals to that tribe that were instrumental to their creation of the earth story. That's not to mention the sizable ultra-aggressive grizzly bear population that lived in the area and made quick work of more than a few trappers and settlers.

Deedra said she had something really awesome to see

that I'd truly appreciate.

We parked our car out of sight on a secluded fenced up road that looked like it hadn't been used in years judging by the tall grass growing wildly all over it. Most people wouldn't have noticed it even in daylight. I can't describe the location fully for reasons to come, but Deedra did have a plan. We stood on perhaps the only vantage point around, as the thick timberline would obstruct one's vision anywhere else. She put her hair in a ponytail, and put on a baseball cap she got out of the trunk. I liked a girl in a hat. She said in regards to my own cap, "I wouldn't lose your hat during the next few days. You'll need it. You want to go camping?"

"Well, yeah," I said. "I'd never lose my hat. I always have to have one when I'm out here. Good for rain, sun, everything. As for camping? Of course. I've been cooped up in my little house for a long while, so I have serious cabin fever, yo."

"I bet. We got to do a lot of hiking, dude. Good for the sun, eh?

I'll have to remember that."

"It is. How far we going?" "Until dusk. See that ridge?"

I looked at where she was pointing in the east, a faint mound that I knew to be a fairly sizable mountain loomed. "Damn. That's like 20 miles."

"Yeah, there. I thought you liked hiking."

"Not in the dark...not straight through the creepy woods with all the bears, and the mean moose, and, and...the angry rabid chipmunks chippering at me."

"Well, you won't like this then, either. Put your senses on full alert. Just trust me in that respect, follow, and try to keep close. On second thought, you lead the way. You're probably better at traversing this territory and terrain than I am."

"Yeah, right. More foolish, you mean. Well, just point the way or yell at me if I start drifting the wrong direction. But I think I know where I'm going. The stars will guide me. Or The Force. I won't even be able to see stars in this forest, and we may end up walking in circles. But seriously just watch the moss on trees and you usually don't need a compass."

"I know."

"It annoys me to no end in movies when a person has a supposed hint of survival skills—cough Blair Witch cough—does not know that moss thing or have the sense to follow a bleeding creek. Northeast, we go!"

I walked into the abysmally dark woods, and mentally prepared myself for the task. I wasn't intimidated, but quickly found out it was going to be difficult when I started running. The flat part of the forest wasn't so bad as we trudged along at a powerfully fast pace, and it was mostly the large trees we had to watch out for. My natural night vision, which seemed to reflect the moon and starlight, wasn't as strong. It was just too thick of a forest, and most treetops reached up high and blocked any incoming light. Try running at full speed through dense woods at night with no light, and like an unlucky downhill skier you'll soon taste tree bark. I darted as best I could, however, mostly high stepping around shrubs and avoiding thickets of trees, especially near creeks. Going up the base of mountains was the worst as the shrubs thickened and grabbed at our feet. Deedra and I both tripped at least a few times, and 'shouldered' a few trees hard as well, like slalom racers. But those big ski poles did not give much leeway and reminded us why we had to be on full alert when we went extra fast, even through seemingly less thick areas.

Fortunately, I did feel an extra guidance, a sort of radar. It was what Deedra probably meant by 'full alert.' We were part mammalian, and bats had radar, and dolphins had sonar, so it was almost only natural that we'd partially obtained this radar/sonar/whatever trick. It gave me extra time to react. It was mostly my feet that

I had to worry about. Tripping sucked, and we'd spill hard because we were going so fast. Deedra actually banged her head into one tree really hard after tripping, and we had to wait a minute while she regained her marbles and I made sure she was fit to go again. It was funny, yet it wasn't. So I'd yell out warnings as well if a tree just seemed to pop out. Most of the time we kept a hand forward to shield and block smaller hanging tree limbs and branches.

Deedra said it was necessary that we move fast, however, otherwise we'd have to dig ourselves graves and lay there for the day.

"That's probably why you're fingernails sort of look like shiny 'press-ons,'" she said, helping me up after I fell. We caught our breath. "It's no big deal really, burying yourself. It's just a bit tricky is all. It's an essential thing to learn anyway. The hat's perfect to cover your face when you have to do it."

I picked up the pace even more when I finally saw an open rocky ridge with stars behind it seeping through the gauntlet of forest. After I busted out of the woods, I boulder hopped to the top of the ridge. Boulder hop hiking was what I was more accustomed to from the higher elevation mountains not to far from my hometown. Deedra was soon next to me.

"Good timing so far," she said as she caught her breath. "You kill me."

"Well, I'm not going to bury myself alive tonight. It's not a skill I'm eager to learn. That's where we're going, right?" I said, and pointed to the next mountain over. We had to go down a valley, then come back up a steep mountainside. "You leading now?"

"Yeah, I gotta remember where I'm going specifically. Don't worry, I can't draw a map of it, but I know where I'm going by...whatever landmarks and whatnot." "I know how that is."

On the bottom of the valley was a creek, so I stopped

and soaked my head in it. "I'm sweating dude, hold up," I said.

"Blood-droplet sweat."

"Don't remind me." I poured water over my neck, looked at the sky, got a mouthful of water, rinsed it, and spit. I dunked my head in again. Fresh. Deedra did the same. "We're going to make it easily, right? That's the mountain right there?"

"Oh yeah, we're like there, dude. It's just like up this steep hill." "You call that rockslide infested, 5,000 feet up, boulder field of a mountainside a 'hill?' I'm burnt out. I need some nourishment."

"See why we drank Angela? She helps."

After carefully climbing the last grueling mountain, we reached the very top of the mountain's highest peak after a bit of Spider Man scaling.

She walked with her arms off to the side as if it were helping her keep her balance right along the narrow, ridgeline peak. It'd been a scorcher of a summer so far, but there were still snow banks all around. It was pretty dangerous, and I was cautious. I wasn't afraid of heights or anything, just the sudden landing from the 500 foot or higher drop-off on the other side. The ridge we were on connected to the other mountain, creating a v-shaped valley just below. "It's just over there," Deedra said. "We're staying almost right under where we stand. Well, about 200 yards more to get down."

I looked over the precipice and saw nothing but a sharp drop-off. "What is it, a cave down there? We're going to be bat cave people?"

"Yup. But there are no bats."

We were almost at the base of the 'v' and Deedra said excitedly, "That's it," and proudly pointed down below her.

I looked, and was quite simply astonished at what was on the bottom of the 30 foot or so high ledge we were standing on. It was a Medicine Wheel, a symbol from the

Native Americans that many thought represented a calendar of sorts, or a shrine of great deeds by someone or some people. Maybe either or, depending on the individual wheel.

This wheel was a circle of stones sitting on green grass about 10 feet in diameter, and had stone 'beams' protruding from it that were connected by a larger circle. It looked like a little kid's sun drawing with beams, only it was done carefully and intricately with rocks.

Deedra later told me it was specifically a 'type six' Medicine Wheel, meaning the design had eight 'spokes,' and the most elaborate of these 'spokes' faced southwest. It was a distinctive, breathtaking find, and the most western Medicine Wheel I knew of. 'Medicine' was just the word whites used to define Native powers and practices they couldn't comprehend. How many centuries had it been there unnoticed by other men?

No one actually knew the exact North American Medicine Wheel's original significance, but I had a strong hunch for this particular one. Some of them, including a very famous one in northern Wyoming about 150 miles from where I grew up, lined up perfectly with the Summer Solstice, the longest day of the year. It was no coincidence. That one was odd, as it was just south of Montana, and all of the known Medicine Wheels were in northwest Montana (albeit little more east than we where we were) and Alberta, Canada, as well as further east in Saskatchewan. The Blackfeet Montana and Canadian lands had a few of these Medicine Wheels that dated from 2,000 years ago.

The Wyoming one was made perhaps as late as the late 17th century, and had 28 'spokes'—one for each of the 28 moon days in a lunar month. In addition, it also gave the Plains Indians directions for the sacred and grueling Sun Dance that the U.S. Government officially abolished in 1904. It's been brought back since, though.

"This is...this is...mind blowing," is all I could say to

Deedra as I saw that the 'spokes' were made from little white shiny rocks. I called them 'beams' though. It looked like someone had done a meticulous job all right, although a lot of the stones were sunken. "And you found this, right?"

Deedra pulled me close and squeezed my opposite shoulder. "I knew you'd like it."

"That I do."

"But I didn't find it, Joan did." "Does anyone else know about this?"

"No one that's alive, at least we presume. Let's go down there."

She suddenly hopped off of the ledge, and about made my heart stop in doing so, but landed cleanly on her feet as she touched the ground with her hand. "Come on!" she waved.

Lest I become scared, I didn't hesitate and aimed for a grassy looking spot below. The free fall was fun and I rolled after I landed. I carefully started studying the design. The specifically patterned lined white rocks made a glow in the moonlight. The most perplexing of these were two lines together that faced...

"Do these two face the western Solstice high point or whatever?" I asked.

"How am I supposed to know? I've never seen it in the day!

Kidding. But based on my calculations, I think they do." "Awesome. Say, when is the Summer Solstice?"

"Three days from now. Why, are you planning on celebrating it?"

"I know Natives do use that date for the Sun Dance, but do others celebrate it still?"

"Oh, they certainly do. Don't ask now, but we'll go to this celebration I've always wanted to hit."

"Apollonian celebration in three days? Celebrating the Sun God Apollos? Sounds pagan."

"Very. More like Apollyon celebration."

I didn't even know what that meant. Deedra rested her weary legs, and watched me do my own studies. It was marvelous to me. I could describe it forever, but let's just say I'd rather take a picture, and that I planned on doing just that the next time. I was surprised it was still so intact. I would've expected it to be continually covered by a snowbank, but I guess the little walls situated around it wouldn't have exactly shielded it from the Sun most of the day. Hence, the reason whoever put it right at this spot.

I looked eastwards, across the Rocky Mountains where the sunlight would be illuminating the area in less than an hour. This was the marrow of the world. I stared for a long while, just seeping it all in. Deedra soon joined me.

"What's the matter?" Deedra said.

"Just wish I could see the sunrise here," I said. "It's got me all sentimental!"

"I know, me too. Me too. This particular place makes you think hard about that."

"So you come here often I take it? Lucky."

"A couple times I did to get away. Nice night out. We're lucky because last time I was here it rained the whole time. But I still liked it."

"Damn, and you still hiked in the rain?"

"Well, I wasn't doing anything else! I have to come here to replenish my soul. This place is pure and unpolluted by modern man. It's been that way for a very long time. This very place was something special to someone, and now it is to me, and I hope it is to you, too. Promise me you'll never tell anyone about this place."

The thing was, I did have the urge to tell an archaeologist or friend about this place. I pushed that thought away. If it was found, it was found, and it wasn't mine to give away.

"I promise. But what about that cave?" "You and your studies. Let's go."

When I got to the cave I was excited to see a knoll of pebbles and grass in front of an entrance that was about five feet high and ten feet across. You wouldn't have been able to see the cave from a helicopter, and that would buy this area more time to be free of man if you excluded us.

"That's cool, innit?" Deedra said pointing to a pestle and mortar; that is a little baseball bat shaped rock used for mixing, and a stone bowl.

"Heck yes. This place is a living museum."

"There's red stuff in that bowl, too. Or a stain anyway. And look at the wall."

The wall had drawings of bison being hunted by men, as well as a Sun. Holy shit. This was too eerily good, and that in my opinion made it superior to the other Medicine Wheels in the scope of archaeological significance. I must've been dreaming. I almost felt selfish keeping this site to ourselves, but I had made a promise Deedra, and I was a man of my word. Besides, this place looked so cozy, and I didn't want a bunch of archaeologists digging the ground out all around the area, robbing it, and then have government officials telling me I couldn't go on the land anymore where perhaps my own ancestors once breathed and prayed. That's what they did. Forty years ago one could do private ceremonies on the Medicine Wheel in Wyoming, and now it seemed it was for tourists only, most of who could never appreciate or even begin to grasp its meaning.

I looked up to the right and saw that there was a slit going further into the mountain. It only looked like about a foot and a half high, and I walked over to take a closer look.

Deedra said, "That's where we're sleeping."

I'd almost forgotten about rest, although I don't know how I could've seeing as I was so physically tired. My brain was running too fast. "No way, dude. I can't even fit in there. Nuh, uh."

"Yeah you can. You can bury yourself if you want to, though, down in softer soil in the valley in the tree line. You better move fast, though. But the cave is better and cleaner."

I looked inside the black slit, and did seriously consider burying myself. I sat down, and patiently rested and waited for the last few moments until the sun came up. I wasn't going inside a crack in the rock with an entire mountaintop above me any longer than I had to. We were both too tired to say anything more as we scooted next to each other and held hands. All that mattered was we were there.

I imagined the last person who had used that mortar and pestle. I wondered if he had a family. I bet he was devoted, seeing as he made the cave paintings. I bet he was a good man.

Some figured it was the earliest of the Mayans who had made the first Medicine Wheels when they passed through on their way to South America, not extraterrestrials as some people thought. They just can't give Native people of the Americas any credit! Deedra was talking about Mayans and said they had a calendar more accurate than the one we used today that dated back to the origin of 3114 BCE, and they needed none of that leap year stuff. So many things to ponder.

"Ready?" Deedra said lazily. "I guess."

"Just follow me."

I watched her situate herself into the crack and start slithering herself like a snake further and further underneath the stone until she disappeared. I hopped up and copied her. Man, talk about being claustrophobic suddenly. I made it in until I was enveloped in complete darkness, went another body length, and started panicking and would've hyperventilated until I heard the soothing noise of water trickling. "Deedra, where are you?"

"A little further."

I hesitantly inched to the voice, and tried not think about the fact I couldn't turn on my back. *Dark. Nothingness.* There was hardness above and below me, although I noticed the ceiling getting a bit bigger. *The mountain's going to fall on me*, I panicked. I thought I was going to get stuck before Deedra lit a lighter. *Thank God.* She was close by, and it must've been dawn as I suddenly fell asleep.

Chapter 14—To the Clouds

I HAD TO GET OUT of that bloody hole.

I anxiously and laboriously started my 'worm squirm' to where I guessed the entrance was. Something grabbed my leg hard, jerked me back, growled crazily, and made me about cry. I swore and tried to kick it, but it said, "Chill!" and then laughed at me.

I really cursed Deedra for doing that. It wasn't very funny, but it was for her. She lit her lighter and told me the area above our heads got thinner, so it was better if I tried to crawl more towards our feet than our heads, because one time she went too high and couldn't crawl downwards very well once she hit the wall, and was above the crack. She had to do a 180 circle and it drove her nearly insane. It would've been hard to crawl downwards like that. Still, it was comforting hearing a voice during my crawl out of there at least, even if she told me a less than comforting story.

We got out of the cave not a moment too soon for my tastes, and Deedra asked if she could talk to me in seriously, as there was something that was bothering her. I of course said I'd oblige.

Overlooking the western ridge was the metaphorical painting I'd been looking for and I was fortunate to find it so early in my young life. The expansive Montana 'Big Sky State' dusk skyline was a vast watercolor painting that covered the mountain tops like a comforting violet blanket rimmed with the orange warmth of the set sun. It was enough to humble anyone and make them thankful just to be breathing. There was no hurry. This was life at its fullest and most complete. At full starry darkness we went and sat down in the softer grassy area near the Wheel, glad the weather was perfectly pleasant.

The erratically patterned small clouds gathered and grew denser perhaps only a few hundred feet above us on the mountaintop amidst the cool rejuvenating air, wandering with a continual purpose to help renew the life of the Earth. The stars that darted behind them and then reappeared like fireflies seemed close enough to touch. Besides us, the steady song of the wind swishing in the tree line below was the only noise.

"You don't...know me well, yet you've told me things about you that only you know," Deedra said as if she wanted to continue, but stopped.

"Yes?"

"I feel that you deserve to know all there is to know about me, since we're together like this. I've never told anyone before, not even Joan, though I think she somewhat knew the events. Not even psychologists, although they did drill me like the KGB. They even shocked me! Funny. I just put it away, I knew they wouldn't understand. They'd listen just to take notes, conclude what kind of med prescription they guessed I needed to dull my brain from it, and that would be that. I never wanted anyone to understand, I just wanted someone who cared to listen. That's all I asked for."

I was intrigued. Deedra was obviously revealing herself so I'd truly know where the young looking woman who I'd forever be linked with came from. I'd been waiting for her to do just that all the little yet seemingly infinite time I had known her, but I wasn't impatient. People need time. She'd told me countless stories, but never her story.

"I wanted someone to listen. No one seemed right. I told it out loud once before, here at this same spot. I told God, then I asked him why he never heard me. I was just a little girl. My mom...the last time I saw her, she..."

Deedra looked at her fingernails, then mine, as if to distract herself, and sighed uncomfortably. I moved in close and put my arm around her. She put her head down and her hair fell over her face. I moved it with a sweeping gesture and she looked at me, scared. Her eyes were fully misted over and red. "I'm sorry," she sobbed.

I could've cried for her as I saw the little girl she spoke of in her remembering her mother. I fought the urge, and smiled at her. "It's okay. You must let it go." I gave her a rub on the shoulder. "This is like your favorite spot, remember? There's only me here, you're comfortable. Do it for that little girl, for her, please. You'll feel better."

"Hey," I gave her a hug and kissed her on the cheek. I smiled to her. "I'm a good listener."

A certain glint came to be in her eye that only those with a love of life possess. "I know you are," she said.

I backed away, content to listen. "What do you remember of her?"

"You're right," she said, and pulled her hair back behind her shoulders. "She taught me how to read. I had just turned four. I could read some. Hardly remember having to learn the ABC song, just knew that I always knew it.

"Letter recognition, she must have drilled that into me. How the hell do you teach a kid that? Who knows? I guess it was always just Mom and me though. She must've been really bored to teach me how to read. She would make me repeat every letter in a word. Spell it out, then point to each letter on her little hand-made chart. H-A-N-D, hand. She'd make me sound out the letters. I caught on easy enough, I guess. Do it for everything.

"B-E-D, bed. Drill it. Colors helped me recognize, although I think I knew how to spell them before I knew what they were! I caught on before whatever happened.

"That's when we went to that church. The church people said 'hello,' and even gave me a donut and juice.

They were really nice. We drove away and my mom was different."

Deedra pulled off her ever-present hooded sweatshirt and laid it down as a pillow. She laid back, closed her eyes, and let out a deep breath, and spoke again as if she'd played it in her head a thousand times.

"We packed our stuff, or my stuff, when we got home to our motel room. I started folding her clothes to put in her bag, but she shook her head and said, 'No.' I was used to moving and helping her pack. We did it together.

"This time was different, only my bag was packed. Mom sat at the table, writing something in her notebook. I wanted to read it, but she said it was only a poem and we'd read it together later.

"So, we hopped in our little beat-up car and drove off. She was crying for some time after that. I didn't like it, obviously, being on a back road somewhere with my mom crying. 'No Mommy,' I told her.

"'I'm sorry," she said.

"'No more crying,' I said. 'Where are we going?'

"'We're going to the nice people's house from the church.'

"'Are we staying there, Mommy?'

"'Yes, we are, darling. But they're going to give you food, something to eat, okay?'

"Are you eating?"

Deedra opened her eyes. "Food was a problem for her, I remember. She'd always feed me, hardly herself. Poor, we were."

She closed her eyes again and continued. "Mom said, 'I have to leave you, babe. I have to go see your Daddy.'

"I don't have a daddy anymore, Mommy. You said.'

"'You do, hon. Daddy is in Heaven, now. Daddy lives in the clouds. We will all be in the clouds someday, a family.'

"That was a weird concept at four, someone in the clouds. My mom started crying to herself again.

"'Clouds. C-L-O-W-D. Cloud... s-s-s. S.'

"C-L-O-*U*-D-S, darling.'

"She gave me a one-armed hug. She'd pulled over by then, and off to the right I saw a farmhouse with a real red barn and other ranch stuff.

"I noticed Mom had regained some of her composure, or at least she was not crying and had dried her eyes. She gave me a warming smile and touched my cheek.

"'Listen, Deedra,' she was serious. 'I must leave you here with these nice people. They'll take care of you awhile, okay? Don't be afraid. Mommy has to leave for a bit.'

"'To the clouds, Mommy?'

"A flood of guilty sadness rolled over her face. 'No, Deedra, I don't know. But I can't take care of you anymore. You must understand.'

"Of course I could never understand, and nor did she expect me to.

"'I'm so sorry Deedra,' she choked. 'It's the best thing I can do for you. Please forgive me.'

"C-L-O-U-D-S, Mommy. I will get it right for you. I was wrong, that is all.'

"She had started to pull in towards the driveway and through the gate, but she hit the brakes. 'No, Deedra. You're not wrong. It's me.' She was very stern and held my face. 'You must never, ever think that you were wrong! You are not wrong. Nobody is wrong. It's just the way it is, understood?'

"My heart knew we were over then, but I still tried to be a big girl for my mother.

"'Okay, mommy, understood.'

"She tousled my hair, leaned back, and put her hands together as if she was praying, and breathed heavy once. I did the same. I prayed my fate would be well, since I knew it would never be the same life. I felt my soul rise above my body for the last few feet of the long driveway as the car finally drifted along. My mother stopped and waited for a minute in silence. The hefty woman that gave me the donut earlier at the church approached. I saw my body through the car's windshield. My eyes were closed. I had noticed from my new view of me that my mother had put on my prettiest flower dress that day. 'D-E-A-D, dead,' I thought of the little girl with the closed eyes and limp body. "Mother and the hefty woman were talking to that little girl. 'Wake up!' they said. They shook her. 'Deedra—'

"I climbed back into her and said, 'Yes, Mommy?'

"She sat me down on the prairie grass and crouched to me eye level. 'Deedra, this is where you will live now, okay? Your new house! You've always wanted a house, haven't you?'

"'You're leaving me.'

"She looked at the other woman, then me. The tears I had still not grown used to came back to life in her. 'Only for a while.'

"But even at that early age, I knew it would not be only for a while; that I sensed in her eyes. She hugged me for the last time.

"'Remember, I'll always love you. We'll meet again someday, I promise. Please forgive me, little Deedra, please.'

"'It's okay, Mommy. I love you.' "'I love you too, darling.'

"She kissed me on the lips, got up, and walked back to the car. The big church lady grabbed my hand to comfort me. I think it worked.

I saw my mom at the end of the long driveway one last time. I could barely see her, but she blew a kiss and pointed up—to the clouds.

"Then that little word that happens to everything but the mountains and sky came to mind—gone."

Chapter 15—Dead Flowers

SOMEONE WAS FINALLY REALLY LISTENING.

I waited a few moments for what she'd told me to sink in. That was perhaps the paramount moment in her life. What went on in her life from that point would probably somehow always link back to that moment in time. She looked at me and her eyes were serene, despite the memory.

"Then what?" I asked. "I'm sorry!"

"No, I was rude. Take your time."

"All right," she sat up again. "I hope I can tell this okay." "You're a master storyteller. You're doing fine."

"I know," she laughed. "I sound conceited. I mean, I've had it going through my head constantly forever. It wants out bad!

"Okay. Phew! My mom left me at the lady's house and all was not that bad for a while there actually. I mean, I ate well for once, probably got a little chubby, and I even fed the chickens every morning when I got eggs. They'd let me do that before breakfast cooked every morning. It was a basic farm life that seemed much more different than my previous days with my mom, which were usually spent cooped up in some small apartment or motel room aside from hours spent at the local parks or library as she scribbled away in notebooks. I wish I could read some of those.

"Anyway, I used to help the mom—that hefty church lady—babysit the kids that she had in her sort of foster home. There an assortment of maybe six kids. I helped with the two very youngest kids whenever I could.

One was about two, and the other was a little newborn Mexican baby that had the fullest head of hair that was very cute. My new mom, or Gramma Sarah, told me the baby's parents were migrant workers. They'd come pick him up at night time, and some days I guess he stayed with his mom. That was explained after he'd not shown up for a couple of days.

"I was well liked, and they were amazed that I addictively read everything. They were so proud and would show me off to people, which I didn't like, because I was generally shy around people I didn't know. They'd help me with words and explain things to me like street signs that showed how far a town was and such. We lived around a generally flat area, but the immediate area we were in was filled with low rolling hills.

"When Old Roger would go out—Roger was the husband—to check on his cows or whatever, or just ride his horse sometimes at dusk, he'd often take me with him on his horse named Pal. These are some of my best memories, that all too short summer.

"I even went to church and was the best Sunday school student they had, they said. I just loved learning, and they made those sometimes violent Bible stories like David and Goliath, Daniel and the Lions, Samson, and Jesus' crucifixion, look so cool on that little velvet whatever board with the cut-out paper men. Know what I'm talking about?"

"Yeah, I remember those," I said.

"Well, that was the first exposure I had to Church, and you know, and I liked it a lot. I was especially fascinated by the story of Jesus, when he rose up three days after he was on the cross, then of course I liked the part where he rose up to the clouds after he had shown everyone he was alive. That story I'd always ask the Sunday school teacher about because of my mom, you know? Wait a minute, I jumped ahead a little bit! Let me backtrack. Sorry, I'm not trying to be desultory."

"That's okay," I said. "Much obliged you're telling me, once again."

"Thank you, too. We're such a polite couple—just means we haven't known each other long from what I know about relationships!

"I was trying to skip this over, not on purpose, but it must've been a few days after my mom left that I'd been informed my mother died. Of course, I never could understand the concept of death at that young age, but the news came when some guy in a suit and woman in a dress talked to Gramma Sarah. When they left, Gramma Sarah was on one knee trying to support herself, crying, by the stairway banister. She was crying for a bit when finally I asked her, 'Are you hurt, Gramma? Need a doctor?'

"'No, Deedra,' she told me. 'Gramma's gonna be fine.' She tried to regain her composure much like my mom had done when she'd been crying those few days earlier. 'It's your mom, she's gone. She's gone...to Heaven.'

"'I know,' I said. 'She was going up to the clouds. She told me she was.'

"She got happy. 'Come here,' she motioned. I drew close and she gave me the hardest, most loving hug. 'Poor thing. Poor little girl. You're right, though. She went away, but you'll get to see her again in two days. She's sleeping though. We'll say good bye again. You okay, Deedra?'

"I'd only been more sorry for her than I was for myself. She was the one crying, after all. I gave her a hug on my own accord. 'It doesn't hurt anymore Gramma in my chest. I cried last day and now I remember Mom said it'd only be for 'while like she promised. Now I get to say bye bye to her again.'

"It was true though, I'd cried the same night after my mom had left just because I missed her already. The next day after she left, I was so busy having fun, and they did their best to keep me occupied and such, I couldn't think about her until that night when I was lying there awake in my bunk. Then it all hit me. It felt like something attacked my soul, and the whole bedroom got cold. I got really scared. I wanted to cry out for my momma and then...fully realized that she was not there.

"She was all that I knew, and she was gone.

"I put my head in my covers, and cried. It was the same night my mom had died too, I would later find out. I don't know how long I cried, but I do remember Gramma Sarah picking me up and laying me in her bed so I could sleep. She kept running her fingers through my hair and telling me it'd be fine. 'It'll be fine.' Hmm. I finally dozed off and felt swell and well and refreshed in the morning. For some reason, I think my mind and body came to accept my new destiny as it was determined to enjoy my new life that day.

"Of course, a couple of days after the guy in the suit had come to talk to Sarah, we were to go to my mom's funeral."

Deedra paused. She was thinking, but I got no vibes that she wanted to skip over the funeral part. After ten seconds or so, she started speaking again.

"Yeah, I was just trying to put things in order. I realized I've been skipping around a bit. You follow me still?"

"I do," I said. "It's been awhile for you. Don't sweat nothin'."

"All right-y then," she breathed heavily. "We went to the funeral and all in town, and there were about two dozen people present who I'd later find out belonged to the same church we would go to. Of course, the peculiar thing about that I'd never notice at my young age and social isolation was that none of them were my relatives. Years later, I'd find out that Gramma Sarah and Old Roger had footed the entire funeral expense. It was the least they could do for the daughter they were going to adopt, they probably figured."

That was a change in the story.

"Yup, they were going to adopt me," she said proudly. "I think maybe that was a deal or promise they'd made to my mom before she left me with them. I'm not sure. Not the funeral expenses, but the adoption!

"Anyway, we get to the funeral and everyone is solemn and kept giving me hugs and telling me 'how beautiful' I looked. I was wearing the exact same flower dress that I'd worn when I'd last seen my mom."

Deedra chuckled and said, "Kind of a snazzy, cheerful dress to wear to a funeral, now that I think about it! I guess it was my nicest one. Hmm. The service went by and I was not really paying attention to what was being said as it all sounded a bit too somber for me.

"The real excitement came when I was to finally see what was in that wooden, black box up front. Everyone was walking up to it, looking into it, then some people were crying, and then they'd always look towards me and smile real generic through teary eyes. 'We gotta say bye to your mom now,' Gramma Sarah whispered to me.

"She was pulling me up towards the front—towards the box— and I was scared of what I might see. Everyone was crying or getting sad when they looked at it! Would it hurt?

"Gramma Sarah put a flower in my hand and told me, 'Put this in your momma's hand.'

"I'd never been to a funeral and had no concept of death aside from seeing a few dead animals and bugs. And when I saw my mother it was the happiest moment of my life, just so unexpectedly seeing her again. 'She's sleeping,' I said after I stepped up to the little stand they'd pulled out just for me. 'Put the flower in her hand, Gramma?'

"'Yes, Deedra.'

"I put the flower in her hand, careful not to wake her, and observed how pretty she looked. I remembered the day she'd left me, and I saw myself as I floated above everyone in the car. I wondered if she could've seen me then, too. I looked up around towards the ceiling for her. Nothing, but I knew she was there. A total calm rushed over me. Someday, Deedra, someday.

"I don't know how long I stood looking at her and around her, but no one said anything to make me move along, though some people had started crying more loudly, I noticed. I didn't want them to be sad anymore. Some of my mom's last words popped in my head, We'll meet again someday, promise.

"I leaned far over on my tiptoes and kissed her forehead gently. 'Night, night, Momma.'

"I told the people crying in the small congregation, 'It's okay. She doesn't hurt anymore. She said she promised to see me again...in the clouds.'

"There was silence for a bit, and then everyone started murmuring. I think they were trying to decide if I actually said what I just had said. Someone started clapping, and others followed the lead. Then the ladies started crowding and hugging me and one distinct word I heard a few times among the murmurs was 'miracle.'

"They thought it was a miracle, but it was only the truth. That's what my mom said. Of course, they were very conservative Christians and saw it as a sign that an angel had spoken to me. But, you know, any kid that went to a Sunday school class a couple of times would have said this, too. Everyone was calmer and happier after that. I didn't like the mournful mood, and only wanted to be happy too, if only to make the grown-ups not so depressed.

"The burial was very weird to me, as you'd imagine. My mom was in that now closed box, and they asked me to throw a handful of dirt on top of it, and some more flowers. After more prayers they led me away, and I didn't get to see the actual burying process, just heard some singing. 'Amazing Grace,' it was. I glanced up into the darkening clouds. 'Is it going to rain?'

"'Looks like it,' Old Roger said, putting his rough yet gentle hand on my shoulder. 'He's going to make all things new again, Deedra. All things anew.'

"Jesus is?'

"Why yes, he is. For you and me. For everyone."

"Wow, so it rained that day," I said cautiously after Deedra sat silent a spell. "You ever think that...God was like crying for you?"

"Sometimes. Most times, no. That would imply fate—what happened. I don't believe in fate a whole lot, and was angry at it if there ever was such a thing, especially after what happened to me. Go ahead, ask! Heh."

"All right. What happened to you then?" "No, it sucks."

"Then you don't have to tell me, then." "Nah, just kidding. Yes, I do."

She rolled her neck a couple of times, and continued.

"I was content all summer. Those people truly loved me with all of their heart. They loved the other kids around, but I knew they favored me. I never made any show off of it to the other kids though, as I loved them, too. Roger And Sarah would tell me that 'God had a special calling for me,' when they tucked me into bed sometimes. They said I'd grow up and do great things for God someday. Imagine that."

"Imagine."

Chapter 16—The Diary of Dust

"I COULD GO ON FOREVER about the countless little details I remember about that summer and all, but I'll just go ahead and get on with it," Deedra said.

"No. Tell me at least a few."

"Alright, if you insist. It was just mostly trivial poetic things, you know? The way the wild flowers swayed in the field, just as the prairie grass did as if it were a harp with the wind playing it. I always pretended they were dancing, and I loved the music it made. I used to think that sunflowers were the prettiest flowers of them all just because some were twice as tall as me. Petting the horses every day. I even petted the cow, too. I don't know, I just loved everything about that unembellished life. I liked my chores. I loved getting my own eggs every morning, and then eating them as a reward. I'd always have this stick I'd walk in with to chase the chickens off with. That was fun. I thought I was so tough.

"There were a couple of chickens that they let keep their eggs to let the chicks hatch and I watched it, but I never grew sentimental over the idea that's what eggs grew to be, you know, cute little chicks or whatever. I had a job to do, damn it! Those chickens dreaded me— although I was not much bigger than they were —when I got part of our breakfast each morning."

"Not a natural vegan, eh?" I said. I could imagine her as a little girl all ardent on getting the breakfast eggs. It seemed the cutest thing.

"I still drink animals at times. Anyway, life was of course too good, and I was going to be adopted by these nice people. They had me start calling them gramma and grandpa instead of 'Old Roger' and 'Sarah.' Grandpa Roger and Grandma Sarah. I think they wanted me to call them grandma and grandpa out of respect for my parents."

"Oh."

"So...yeah, I was with them and was to start kindergarten and all, but actually it was first grade since I was advanced and it was a smaller school system, and I looked forward to it. Grandma had me all set and was proud to send me off in my new school dress that she'd made herself. I was to be accompanied on the bus by an older sister of mine who was a few grades higher than me, and she'd help me adjust or whatever. I mean, it was a small school, so I guess you had all the attention you'd need.

"There was not much to remember of those first few days of school, other than it was school, I guess. They were trying to assess exactly where I'd be as far as my curriculum went, though they'd done some testing earlier and were impressed. I'm not trying to brag or anything."

"Of course not."

"But that's when it all went downhill. Turns out my mom had not tied up all the loose ends and I still had supposed family, a great uncle, that was still alive and could get technical legal custody of me since I was part-Indian and he was on my mother's side. Native American family ties over the welfare of the child deal. I thank the Indian Child Welfare Act for that.

"Why they wanted me suddenly, I don't know. I was in the middle of being adopted and was cared for. I mean, this was despite the fact that my mom had explicitly told Sarah and Old Roger that she did not want me ever going to the uncle's home. She'd written this letter that I suppose was her non-binding legal will basically, and her last wish was that I not go to the uncle's at all costs. But it was going to happen because my mom was considered unstable since she'd committed suicide, and was a druggie. I mean, what good is the word of a suicidal addled junkie anyway? They couldn't just listen to her. Bastards.

"Although I'm still mad at my mom for being that way and abandoning me, I never lived her life, but I was about to find out what it was probably like.

"The court rulings and all that my adopted family did for me had no legal sway in whatever the decision was. I was to go to live with my supposed great uncle, and that was that. He wasn't even a first uncle, but a 'second cousin.' It was fucked that he even wanted me."

"How did they find out where you were in the first place?" I said.

"School enrollment and all. They found out once they checked my name. Supposedly, my mom had tried running away from her leftover worthless family when she was a minor teen, and they'd always been sort of looking for her when she left."

"Oh, that sucks. They sucked too, huh? You seem to hate them.

I can tell by your voice!"

"Hate...I don't fully hate anyone, I tell myself, except them. I got taken from the only stable home I knew and was suddenly living in a shit hole tiny trailer house. I have nothing against trailer houses, but this one was surrounded by the most gawd awful scenery of overgrown weeds and junker cars. We were in Nebraska, and the rest of the surrounding area was just plain old...nothing. It was just prairie and a little shitty trailer off the side of a dirt road. Nothing against Nebraska either, but this particular area, another Great Depression and Dust Bowl Era couldn't have made this place anymore depressing than it already was. A tornado would've been a blessing. Well, to me anyway, although I'm obviously inclined to having proclivities with my not so fond memories.

"So...I'm living there with the uncle fucker, the wife, and the older kid who was somehow my other relative, I suppose. These people were total alcoholics, all of them. I'm sure they only kept me around for extra welfare or foster kid state money or whatever—nothing to do with love. The son moved out shortly after I moved in. He was sort of nice to me, and tried to make me somewhat comfortable, which was probably not possible then.

"I went to a new school while the uncle worked, and that was my getaway. At first I never tried hard with my reading or spelling at my new school. I was just really depressed and didn't care.

"I had to escape that terrible place. I was going to try to go somewhere, anywhere, to get out of that place. The wife did nothing but watch soap operas on TV, and would feed me the minimal amount of government commodity food every once in a while, but I ate whatever was laying around; mostly a lot of the oatmeal farina stuff. That was all the rage back then for me. That and government cheese! I do think I started getting skinnier, but at least I wasn't starving. Every night there seemed to be a party with who knows who, so I could rarely sleep well when I had to go to school. Once, I never woke up for school after a particularly loud night, and missed the school bus. On the way to school when the uncle gave me a ride, he slapped me hard upside the head a few times for missing the bus, even though it was his wife who usually woke me up but was probably still passed out that time. It was right on the guy's way to work or something, too. It's not like it was out of his way.

"Just understand the place: I hated it. "Got ya."

"So I took off walking one day after school as far as I could over the horizon until I reached some hills, and kept on walking and walking into the dark. I finally came out on some little two lane highway, and immediately someone picked me up despite my protests and physical fighting with them, and they took me to the police. I even tried to escape the police station in the meanwhile until that irascible idiot of an uncle came and picked me up.

"Of course, he was perturbed and knew he could get in trouble for me leaving through child endangerment laws, but the police or no one asked why I'd left in the first place. I remember the uncle playing it off as if I was lost, and how he was going to thank whoever personally for finding me.

"When he got me he goes, 'I missed you so much, you had us all worried,' in the most fake voice ever. I knew better.

"On the way back to the trailer, he and the wife both beat me. First they slapped me around a bit, told me what a bad girl I was, and even said something like how I was worthless like my mother. They were more concerned about themselves getting in trouble than me being okay, obviously. If I cried during the ride, they'd hit and pound on me more until I stopped, yet they seemed to get mad if I showed no painful reaction to the abuse." Her voice cracked. "It was fucked up, bad. I didn't know what to do, so I started praying to myself. I did start praying out loud briefly, and all that got me was a handful of hair pulled out, and a few hard pinches on my ribs."

To this, I could see in Deedra a strong sense of loathing and just plain fright. She was not trying to feel sorry for herself or make me feel sorry for her, see was just telling me what was, and I could feel my own anger start to rise.

She continued.

"The uncle even said once to the wife not to hit me so hard in the face, because I 'might bruise.' But when we got home, that was the worst of it. He took me into the room and hit me hard all over my back with his belt...and then told me I was, 'just like my no good whore of a mother,' and needed to be treated like her. I had no idea what this meant. But then...then he started...touching me...all over inside. Molesting and hurting me real bad."

Deedra's face, which had been steadily growing more distant suddenly lost all composure, and she let out an unearthly piercing wail at the sky. Her anguish eerily echoed throughout the mountains for all of God's creations to hear, scaring even me. Then she tucked her head in her arms as if to hide from the world, rocking herself. Shaken from the shrill scream, I was unsure of what I should do then. What can you do when someone so close to you tells you something that deep, personal, and intense? I let her be for a moment, and then held her hard. Unlike the movies, there are some things a simple hug can't fix, but I had to let my friend know I was there for her.

"I'm sorry," Deedra said after a long minute. "Some kids have had it worse and—"

"No, don't be," I said sternly. Part of what Deedra's mother told her when she had to leave her came into my mind—that it was no one's fault—but this time it was someone's fault. I breathed hard, looked at the same sky Deedra yelled at, and silently asked The Creator for wisdom. "That guy is a fucking asshole. Look at me Deedra, please."

I had to let something be known. She did look at me with her face then all smeared with blood from her tears. I ignored her somewhat frightening appearance, and told her what was on my mind. I had to tell her what she needed to hear.

"Remember your mom's words, 'You must never, ever think that you were wrong! You are not wrong,'" I said. "You say you're 'sorry,' and that's how I can tell you still have it in your head somewhere that you think you're wrong for feeling the way you do about it. I'm sorry that it happened to you, I really am, but remember, you couldn't control it. You could not control it, Deedra. For the bright, little, innocent girl that you were, you were betrayed by those who were supposed to take care of you.

You know that. Remember that. You could not control it."

I pulled her closer, and let her cry on me. I kept telling her something like, "Never be sorry, okay? You never did anything to deserve that. No one does. You're not wrong," over and over as I rocked her gently. For a brief moment I felt like the mother she needed while growing up. Perhaps her mother moved through me. Deedra was the most precious thing in the world. I had a flashback of us in the car as I laid my head on her shoulder. Now it was her turn to rest upon me, and realize that she didn't have to bear her burdens alone. Although it wasn't possible, I just wanted to take that awful cancerous hurt out of her mind forever.

She wanted to continue her story after she regained some composure.

"I have to tell the rest," she said. "You probably want to know right?" She let out a nervous peal of laughter.

"Uh, sure. Please. Whatever suits you."

"He was always doing that to me after that. It was almost routine that he'd do it a few times a week...but who really keeps track of that? The wife didn't even care nor raise a finger to do anything. I think he must've kept it half out of her sight, but how could she not know? I'm going to go on before I start getting pissed at her like always. I don't know about the son though, he may have been naive about it. He was somewhat nice to me when he came around, and brought me candy. He was all right, actually, but he talked to me like I was a baby. I don't think he knew much about kids.

"So the uncle, or whatever—I don't want to call him my relative—was always abusing and molesting me. My teacher seemed concerned, so I must've looked too withdrawn or something. That's how I felt anyway. She was always asking me if everything was all right. She even went so far as to contact my new so-called guardians much to my protest, and I guess they just told them I was bound to be a bit depressed since my mom had just died. I guess that was sort of true in a way, but what could I do? I didn't think I had a choice in anything. I wanted to stay at grandmas and grandpas, or Old Roger and Sarah's, but that's about all I told the teacher who questioned me about being depressed or whatever. I guess you could say I had a great deal of mistrust for grown-ups."

"I don't doubt it," I said. "If I can briefly interrupt, what was the teacher like?"

"Hmm. She was very young, Ms. Miller was her name. She stuck with me and even worked as my tutor to push me when I got put into a higher grade. She was going to make sure my potential or whatever was fulfilled. She really cared. But let me digress a bit again.

"The school had like 10 kids or less per grade, and I guess I had a couple of friends. School was still far from my mind. I started missing my mom more and more. I continually longed and dreamed that I could go back to Sarah and Roger's house, be stable and not have to go to bed wondering if I was going to be interrupted in my sleep in the middle of the night. Life really sucked. I hated my existence. I started asking God why I had to live like I was. I started blaming God in my head whenever I felt that uncomfortable grotesque touch and foul sour whiskey breath by my ear in the middle of the night. I'd go to sleep cursing God after it happened, but I knew He helped me get through it somehow later on, so I tend to believe at times.

"Well, I don't know. I felt abandoned by Him. I sort of lost my lingering faith a few years later, and still hated God if there was one, but I did recall I didn't remember very much of the actual act of being molested after that first time. Call it a natural defense or 'suppressed memory' whatever, but after the first time it happened, I prayed to Jesus real hard that he'd help me if it happened again, although mostly I prayed that it wouldn't. It did happen sooner than later, but the thing was I went away while it happened. It was not like floating out of my body going away, but I was back to Old Roger's farm and places like it. Dreamlike. That meadow of swaying grass, the horseback rides, but no one was on the horse but me, and I felt no more pain. I was always alone in these dreams or whatever, but at least I was away. I'd always daydream and try to recreate those places everyday all the time. It helped me cope with life a little better.

"I mean, these gawd awful things were happening, and I was beat all the time for no reason, but I wouldn't let them beat my soul. I kept that resolve they'd never beat my heart, though I probably did it unconsciously; my not wanting to give up hope in life so that perhaps one day I'd be reunited with Grandma Sarah and Old Roger, since I became bitter over the thought of my dead mom when I saw other kids with their moms.

"Then one day I started trying harder in school. I really applied myself, and Ms. Miller was amazed by the seemingly effortless ways I picked up on and remembered bigger words while reading 'older kids books,' and then finding them in a dictionary if I didn't know them. She often told me how to pronounce them, explain what they meant, and I'd repeat them in my head dozens of times to make them stick. I was smart, I know, but I was no natural genius as some kids like you are."

"Hah!" I said. "'Genius' is a bit too liberal of a term to use for me. I just like reading a lot is all, just like you. It takes me forever to comprehend a difficult mathematic theorem, and that's universal."

"You're too humble. And you just have an artistically abstract mind, that's why math is weird for you. Me? I just tried hard, and in reading I had a head start on everyone else. Being able to read at an early age does not make one smarter, and I see parents unnecessarily push their kids too hard trying to achieve that. In fact, you might make them sick of reading and do more harm than good if the kid just doesn't want to read early.

"But Ms. Miller started giving me harder and harder books to read, and would have me circle the words I didn't know for homework. I mean, there were no advanced classes for kids like me in a school as small as that, but the teacher tried her best to accommodate my new found lust for learning, and bless her for it. It really helped, and eventually in a fucked up way it was the reason that made me leave my life. It was my key out of the uncle's house. Heh heh.

"Okay, I was at that house until I was seven, I remember, and I was to start second grade. I remember that summer all I got for my birthday was an excuse for the grown-ups to party and another late night visit from the uncle. Well, at least one of the drunks brought a little cake. The 'visits' were a natural part of life by then, but they were becoming less frequent. I think the uncle's health was starting to fail more. But the most vital event that I remember was that there was a gift my teacher gave to me the day after my birthday while I was out playing. Miss Miller actually showed up at my house very unexpectedly and said, 'I feel compelled to give you this book, Deedra.'

"I of course was looking around to see if the wife was looking, and she must've been as I later found out, but I took the book without even looking at it, and told Ms. Miller, 'You have to go now. I'll get in trouble.'

"The thing was, Ms. Miller understood and left without even asking questions. She just knew or presumed my family life was not the best. What could she do but leave or risk making my so-called guardians suspicious? She got in her car and said, 'Oh, and Deedra?'

"'Yes, Ms. Miller?'

"'Happy birthday,' she said, half smiling sadly, and left.

"That simple gesture restored my little faith in

humanity just enough. It really really helped me through the years—her just doing that simple little thing. Just her caring enough on my birthday to come over and do that, even if I was mostly paranoid during her brief visit. It took a sec for me to appreciate her deed, but I did after I went to my favorite spot to read in the shade inside an old but comfortable gutted out junker car seat. I wanted to cry tears of joy. I really did.

"I'd practically grown immune to having any feelings. I forgot what love felt like. It just...honestly touched my heart. I stopped myself from crying though as to not let it ruin my reading fun by tears blurring my vision.

"I remember that feeling though, walking to that little tree shaded area by the junker car, and remembering everything getting blurry just thinking about her saying, 'Happy birthday,' and giving me what I knew to be a wrapped book. I was almost thinking, *What's wrong with my eyes?* Hah hah! I'd pretty much forgotten how to cry, forgotten what it was aside from reading about it! Ms. Miller probably gave me a dozen books before the start of summer vacation, but I'd read all of them a few times by then. The birthday book she gave me was the one I remember the most, obviously. It was *The Diary of Anne Frank*. Needless to say, I really liked it a lot.

"It took me like two days to read it. I wasn't speed reading, either. I actually read it a bit slow as to enjoy the words more. It's just that this book I read for like eight hours straight that next day. I had nothing else to do, and it was a gift. I read and re-read passages. You've read it before haven't you?"

"Yeah," I said. "One play version. I can see how you could sort of relate to it, actually."

"Yeah, trapped there for what seemed like forever. But at least she had people she loved around her. I felt sort of jealous for her having that. Of course she eventually went to a concentration camp and died, but she still had faith in humanity until the end. I was Anne

Frank when I read that book. I really wanted to be her, though most people will tell you the opposite. I imagined her scribbling away in pages just like my mother used to. I wanted to be her even when she died. I just wanted to die with her when it mentioned she did at the end. It was not a suicidal notion, I just musta thought it was romantic in a way, that she had family, and was going to go be with them again in Heaven. Anne at least seemed certain of it, I thought. I was empathetic for her, and dispirited that I couldn't pretend to be her anymore when the book was over.

"So I went back to school again shortly thereafter, and I really was looking forward to the school year, as it was an escape from the constant physical and verbal abuse I got from home. The teachers were very heartened to see me back or whatever, but they were also resolute to make a better life for me. I mean, the uncle I stayed with was not exactly the most reputable person and neither was the wife, so they wanted to see my full potential realized. They kind of really messed that up even though they were trying to help. They contacted whatever child agency, and they came by the place some Friday the week I started school, and of course the guardians were not too pleased by that. Those teachers should've known. Hmm. Oh well, can't blame them. They tried.

"I got home that day, and the uncle's wife grabbed me by my hair as soon as I walked in the door, slapped me around, and threw into my room and told me not to come out. I didn't know what that was for, but I presumed it had something to do with school since I'd just started it. Their beatings hardly even affected me anymore. I took them with a grain of salt and as a part of life, although I'd started becoming bitterer over them as opposed to being afraid.

"I just sat down and read my book again, ignoring the stinging sensation on my face. I musta been in my room for a long time, as I noticed it was soon dark out and I never got to eat anything that night and my stomach wouldn't let me forget that detail. I laid down, and waited for the inevitable whatever that was about to come my way. The uncle was nowhere to be seen that whole night, and finally I heard him coming in late from whatever bar. I knew his molesting of me was wholly wrong since they had a specific word for it that meant it was especially negative, but I was just content he'd been doing it less and less as of late. He awfully called it, 'Giving me a kiss goodnight.'

"So I hear the wife yelling around to the husband about me and all, and something about the school. The uncle starts yelling around too, and they were both really worked up and I knew I was in trouble then. He barges into my room and I immediately sit up. 'What the hell you telling those teachers at the school?' he goes.

"'Nothin'',' I said, which was true.

"'You lying little bitch. You telling them we ain't taking care of you?'

"'I never said nothin' to them!' I yelled defiantly.

"He started taking off his belt right then and I knew what was coming no matter what I did. I braced myself, looked him in the eye, and said again, 'I didn't say nothin'.'

"Him, 'We'll see about that,' and then he whacks me real hard across the shoulder with the belt. I don't even think I flinched, I was so sick of him and determined to stand up for myself.

"'What about that teacher coming by that day, huh? What about her coming by, and what'd she say?' the wife said.

"I hated her for saying that, for seeing me and the teacher that day. It nearly negated every positive memory I had of that day, just knowing that I was being watched by that stupid cunt.

"I never answered the question, and the uncle jerked me by my hair so I fell forward, and then he started hitting me with the belt and it went on for a long time. I thought he was going to kill me, and I don't think I would've cared if I died right then, too, it was that bad. He's hitting me all over with that belt, and then kicking me until a couple of my teeth were knocked loose, but I wasn't scared. If I was going to die, I wouldn't give them the satisfaction of letting them know they'd really beaten me where it mattered: in my soul. He probably was gonna kill me until the wife finally intervened some way, and then he let up. 'What did she say, you dumb little bitch? That teacher?' he said to me.

"He whacked me across the back of the head with the buckle of his belt. I put my hand to where he hit me, and felt something wet that was blood, and my head became numb and light. He then whacked my hand holding my head, too, and that stun and hurt even more. The wife—sounding for once concerned for me—said, 'Answer him, Deedra, please!'

She must've started getting worried for me, but they were not leaving without the answer, so I told them coldly, 'I said she said nothing. She gave me a book. That's all. For my birthday.'

"I started crying then despite my not wanting to. They were ruining one of the only good things that happened to my life in a long time. I could think about getting that birthday book during the most foreboding of times, and I'd go away in my head. I even looked at the wrapping paper every day, and sometimes rewrapped it. Now they were exposing that moment as if to drag it out and stomp on it, or at least I thought that and that's why I was crying.

"'She didn't give you no book. Now where is it if that's all she done?' he said.

"Not even bothering to look up, sitting there with my head in my arms, I just pointed to the end of the bed. I heard him grab the book, say something about 'stupid Jews,' and then the most horrid thing possible happened:

the fucker started ripping up the book.

"Of anything he could've done, that was the worst. I didn't even care then, about me, about him, about everything. I jumped up and tried rescuing the book and yelled 'No!' at the top of my lungs, but of course that was to no avail. He was too strong, and back-handed and knocked me down. I got up again anyway, and I don't know what I was trying to do, but I ran at him and then clawed, scratched, bit him— whatever. I was possessed. I was knocked unconscious shortly after. I woke up later towards dawn, and I had blood caked all over my face, clothes, bed. My head hurt all over, too."

Deedra started laughing maniacally. "You know the funniest thing?" she said.

"What's that?" I had no idea about what she could've found humorous about the brutally morbid story she'd been telling me.

"I felt dandy. Screw the physical pain, my heart felt the best, my mind felt at ease, my conscience was clear. I'd fought back. I saw some of the pages of my book ripped up on the floor and I was again disheartened, but not all the way. Him destroying my book would be remedied."

Chapter 17—Paper, Rock, I Win

"PHEW," SHE LET OUT A BREATH as if she were relieved to be done with the difficult part of her story. She seemed eager, yet calm, when she started talking again. "It all happened very methodical, the events that occurred next. I knew what I had to do. I was going to kill that bastard uncle of mine. Realize, that by then I knew what he'd done to me was very bad and totally wrong. It's not like I didn't know what he meant by 'punishing me like that whore mother of mine' by then. I'd thought about it plenty of times, and I knew what pedophile meant. In a strange, incongruous way it kind of gave me a little comfort, just knowing that my mom had gone through the same thing with this pedo creep.

"It's weird to explain, but I was like, *This used to happen to mom, too.* She went through it and ended up nice, every little while whenever the hurt and disconsolateness of it all seeped into my heart and threatened to make it forever black. I knew I wasn't alone at the very least. Very fucked rationalizing, but you got to tell yourself something to help you pass through those times. I knew I wasn't the only person that this awful thing had happened to. There was an actual word for it, so others must've had this happen to them, too. Why God didn't punish all of these big people like in Moses' day I didn't know, and I often asked Him why.

"Right then, though, I was more than upset, but I couldn't stop grinning. Simply quite mad, really. Something was telling me to do something, and I was going to listen to it. No matter what happened, I'd listen to this voice or whatever in me and ride it out because it was making me happy despite the disconsolation I felt my book being ripped up. I must've thought it was my mom, this voice, because I whispered, 'I'll do it Mom. I'll be a good girl.' There was no turning back.

"So I sneak out of my room, and it's dawn out so I don't need to turn on any lights. I went to the kitchen as quite as I could be, then start pulling out the drawers. Ah ha! Knives. No, I'm thinking, something else. I intuitively pull open another drawer, the bottom one, and there is a pair of pretty hefty and sharp heavy duty scissors in there. They're like daggers. I knew the lady used them for sewing or something once in a great while for patches on jeans. But yeah, those were what I needed. Grab a steak knife, too. I taped the scissor blades so it's sort of at a right angle and only one blade is protruding straight away. I also grabbed a short knife for good measure.

"I walk down the hallway, it's building up inside me, all this tension, it wants a release. Whatever was going to happen was going to happen. It's not a long hallway. It's a very short trailer. I peek inside the half-open door. They're both sleeping. Alright. Bre-e-eathe. I walk up to the bed as quite as possible. The floor creaks a little too loudly and I stop. The wife is stirring a bit. She actually has her arm around that bastard. I move forward again until I am right next to him. I can smell that detestable breath through his heavy snoring. He's lying on his side, so his face is about a two feet from my right hand—the hand with the scissors in them. The left hand has a short, stout steak knife in it. I breathe deeply, and for the first time I'm losing some of the intensity. It's starting to leak out but the voice comes back to me. Do it, now. I'm having second thoughts about doing whatever it was I was going to do, until I picture the ripped up pages of my book scattered all over in that little prison cell room of mine. Maybe I can fix it, I thought briefly. No, someone has to pay for that. It's Saturday and they're going to be here all day. I know I'm probably going to be confined to my room and be beat every little while for attacking the uncle amongst other things. I raise my right hand slowly, and my left hand—my hand with the knife—wants some revenge, too. I look at the bastard's closed eyes. There.

"My hand is about shoulder level, and I'm not even thinking anymore. My vision is getting blurry because of the tears clouding my eyes. This was it. I'll be a good girl for you, Mommy.

"I sniffle a bit as I'm crying silently, and the wife I know is starting to wake up. She opens her eyes, and instantly I'm resolute again. The scissors plunge with all of my strength into the eye area of the husband as she sees it all. The audience made it better, especially since it was her. It made sense. She stood by and watched me be tortured by this man, now she could watch this too since that was all she was good for. The scissors stopped after they mostly ripped through the eyeball and upper nose area, and the site of the blood and the sound of the uncle and wife screaming means nothing to me. My left hand remembers what it wanted to do and thrusts into the uncle's stomach twice, but I know it's not deep enough for a kill. I know he feels it though. His arms flail wildly forward, trying to protect himself and hit me. I'm too quick and hop back towards the doorway when he lunges and falls off the bed. He never hits me that time as he holds his stomach. My eyes dart the room. I'm also preparing to run, though I'm still rabid with anger. The fight mechanism wants it more than the flight. The lady has stood up and has the audacity to act like what I was doing was somehow wrong. I still don't hear her, but she's yelling and condemning me as the hunched over uncle suffers justice, and she's dared taken a step towards me. She's wrong, I'm right.

"Shut up!' I say, and throw the scissors with all of my strength at her. I can throw well, as I threw rocks at set-up targets and birds if possible many times a day when I wasn't reading. The scissors bounce off her stupid face and graze her. She's bleeding pretty good. Excellent. But she's not down. I made her mad, and she's charging towards me a bit until I charge her back and swipe crazily with my knife. She wisely turns her attention to the sobbing, screaming, cursing uncle, and I have the urge to stab her in the back of the head as she scrambles and stoops to put a pillow case on his wounds.

"But I take off running instead. Down the hallway, out the front door, across the field. I still have the knife in my hand. I'm going to go to that town. I'm hungry, and my stomach is growling. I recall counting mile markers and it was seven of them. I'll stay out of sight of the road, but walk along it behind the rolling hill off to the side.

"I walk, not even thinking about what I had done for the first few miles, but then I start laughing to myself as I picture the uncle lying there in his own reap, not being able to see and in agonizing pain.

"'I told you I'd be a good girl for you, Mommy,' I said. I'm sort of sad that I didn't kill him, but if they send me back there, I'll tell them I'll do it again without hesitation. H-E-S-I-T-A-T-I-O-N. Hesitation."

***

DEEDRA HAD A SLY GRIN ON HER FACE. "You like that?" she said.

"Uh, yeah," I said. "Very good story. Trippy. Hollywood ending, too. Well, sort of. Geezus! Fucking crazy. I can't believe you did that. Amazing."

"Yeah, it's pretty funny."

"Hilarious," I said half-sarcastically as I winked to her. "Fate."

"I thought you didn't believe in fate."

"Well, I sort of do when it's convenient. But like I said, if there is fate I'm not going to be like some Hindu living on the lowest levels of the caste system sweeping streets and lying down and taking it. I have to fight it. And that's what I did. I refuse to accept the notion that all is game, set, match predetermined. You must create fate."

She waited for my response. "Well done," is all I could say. I was still in listening mode.

"Being trapped in that house like it was some damned jail...sucked. And my mom, who knows, her circumstances might've even been worse. I don't want to think about that though. I never did kill the bastard, but he probably learned his lesson, though not well enough for me. I was hoping to send him to visit God, you know? He could have a chit-chat."

"Yeah," I said. "But, you know, I see you're a very...I don't know how to perceive your personality, and I don't want to judge, but where you ever like, an 'angry kid' following that episode? I don't want to push into it too far and be your shrink. I'm just curious."

"No, it's all right. It's a very logical question. I can see how you probably think I'm heartless and cold sometimes, and I can be. But as far as my childhood after that, it's really tough to say. I got locked up in a mental institute and I was fed and experimented on with all sorts of drugs I never wanted to take. Lab rat for kids that hardly ever talked or something. The bad kid beyond help.

"But yeah, I was prone to violent episodes just as the doctors' notes read to tell the truth, though I doubt I would've been if the circumstances of my life hadn't been like that. I mean, I think I have a good heart somewhere in me."

"And you do...somewhere. Kidding."

"Gee, thanks." She wasn't offended. "Heh. I could be crazy though, I guess. This one time I didn't want to take the shot of whatever they were giving me, and I grabbed the needle right from the nurse, stabbed her with it in the chest, bit her, and tried to fight her. Even while I was doing the act I knew it was wrong, but I just hated grown-ups or something. I felt sorry for the nurse and everything as soon as I did it, but I still would've shoved that needle right into her eye given a second chance, because I knew whatever was in it would not make me feel like me, even though I myself knew I needed help. Help wasn't in an injection or meds, yet I wouldn't talk to them, tell them that."

I said, "They're even more quick these days to feed any kid with a psyche problem 'happy pills' rather than get to the root of the problem. That's not exactly soul-searching."

"That same nurse though, God bless her, she came by one day and showed me her daughter about my age, and it did kind of make me trust her a little bit after that. Who brings her daughter to a mental institute to gawk at some girl like me sitting in a padded room cell with a straight jacket, because I'd acted out that day? Honestly! Oh my God, I bet that girl can never get that image out of her head! She looked all spooked. Obviously, I couldn't wave back so I just nodded! Hah!"

"Yeah, I bet her mom told her, 'You see what happens when you don't listen? Do you see what happens? This is where they send the bad kids who don't make their beds!' Hah hah!"

"Probably. She had a good heart in her, just doing her job, that woman. She brought me books and magazines even after that stab incident. That's why I remember her. That and her bringing her daughter to see me and wave nervously."

"I get bored just thinking about those places though. I don't want to talk about them really. It's like asking an inmate, 'How was prison?'

"'Well, it sucked, obviously. Prison is prison,' is all you can say." "Cool," I said. "Probably was boring. But I must ask, how long

were you there in those places? When did you get out?"

"Briefly, a few times. But I always got sent back if I

went to a foster home or group home. I wouldn't talk among other things, plus I became institutionalized. I only felt comfortable in those psyche wards. There I could just read all day and not worry about anything but stupid group. There was a sense of security there. I think I actually helped others there, but never myself. I did start accepting whatever drugs they gave me just to break the monotony, probably became addicted to them, and that was life. Made a few friends here and there, nothing intensely intricate. Had a girlfriend briefly when I was about 16 until I discovered I wasn't a lesbian. What the hell though, I was only human and had only come into contact with people my age that were the same sex. We were watched carefully, so we attacked each other with great lust whenever possible. She gave me head and vice versa. Hormones."

"You big dyke, you."

"Oh yeah, I was! I thought she was pretty, but I guessed I was just going to appreciate beauty and not become a lesbian rather than force myself to become what I wasn't just because I was under extenuating circumstances. I'd read about that happening amongst prisoners or something, and certainly didn't want to be known as 'Bull' or 'Butch!' I was just looking forward to 18. That was my magic number, because that's when they let me out if only I'd behave, and I started to. I even got my GED. Woo hoo! I was free."

"Where you reformed? You must have been." She laughed and said, "That's what I told them." "Then what, you just drift?"

"Yeah, sorta kinda. But I'll tell you details of whatever some other time. About Joan or whoever and how I met her. Or, more accurately, how she found me. But I'm drained emotionally right now. You should start a fire or something. Aren't you chilly?"

"Not really," I said, and looked at the sky. It looked as if it might rain a bit as the stars became less visible as the clouds density increased. "I'll start a fire for you though. Give me something to do. I'm starving. Maybe I should go and scrounge around for a chipmunk."

"That's mean! If you see something, go ahead and drink it, I don't care. Just, uh, don't think about your hunger too much. I have a huge surprise for you like I said."

"Righty-o!" I said.

I had to do something to keep my mind off the gnawing hunger and zig-zagging down the side of the steep mountainside to the tree line in the dark seemed entertaining enough. I gathered a couple big pieces of dry, dead wood and went back up towards our little cave hideout, and busted them up. Deedra had moved from the open area of the 'medicine wheel' area to the cave area. She had a lighter, but I rubbed a few sticks together and started the fire the very old fashioned way. I'd actually done it that way before after a great struggle. Try it, it's hard. It's easier if you can move like a superhuman blur though. Camping at a place where we were probably the only ones alive on Earth that knew about it was simply choice.

"Do me a favor, okay dude?" she said. "What's that?"

"Thanks for the fire, by the way, but...just don't like ever think of me as 'that kid that was molested,' or whatever. I hate that. Think of me as me. Know'm saying?"

"Yeah, I do," I said. "I won't think of you as anyone but the intelligent and beautiful young lady in front of me, because that's what you are right now. You made it, and you are who you are. That's all that matters right now. It's good to know where you're coming from so I don't judge you. Not that I would anyway. But you may not ever completely overcome it or stop mourning your losses, ya know? I don't think anyone could." I threw some more wood on the fire. "But I have a sincere feeling that after tonight, you'll put a lot of it behind you, and both of us will move forward."

Later, I reluctantly followed Deedra back into our slit in the cave. I really hated sleeping there.

Chapter 18—Iconoclast

THE SUMMER SOLSTICE was the next day, and Deedra was adamant that we had to "leave now!" I didn't really care for the idea, but she convincingly asked, "Don't you want to feed, man?"

I really did, as I hadn't drank in three going on four days. So I scoured the land for a faster way back with the help of the dusk's remaining light, and we left. We were both sort of too weak to move speedily through the thick timber, so I navigated a route that would have us not going directly to our car and it was actually more than a few miles longer, but it was mostly on the higher elevations where there would be less trees obstructing our brisk travel. The route easily made us have better timing than before, plus it was mostly downhill, and we arrived to our hidden vehicle without incident. I wanted to drive, but Deedra again insisted on driving because she was going to find us a place to sleep and only she knew where we were going for my "next surprise." She was full of surprises, I guess.

I wasn't hurt by her wanting to drive as I leaned the seat all the way back, stretched my legs, relaxed, and rocked out.

We discussed how so many rock and cultural icons had died before their time. We both loved The Doors, and singer Jim Morrison, who was considered The God of Rock, had died young. Good old Jim, anyway. Cause of death: Burnt out as he shone too brightly for a brief while, as did Kurt Cobain of Nirvana before he passed away.

And there was obviously 'The King,' Elvis Presley. He'd lived the life most people only dreamt, and yet was perhaps so lonely he could die when he did. Rock and roll purist band AC/DC's Bon Scott predicted his own demise on his "Highway to Hell." Perhaps the greatest guitar player of all time—who was buried in Seattle—Jimmy Hendrix, was bound to die, right? As was the soulful Janis Joplin, and even the Sex Pistol's iconic punk rocker Sid Vicious.

Sure there were numerous rock stars that never lived out their life span and died young. Many had survived the test of time, some had members die and moved on, but these names in particular stood out because their deaths were pretty much self-induced in one way or another while at the top, and they took a big part of the arts and society with them as they found their dreams early and chased death shortly thereafter.

"Lucifer was head of the Seraphim, and leader of the highest of the Nine Orders of the Choir in Heaven. He fell from the Heavens. Think about that in relation to our modern rock Gods," Deedra said.

That was a weird point. "I don't know if that means there's a connection, but it certainly makes the deaths seem less coincidental for some reason," I said. "People used to think Old Jim Morrison was possessed. He'd just like, hoot and holler for a long time without even singing or saying words during entire supposed songs. It's gotta be weird after a while. People are like, 'I actually paid for that concert?' Hah hah!"

We passed through a few small Montana towns whose primary income had been logging, and I explained to Deedra that a lot of the logging industry had been shut down due to political pressure from outside groups, and thus a lot of the entire region became unemployed. On top of that, many people died because of mining that poisoned the water.

"But these trees," Deedra exclaimed. "They're so

thick! They can't spare any of these trees? The pine needles alone are like a foot deep in some places. That constitutes a serious fire hazard. Have they ever seen this area? "

"Probably not. Environmental lobbyists or something and even nearby college tree huggers. I don't know. You know, I'm not for clearcutting or anything as no one in their right mind is, but it's just ridiculous to wait for all of this to burn the hell up in forest fires anyway, and then try to put the fires out over and over. They just save them for the next fire season, and spend another 30 million putting them out. We shouldn't regulate nature, it will have its way anyway, but logging some of this out helps in a way if you plant new trees, et cetera, et cetera. It's not like we're in South America where we'd slash and burn and then leave it to erosion. These particular trees are not made to be a hundreds of years old, they need to be replenished one way or another. The Native Americans would purposely set controlled fires so that they'd cleanse themselves out. That's how the new seeds come out: they pop in the fire. They understood the need for fresh life. You create lush undergrowth and thereby more abundant animal forage, not a pile of pine needles like you said. These so-called environmentalists, they often mean well, but don't usually know the real ground situation. And if you know me, I'm as environmental as you can get, I just get mad at people from out of state or even here who don't know the facts saying, 'logging is evil, yadda yadda yadda!' Sorry about the rant."

"You're so passionate. Joking."

"I know, and I'm on the supposedly wrong side of the 'passionate' cause!"

"You won't gain any fans that way."

"I don't care. They've never been in the extreme northwest part of this state. Besides, it's not like I'm advocating cutting down an entire National Park. It's common sense."

"We're in Idaho now."

"We are?"

We jammed some Nine Inch Nails, and it was nearly time to sleep again. Deedra was right when she said 'curse these short summer nights,' because they were. I asked her when we we're going to feed and she said the next night. "Come on!" I said. "I'm a newbie vampire. You're killing me. Can't we just find an old person or something? You said so yourself, 'to go this long without nourishment would be torture.' Look at my face, it's all caved in and hollow looking like a crack head."

"As much as I know how you feel, I wish you'd stop your whining. It's only one more day, and you've already made it through this night, so just try not to think about it. I promise you tomorrow you'll be fed well. Tomorrow."

"Always die another day. We need a sacrifice to the Moon God. Hey! You and I are like Apollo and Artemis. You're like the Goddess of the Hunt and Moon. That fits you perfect. I guess I couldn't be Apollo, though. But remember, you said we were twins to those girls just like Apollo and Artemis were? I just remembered that. Sorry, I'm being busy brained."

"You're an Adonis!"

"Just not like that 80's wrestler Adrian Adonis!"

"But recall, Apollo was also the God of Poetry too, and you write."

"I consider myself just a simple writer and perhaps someday a keeper of history slash writer, not a 'Poetry God,' that's for sure!"

"You have a poet's soul. Anyway, the Sun God hates us, therefore we don't believe in him. We're against him."

"Damn right!"

Deedra said we were almost there. *Almost where?* She slowed down and pulled over into a campground area, paid the fee for two days, and said we had to hike again. I was too tired for that, but what choice did I have?

When we'd gone about 10 miles into nothingness

forest wilderness and small steep mountains, Deedra finally said, "This is it."

"This is what?"

"It. This is where we camp."

I looked around us. There was a small clearing and I heard a creek somewhere, but other than that there was nothing but very tall trees around us. "So...?"

"Sorry dude! You gotta dig."

"Blast. I had a feeling that's where you were going. I miss the days of tents."

We started pulling out the earth for our graves in rapid dog-like strokes with our bare hands. Deedra said pile the dirt next to the hole so it would be easy to sweep it over one's self. I stopped once as a chipmunk tested my hunger's will as he chirped and stared at us. I menacingly hissed at him like a true movie vampire, but he never flinched.

"Leave the little guy alone, A.D. I told you we'd have something tomorrow. I promise you so much. I've been wanting to get these people, but I saved them for a special occasion. You can drink some of me if want."

"I'm cool. It's tomorrow here already anyway," I said, then lazily threw a dirt clod at the chipmunk. He ran up a tree. "You saved them for the solstice, and that's the special occasion?"

"Yeah. Don't worry, and dig a little deeper."

I did, and hopped in my hole. It felt pretty natural, actually. I asked if animals would try to bother us during the day, but Deedra said they paid no heed to us, and when they did get close enough to smell us, they were afraid of the our scent. *Comforting enough.*

When the time came for me to cover myself, I never even thought about it. I was so tired and just wanted to sleep, wake up, and eat. The sooner I fell asleep the better. I closed my eyes, put my hat over my face, and Deedra covered me rapidly. The dirt felt cool and comfortable. I wasn't scared at all. It was a quilt. It was definitely better than the cave. I couldn't breathe freely, but that didn't matter much.

The Solstice and shortest day of the year for us vampires was the next day. Rest well.

Chapter 19—Diana Hades

"THAT WASN'T TOO BAD," I said and shook off some of the dirt. "It was a trip coming out of there, though. Imagine if you walked by and us coming out of the dirt like that! Zombies!"

I asked Deedra how she buried herself, seeing as she'd done my covering up for me. She said she buried herself really well from the waist down as she made a big pile right at her waistline, then laid back, and pulled the excess dirt on top of herself as best as she could. Her hands poked up through the dirt, and then she'd pull them in. Lastly, she shook very rapidly—which we could certainly do—underneath the ground to settle the dirt.

"Wow," I said. "Hey, mind if I wash up before we finally eat?" "Go ahead, but hurry since we only got like an hour before the big Midnight extravaganza. I'll wash up with you, too."

I walked to the small creek and started splashing water on myself by hand; complaining about forgetting to bring a change of clothes. I was really dirty. The sudden sight of Deedra joining me completely nude made me...something. What the hell, no one is going to see us anyway. I shed my clothes and joined her in the little pool she was in. Shrinkage, dude! I laid my head back, submerging my head completely underwater with my eyes open, looking at the three-quarter moon. For that brief time my aches from my hunger and fatigue went away. Sure the water was freezing, but it felt too fresh.

Deedra had basically just dipped, washed her hair, and got out. She told me to hurry up. We still had more hiking to do. As much as I liked hiking, right then I was getting pretty annoyed with it. Well, at least she'd selected the right person who could actually handle the physical and sometimes emotionally draining toll of it. The northern Idaho terrain was often steep, dense with trees, and no less forgiving than Montana's, but the elevation was lower, although I don't think that mattered much aside from the trees getting bigger.

So hike we did with me following Deedra. I was very curious about our 'Solstice celebration.' "Tell me a little about this rendezvous we're going to Deedra," I said after I asked for a breather. "They aren't really celebrating the Solstice, are they?—for the tenth time."

"They are, dude. It's one of their birthday's coincidentally, but they are celebrating the Solstice, believe it or not."

"I sorta thought you were joking all this while. And you said Apolloyons? What's that? Huh, my memory seems photographic now."

"Your memory will be better, yes. Let's just say these people you won't like, knowing your good moral Christian inclinations. Heh. They're actual Satan worshipers, dude!"

"No way. Satanists don't celebrate the Solstice, do they?"

"They celebrate a lot of things, especially that which is pagan and 'un-Christian.' They're offended that Christians hijacked their holiday dates as their own Easter and Christmas. But this Solstice in particular, it's also like the leader's birthday, and a birthday is of great significance to them. If I know these crazy mofos like I think I do, they'll have something supremely appalling planned."

"You think?"

"I'm sure of it. Let's go."

We came up over a ridge, and I knew there was a house down in the valley somewhere, or I should say I could sense people. Maybe it wasn't people, actually, as it was something far more portentous, immediately causing me to be on my mental guard. Deedra asked, "Feel that?"

"Yeah. Something evil is stirring down there alright. It gives me the creeps, and nothing really scares me, 'cept for sleeping in that cave. That was just awful."

We went for about a half-mile before we saw the object of our infatuation: a cabin with a bonfire lit beside it. Deedra had warned me to keep myself 'cloaked' as well as possible as we cautiously crept forward. Nothing must escape my thought process she said, lest they hear me for they did have powers as well. She said to watch for unseen forces that just could not be comprehended, for they controlled them also. I was curious to know who 'they' was.

It was a fairly large and pretty nice cabin from what I could tell upon closer look. It was not new or fancy, but it was bigger than my house. There was a van and pick-up truck in the dirt driveway. We crept closer, and a stick cracked under Deedra's foot. She cursed under her breath, stopped, knelt low, and so did I. We waited a few tense seconds before moving on. She pointed to a large Rottweiler dog in front of the house with his ears on full alert. Deedra slid the large knife out from her leg sheath. I knew where she was going with it. *Poor dog.*

She shot off like a cannon and the dog barely had time to yelp as his throat was cut hard, deep, and fast. She gave the 'come' signal. I went to the door but had urge to listen to what was going on, or that is, try to read their minds to see what we were up against. I gave Deedra the 'hold it' signal just before she kicked the door. She understood what I was doing, and did the same.

They were doing a ceremony, yes. It was sacrificial. I thought that Satanic stuff was mythical and invented back in the Dark Ages, and then re-introduced 1980's to scare impressionable church people as they preached against the evils of heavy metal. Historically, most of the intimate 'details' they'd supposedly gotten about Black Masses were extracted under severe torture in those Dark Ages, which were basically the Catholic torturer's imaginings, so I never took them seriously. Those torturers were so cruelly efficient they could get someone to confess that they killed their still breathing mother and Jesus if they wanted. And they did. In the 1980's there was an inexplicable wave of kidnappings and missing people, and most of those victims were never found again. Although there was no proof, most hysterical Christians assumed it was somehow the work of Satanists.

"They're finishing up," Deedra said.

I concentrated some more. I could hear what they were saying...

"Our Father which wert in Heaven, hallowed be thy name. In Heaven as it is on Earth. Give us this day our ecstasy. And deliver us to evil as well as temptation.

"For we are your kingdom for eons and eons."

It gave me a headache to hear that. It was an interesting play on Biblical words to say the least. They all said something in unison that was maybe, 'Amen,' and there was an awful, loud, prolonged moan of pain, begging, and crying. Deedra had her hand on my chest as if to hold me back. I wasn't going anywhere anyway.

The distinctive smell of blood deliciously filled the air, and a grotesque painful wail shook the air shortly thereafter. The pleading, begging for mercy, and crying continued. What the hell or who was that? Deedra looked at me with raised eyebrows and we shrugged. Then there was a gurgling scream of death, and a flurry of malignant invisible forces pelted me at once from every direction. I was fighting ghosts. "Shit!" Deedra said. "One of them senses us. Be calm. There's six of them in there, plus one more."

I could tell she was spooked by the demons or whatever the scream represented, but she tried to keep her calm as I swatted in the air at invisible entities that wanted us away. It seemed they could actually harm me physically, or at least make my head hurt. The rootless hands that prodded my body and seemed to even thrust through me were disturbingly annoying and gave me quivers.

Deedra said, "A little of your Christian whatever faith would help now. We're going in."

"As if you can't say a quick prayer, too?"

I kicked in the door, and Deedra went in before a heavy gust of heathen forces literally pushed her back into me. She moved ahead, more determined, angry, and ignoring whatever force had forced her back. Inside there was a collective gasp. How dare us. I of course naturally said my prayers, crossed my heart although I was not Catholic, and asked for God's protection as my hat blew off behind me with a another wave of preternatural wind that tried to dive into my innards, and I assume possess me. I picked up my hat, and put it on backwards. Not happening tonight, fellow demons. I'm already possessed by some other blasphemous DNA demon called 'fucking vampire.'

I got into pissed off mode, and moved towards the back room amidst a gauntlet of demons with Deedra as she turned once to me once to flash me her ravishing, sneering smile and fangs. *Hell yeah. No denying what we are now. This is unholy war!* Somebody popped in front of us with a gun. "Stop," he coolly said, and had it pointed with one hand.

In a blur Deedra snapped his wrist back. A spark of a gun flashed as it fired into the ceiling, briefly illuminating the dark room with a white light. She pocketed the clip, and rendered the pistol useless. The man cursed, and Deedra punched him aside. He looked unconscious and down for the count. *What a hook.*

One of them started to speak as we nosily went to the room where the action was. People in clean, white garments were astonished.

"Who are—"

"Satan," I said. "You guys called me, and here I am. Sur-preezed? 'Deliver us to evil,' you wanted!" I noticed some obviously dead lady tied-down with her throat slit, spread eagled on a large sturdy wooden table with a white cloth. The cloth looked like it had a red pentagram painted on it with what I presumed was blood. Around each corner of the pentagram was a candle. There were lots of other candles throughout the room, and it gave off a strong light. "Why?" I continued mocking. "After all the trouble you went through to get to me, I would've thought you'd be overjoyed to see me."

"And you guys even saved me some blood!" Deedra said a little over ecstatically as she shoved a man aside, grabbed a silver chalice next to the dead woman's vagina, savored the fumes, put it down, then threw an older book out of the way just for spite. "You're too kind."

Deedra grabbed the nearest woman and started sucking her life away. The woman could not have been over 25. The other four people—not counting the knocked out former gunman with the now broken wrist— cowered together in the sacrifice room and watched in horror as Deedra drained their former friend. *Thud*! The woman's head fell with dead weight hard to the wood floor after she crumpled. "My sweet Devil, won't you have any?" Deedra said to me.

I saw that they'd cut the private parts of the dead woman, and there was some bulb shaped pieces of mush near her, too. Man, that was horrible.

"Sure," I said. I was as ready as I would ever get. What they did to that woman made me very indignant. "Any volunteers?"

An older, gentlemanly looking, bearded man—the leader I presumed—grabbed the sacrificial knife, and meant to cut my throat with it just as he'd cut the woman's upon our arrival, but I easily caught his knife slashing arm and drank gluttonously. Right before he died, I whispered into his ear, "Seek ye the Devil, find the Devil; in Hell!" I finished him and let him drop. "I wonder if that verse is in the Satanic Bible. It should be. Who's next?"

"No, this isn't real," a middle-aged man said, obviously panicked. "This is not fucking happening! You don't exist!"

"You mean, you don't believe in the Devil?" I asked dumbly. Deedra childishly laughed. We were all blooded-up. "I'm offended. First you call upon me, then I show up. Now, I don't exist. Make up your bloody mind!"

"Yeah," Deedra said. "We're here now, so enjoy it."

"You ain't no fucking Devil." The man was going into the shock. "You...you're fucking vampires!"

"Devil, vampire, whatever. It's all the same," I said and picked up the silver chalice, studied the cool designs, and tried to ignore out of the corner of my eye the dead woman whose privates were hideously mutilated for who knows what reason. I think I would've thrown up if I saw her too closely. Triple-sixes, the stereotypical goat's head, and pentagrams were on the cup. There was blood inside of it, and I actually took a small sip just to be out of hand as I was wrapped up in the mood. It wasn't that bad really, but then I had the most disturbing feeling that the blood maybe came from that women's vagina. "I bet this cup is worth a lot. Looks sort of antique, eh, Deedra? Well, that book you threw probably is, you Nazi!"

The guy continued praying for Lucifer to destroy us, or take us back. For some reason when he said, "Take these creatures Satan and burn them..." it really set me off.

"Curses to you, too!" I said mockingly, then threw the cup with great force at his ribs. The blood in it splattered on him as well as the wall and floor. He lost his wind and doubled over, heaving and panting. "You and your stupid Lucifer Satan God!"

I punted him hard in the face, his head went back too far with a loud crack and he fell silent.

"You killed him already!" Deedra said half amazed.

"So I did. Sorry. Now that's what you call 'splatter punk!'"

He looked gruesome. His jaw barely hung from his face, and his cheek was caved in enough to where his eyeball nearly popped-out, and that hung by that thick veiny thing. A person who had their eye hanging out like that before told others said he could see in two different directions when it happened. That would be confusing to one's brain.

"He's seen better days!" I said, putting a mental note in my head to be aware of my strength. I looked at the two females left in the room. They both cried and cuddled in the corner. I chose the older woman. "Your turn, lady."

"No-o-o!" she gave a genuinely good horror movie impression scream.

Deedra walked over and promptly slapped her hard. "Shut up, wench!"

"How courteous of you, Deedra," I said. The woman did shut up though, and I pulled her to me gently. "I have a confession to make," I told her as I brushed her hair out of her face and smelled it. As I kissed her on the mouth, the other younger teenage-looking girl tried to bolt out of the room. Deedra easily caught her by the hair, and threw her to the corner. "I'm not really the Devil. But don't fret, you'll soon meet him personally, and I'm sure you'll buddy up with him just fine, considering all the services you've done for him and such. I'm sure you'll be living it up famously in hell. Or maybe you'll get lucky and there's nothing."

I sucked hard and fast for half of her life, and threw her to Deedra. The young girl held the side of her head, and was praying and chanting, "Please God, please help me! Please God, save me! Please God, help me!"

"I thought Satan was your Savior," I mocked her. She continued her simple prayers. "See, now Satan's gonna be real pissed off that your loyalty is not to him. And to think, after all the things he's done for you."

Deedra interrupted. "Let's go get that other dude. The one with the gun."

"Oh yeah," I said ignorantly. "He left? Whoa."

"Yes, unfortunately during all of our good fun he left. The party was just getting good."

"Where is he, by the way? Does he have the keys to that truck or van?"

"No, he doesn't. This girl's got the only truck keys, and the guy you kicked has the only set of van keys. Grab them both, will ya?"

The girl threw her truck keys to me out of fear, and told us the other ones were on the table in the living room. She looked fairly pretty, and I wanted to kiss her too, actually.

After I pocketed the keys, Deedra said, "Let the hunt begin!" "Goddess of the Hunt, what about her?" Of course I was referring to the young chick.

"She won't go anywhere, I don't think. But there's some guns in this next room here, so I wonder if she'll touch one. You won't, will ya Kaitlyn?"

"No," she was sobbing by then.

"Good choice. If you do you'll die slowly and painfully. And the guns can't really kill us by the way. They'll just prolong your begging for death if you try it."

We stepped outside, and despite what I had just witnessed, the big Rottweiler whom Deedra had nearly decapitated disturbed me. I told Deedra to let me guess where the guy with the broken arm was. My senses were sharp and I scanned the area. Fear. "Maybe a mile that way," I said while pointing south, proud of myself.

"Good." Deedra was happy for me. "There's a highway about three miles yonder that way. We can't let him get there. Yonder. Hah hah!"

"You sound like a local yokel!"

We blazed south, and the closer we got to him the more I felt his panic vibrate. When we were nearly up to him we stopped. He was jogging slowly, sloppily, and holding his arm. His mumblings were of complete horror, yet amazement of us. "They fucking drank their blood! Fucking vampires! Lucifer, help me now. Take those blood sucking, fucking fiends away..."

Excuse me for his words, for he was not a good Christian. While creeping up on him he stopped quickly, and so did we. He listened in silence for us, then all we could hear was his heavy breathing and complaining, "Fucking bitch broke my fucking arm."

Deedra purposely snapped a tree branch and laughed out loud, her voice echoing throughout the desolate darkness. The man took off in a dead sprint through the thick trees and brush. "Cut him off," Deedra said to me.

I ran ahead of him 50 yards and situated myself behind a tree in front of a small clearing. He came stumbling right towards me. When he was within 10 yards, I moved to the open and waved. His eyes got huge, and he turned around only to run smack dab into Deedra. He fell on his back and put his arms up to shield himself from Deedra as he crawled in a semi-circle.

Deedra wacked his upheld broken arm with the stick she'd broke, and the guy let out a loud curse. "Bitch!"

"Sticks and stones..." Deedra said and laughed.

I got the joke and pointed playfully at her. "Oh, ho, ho! Good one, Deedra!"

I finally got a descent look at the man. He was taller than me, skinny, had a thin face, shoulder-length blond hair, and was probably in his mid-thirties. He still had on his robe. "Fuck you," he said to Deedra. "Fuck the both of you!"

"Fucking watch the fucking language in front of the fucking woman, will ya?" I said. I'd never been one to use curse words much. They show a lack of refinement.

Deedra ignored him, and yet spoke indirectly to him. "Is this about where you buried a couple people, and even a few kidnapped infants before? I think it is. I saw you do it two years ago. Ironic. In the area you sit, there are two souls and some poor babies who want to have a word with you in the afterlife." She turned to me and said, "Shall we re-unite them?"

"Sure," I said nonchalantly. Then I spoke to the ground. "You'll like that, won't you?"

"Fuck you," were the man's last words as Deedra pulled him up, and drained him.

"That's *so* unoriginal," I noted.

I got the second half of his blood. I was so full by then I felt ready to burst. I fell to my back next to the stiff, enjoying the stupor while tripping on the treetop outlines and stars that seemed to twirl and swirl. "The body?" I asked.

"Leave it for the animals."

Chapter 20—Late Charges

STILL WEARING HER ROBE, Kaitlyn walked from the house sobbing and trying to calm herself. We waited down the road, hidden in the thicket. She walked past us and we listened to what she was audibly whimpering about, because we couldn't read her mind. Deedra whispered that she had her thoughts covered. In fact, she was the first one to sense us while we were outside of the house and had informed the coven or whatever of our presence. We were on guard too, knowing what annoying demons she was capable of sending to torment us. The invisible entities still poked and prodded at us, but they'd for the most part given up trying to send us on our way. There was nothing or no one left to direct them, as we'd killed everyone but this young girl in front of us who was resolved about her death. What did it matter if she stayed at that house or not? She walked uncaring of our previous warning and threats. She said, "Oh...my God," and bent over with her hands on her knees, ready to break down.

That was Deedra's cue. She said in a songlike, Valley girl mocking voice, "Like, oh, my God! Oh, my God! Where's your fucking God now?"

I bumped into Deedra. "Sorry," I said, and at last studied Kaitlyn. She was a couple of inches shorter than Deedra, had dirty- blonde hair, was slender under her robe from what I could tell, and had sharp, pretty features on her face. "Say, Kaitlyn, right? What's up?"

Kaitlyn kept her calm, and said, "What's up, guys?"

I couldn't tell what Kaitlyn's game plan was, and I

wasn't sure if she was trying to get on our good side. I think it was genuine relief that we did possess some sort of humanness just by me greeting her politely. Deedra swatted at what would've seemed like a bug to those not in the know, and said, "Will you kindly do me a favor and get these things away from me?"

"Done," Kaitlyn said. "I think. I knew you were nearby because they were acting up. But, well, do me a favor and not kill me, huh?"

"You know we can't do that," Deedra said.

"I know," Kaitlyn said, and sighed. "I know."

"Let's go back inside then," Deedra said. "As much as we like the great outdoors, I've had enough of it for the time being."

Kaitlyn laughed nervously and said, "I can tell. You guys are so dirty! And what's with the baseball hats? You just don't expect that."

"Hats are for the sun," I said.

I looked Deedra and myself up and down, and had to agree with Kaitlyn about us being dirty. It looked like we'd slept in the ground or something, but at least our bodies were clean. It was peculiar that we were communicating with Kaitlyn so offhandedly, but I guess we were sort of curious to know about these people and whatnot. To tell the truth, I think the only reason she was still alive then was that we were too full.

"Do you guys have names? Or what should I call you?" she said. "Sorry to be so informal, but no names," Deedra said. "Just say like, 'Hey you!' or whatever."

"Fair 'nough."

We made it back into the front door of the house. I wanted to sit by the fire so I said, "Hey, that fire is going out! Sorry 'bout your dog."

She seemed sincerely saddened by the big, dead beast. "He wasn't mine, but he was a real good dog. He was my girlfriend's. He was real friend of mine, and loved people."

"Unlike you," Deedra said. "But who am I to judge? But yeah, the dog, that's so sad."

We settled in the living room. A lone lamp decently illuminated the room, but I wanted non-artificial light. I grabbed some of the candles in the 'sacrificial room' to spread them around. "That's better," I said. Kaitlyn said there were more lights and lamps, but I declined their use as the candlelight was more relaxing. I turned off the lamp.

We were all settled in, and Kaitlyn twirled her hair. Deedra and I never said anything, and only looked at each other happily, so Kaitlyn said, "Just curious, but what do you want from me?"

"That's pretty obvious," I said. "Your blood. Whattya think?"

"Duh. Kinda figured that part out."

"But what else do we want from you?" Deedra said. "Just a little friendly conversation is all."

Kaitlyn was bold. Squinting her grey eyes, she said, "And this is after you kill all of my friends? To taunt me like a tortured insect before squashing me?"

"Your friends had nothing to offer to the world," Deedra snapped.

"As if you—whatever you are—'vampires,' pfft! What do you do for the world?"

"We dispose of trash like them," Deedra said. "If you believe in Satan enough, you should know that mercy does not pertain to the weak, or whom you deem unwise. We are the strong."

"Very strong," I said and raised my eyebrows.

Deedra went on. "Look, I know what you guys did and have done. How many victims do they have laying around this area? Two dozen, maybe? And what about you? You made that video just to get in with these fiends last year about this time."

"You do judge," Kaitlyn said, but you could tell she was impressed that Deedra somehow knew whatever secrets she had.

"That I do," Deedra said. "But show my companion the video. You guys keep it here, don't you?"

She nodded.

Deedra said, "Well, get it, please?"

"'Companion,'" I said.

She obeyed, and said while doing it, "Can you please tell me what your names are? I mean, why are we being so secretive if you're going to kill me anyway? I'll open myself up if you do." She meant opening up our minds. "We don't have to be overtly curious about it, just courtesy, you know?"

Deedra nodded that it'd be okay. I hated the concentration involved in having to shut her off. I asked the obvious question, "So, you can do that neat trick, too? Mind reading, or telepathy or whatever? I remember a time not long ago when people talked."

"It would seem," Kaitlyn said.

"How?" I said. "I mean, you seem good at it. Too good."

"So are you guys. I've always been able to do it. These guys, they're my friends and took me under their wing, but I've always known I've had witching-type powers to begin with. I'm a hardcore dark arts pagan from the very old school from my mum. None of this 'New Age' wannabe Wicca, kiddy stuff, fuck around, 'I think I'll cast a spell because it's so-o-o like totally like popular like' shit."

"Clever description," I said. Deedra laughed hard for a second. "So, you like do real magic? Wow."

"Is that why you did that with those babies with that other dude?" Deedra said.

Kaitlyn nodded once a matter-of-fact like.

"Not cool," said Deedra. "You didn't need these guys, so why did you join them?"

"I need a place to live since mum passed. They knew I possessed powers, and like I said they took me under their wing for a confession of loyalty."

"And that would be the videotape," Deedra said.

She pulled forward a small TV, and rewound the tape a bit before pressing play. I saw a poor guy looking scared, sitting in the dark on the forest ground. He looked like a homeless guy or derelict. The camera's light beam focused on him. There was commotion, and someone kicked him. Whoever was videotaping aimed the camera at Kaitlyn, and she flashed a large knife and licked the blade. It looked like the same one used earlier by them for the sacrifice.

"It is the same one," Kaitlyn said. "Sorry, I don't mean to prod your mind. Just telling you."

I focused on the video. The guy was being told to run. He didn't want to. People were kicking him and saying run, but he just sat there and cried. Someone started shooting a gun on the ground around his body, then put the gun to his temple as the camera zoomed in on his tears. I felt real bad for him. The people videotaping laughed at the fact that the poor guy pissed his pants. He finally got up and took off running and yelling as Kaitlyn gave chase. The camera caught up.

It was pretty brutal footage, really. What I saw was the young girl who sat five feet from me in the same room on the TV stabbing the hell out the guy in his back in the same forest vicinity we were in. She turned him over and continued stabbing him not in the vital areas, but in the shoulders, legs, arms, and even in the groin area. What was it with these sick people doing that? The thing that made me want to turn away, however, was when she put the knife in the guy's mouth and said, "I'm going to cut out his tongue!"

She never did right then, but she did pull the knife sideways out of his mouth, slicing the guy's cheek in half.

"Dude," I said. "Stop the video already! What was the point of showing me that?"

"I just wanted to show you what people are capable

of, A.D.," Deedra said.

"Well, I already saw that sacrifice in there. That was enough." I looked at Kaitlyn. "And you! What the hell is wrong with you? Just...why?"

"It's standard to join here."

"'Standard?'" I said. "'Standard' to just stab the hell out of some poor random bastard just because?"

"Well," Kaitlyn said. "It's more complex than that. We gather the power off of it, too. It's like a pep rally of sorts to collect minions and spirits. They listen to you, you know, if you can let them know you're listening and create energies. Like that woman dying in tonight's sacrifice. That brought out strong forces."

"Yeah, mostly like my stomach churning and me ready to puke," I said. "I'll try not to judge, what's done is done and all—yeah, right—but why do you find this so amusing that you'd dedicate your life to it?"

"It's boring out here."

"I guess!" I said. "But other people who are 'bored' don't go out having Black Masses and hacking up poor people just because they're 'bored.'"

Kaitlyn said, "A lot of it is because our leader, the one with the beard as you probably figured, bought this land out here years ago so he could perform these ceremonies. He's from California, and all of these others are from other parts of the country as well. Me? I'm from around here, and I was 'bored,' I impressed them, and I respected them greatly; hence they let me join. I knew who they were before they knew me."

"What about the sacrificed dead girl?" I said. "She's just a prostitute from Oregon. She's no one."

"So sympathetic," I said. "Off, yet on topic, I met someone from Oregon the other day, too."

"Then you also shouldn't be so quick to judge." Kaitlyn gave a knowing, pretty smile. "But I can see what Deedra is asking here. Why would I join this sort of simple 'LaVeyan type' cult or whatever?" she said in reference to Tim Lavey, the writer of the modern Satanic Bible. "See, with them I can fully have the resources to practice my...deep, darker, pagan stuff."

"Does it work?" Deedra said. "The magic?"

"Yup," Kaitlyn said. "Otherwise, it's just a ton of strange coincidences. But I guess I have it in my blood. But we aren't really 'LaVeyan' cult members. That mofo out in the trees you killed helped me in some rituals. Yeah, even the baby one. Before you cast stones, realize that the baby would've been aborted anyway. We paid the females money to carry the babies to term. We met them at the abortion clinic. One was for the coven here, and the other was for me. We've only kidnapped one baby before. Millions of babies have been aborted and killed. Does it make any difference?"

I started laughing. "That's still not exactly what one would call 'pro-choice.' I'm sorry, dude! I just never thought things like that actually happened. This night is too short and crazy."

"Oh, things like this do happen," Kaitlyn said. "Not always for this reason, though. People are evil, you know. Though 95% of the stuff you hear about Satanists is just fairy tales, not all of it is."

"I can see that," I said.

"In fact, many Satanists would disagree with what we do and say, 'You're doing it wrong!' As if they know true demonic powers. Many probably don't even believe in them and are agnostic. But otherwise, what's their point other than they want to rebel because they didn't like going to church or whatever as a kid?"

"Damn, we never have enough time," I said. "You're very interesting to talk to. May I see your wrist, please?"

"Do I have a choice?" she laughed and held it forward, quite calm for someone that may die at any moment. Perhaps she had a card up her sleeve that she'd play. I read into her mind, and it harbored no deceptive feelings. She was just intrigued by us, and was accepting of her fate. She also thought we were both pretty cool to look at. I thought she looked fine, too.

I licked her wrist before piercing it. Deedra walked to the back. At first I thought she was mad and jealous for obvious reasons, but she came back with the silver chalice. "What are you doing with that?" I asked after taking a drink of Kaitlyn. She covered her wrist up.

"We should drink out of it," Deedra said. "I am not drinking out of that," I said.

"I cleaned it out a bit," Deedra said. "Besides, maybe Kaitlyn wants some."

"It's not the sanitation I'm worried about, it's just the thought of drinking from that particular cup. And you mean to actually give her some?"

Kaitlyn was just smiling, and told us if we really needed cups, there was some in the truck. Deedra pulled her knife out, wiped the blade on the couch, cut her wrist, and started dripping some into the silver cup. She said, "We have plenty to spare as of tonight."

I didn't want to watch that heathen cup being filled, so I went outside and grabbed some other coffee cup in the truck. Women, I thought before going in and after throwing a few pieces of wood on the fire outside to keep it going.

"Since she has so little time, Kaitlyn wants to know if you can do her a favor," Deedra said. "I said ask you."

"Yeah?" I said.

"Well," Kaitlyn said. "Usually after our ritual we usually have an orgy and..."

"I don't care to do your ritual," I said. "I'm sorry. What do you want? 'Orgy,' you said?"

"That's what I was getting to. I was expecting to have sex tonight, and now everyone is dead. We've had to practice self-denial for a long while now. I like being with the girl that you two killed inside the other room usually. Deedra says 'no' to woman on woman, but I could ask you. Well?"

"Satanic sex? No way," I said. She pulled up her robe to flash a peek of what she had on underneath: nothing but a red, sheer thong. She'd also shaved herself down there from what I could tell. "On second thought, maybe we'll just see how it goes. Deedra says 'no,' huh? Funny. First, I want to know why you were praying to God."

I sat right next to her as she simply stated that her power was useless against us. She couldn't possess us even temporarily, so of course she turned to the other side. She didn't know anything about Christianity other than you ask Jesus for forgiveness, and she'd heard a few oft used Bible verses. I said forgiveness was indeed a gist of it, as long as you committed your life fully to Him after and strived to cease sinning. Christians were of course considered idiots under Satanic rules, so she never did learn much about them. I took the empty silver cup from her hand and put a gas station coffee mug in its place. I borrowed Deedra's knife, cut myself, and let the blood fill the mug to about half. Kaitlyn sipped it. I asked, "How's it taste?"

"Real good," she said, then killed the rest of it. "With a slight hint of Colombian coffee beans."

She leaned forward to kiss me on the mouth. The witch was bewitching me for certain as she grabbed my hand and placed it under her robe, and started pulling down my pants. I let it be, laid back, and damned myself for letting her take advantage of me in such an atrocious setting. There were six freshly dead bodies in the vicinity, and all I was doing was letting an incredibly sadistic murderer fondle and kiss me!

Deedra just sat there and observed us as if we were entertaining her. Kaitlyn pulled her robe off, and forced my head to her nipple after she laid on her back. I licked it in a swirling motion before I bit into the upper part of her small breast. It was a titillating experience, for sure. Deedra came over and must've been aroused by the dripping blood, or the both of us, as she took off her dirty clothes. Kaitlyn's hand quickly made its way toward Deedra's nether parts, rubbed, and inserted itself. We were three truly diabolical and sinfully beautiful beings after that.

Chapter 21—Greener Pastures

WE SHOULDN'T HAVE DONE IT, but 'shouldn't have' means we did. We'd made a deal with perhaps the foulest person I'd ever met: that little 18-year-old witch named Kaitlyn. We made her promise she'd dispose of the bodies, torch the place with the owner inside, and then wait for us unless she wanted us to make good on our previous 'slow and painful death' statement.

The thing was, she did make good on her promise about getting rid of the bodies, and must've worked hard all day doing just that. We guessed she used the truck to move them. At least the soil was soft to dig if that's what she wanted to do. The place was also mostly torched to the ground as specified. It wasn't fully 'fire season' yet as thunderstorms and ran still fell almost daily in the late afternoon to mostly douse them if they did start, so the fire hadn't spread. That same rain made our sleeping graves turn to mud, but that was the least of our problems after we knew that Kaitlyn was gone. A rock we told her to leave a note under in case of an emergency said, "Sorry! Bless you for your mercy. Talk to you soon." There was also an email address.

And that was it with her. *Bless you*? The truck was gone. Why we never just killed Kaitlyn in the first place before dawn was because of sloth on our behalf. We had an indentured slave to do our bidding. Our unspoken plan was that we'd kill her at dusk even though we told her that we wouldn't. I mean, she was the breakfast I thought about as soon as I woke up, and I'm sure Deedra had that feeling as well. We felt so hollow just listening to more thunder, and knew it'd start raining again. Common sense would've told me to run if I was her, too.

"Oh well," I said. "Nothing much we can do now, unless you want to chase her down right now. We can go get some leads where she lived, but personally, I just want to go to Seattle."

Deedra cursed again. "We should chase her down right now. She's too powerful to know who we are. But I don't know where she'd go. She'll go into the city, though. Probably Denver, but maybe Portland...or Seattle, or fuck, I don't even know. Somewhere in the northwest is my best guess, which ain't much. She could be in Mexico for all I know. Still, what did we expect from a servant of the Prince of Lies? And all because we were too lazy to get rid of the bodies ourselves. Idiots!"

"And she bewitched us, too," I said thinking about the lecherous acts of the early morning, in particular me drinking from her 'sensual areas' as we did what we were doing. "Do you think sex was part of a strategy to stall us and get on our good side?"

"Good side? Maybe. Stall us? No. I mean she just wanted to get laid one last time, obviously, and you remember how right before we left she expected to die? She had no strategy but to get laid. But yeah, we should've just chained her down for the day, because they did have handcuffs and leg irons from that sacrificed lady. Meh, she would've done some demon trick to escape, prolly. It would've taken us an hour or two is all to be rid of the bodies. That was stupid. Argh! Joan would kill me for my incompetence."

"Unless we want to track her down, no one is going to believe her anyway. I mean, what's she going to do?" I lit up a smoke. "Tell people vampires killed off her Satanic fiend friends during a Black Mass ritual in which they sacrificed someone, and spend the rest of her life in a prison mental institute? No way. She's the only suspect! Let her take the blame."

"Yeah, you're right. It's tough to shake you, innit? She's not going to tell anyone—can't tell anyone—otherwise she wouldn't have bothered doing all of that work with the bodies. She'll get a hold of us."

"This is a stupid question, but would you consider that psycho our friend?"

"No way, just a fuck buddy. We still might have to kill her the second we come in contact with her again. At least we have that email. Ooh! Big lead."

We went back to the car through a downpour. It wasn't very fun, and Deedra punched a tree real hard as her rage over Kaitlyn surfaced, but we managed. At least at long last I had a change of clothes. The limited visibility and traction while we drove slowed us down considerably, however. We were planning on getting into Seattle that night, but we figured we'd be just short. The rain did stop after awhile, but we'd already lost too much time just driving the speed limit. Spokane, Washington would be our stop. We killed a prostitute, and buried her on the way to Seattle the next night. I felt like the Green River killer, or Ted Bundy, as that used to be where they operated and did the same thing. I asked Deedra why those types of guys were never singled out by our kind, in particular by Joan, since I assumed she lived or had lived in that area some of the time when these serial murders occurred.

Deedra said, "She killed a couple of them, actually. You'd be shocked to see how many serial murderers have been in the northwest alone. It's uncanny. But the main ones that you hear about, she thinks those people are a necessary part of the human eco-system. I know, sounds awful, but it serves other purposes too as every unsolved missing person or found dead body can be attributed to these psychopaths. It makes our job easier; we can be avaricious in the killing sense."

"Serial killers: a perfected American innovation!" I laughed. "At least the modern ones. There have been others in other countries forever, but still. Like those Satan dudes we killed, and Kaitlyn—straight up bad guys. Man, that was fun, though."

She laughed. "Yup! I was like so-o-o like totally like waiting for that. It was groovy. I don't think we'll quite run across something like that again soon. Seattle's still good though, and Joan holds it. She hasn't even killed as much as the serial killers have these past few decades. I have. Joan did kill a lot when she first got here, I know, which is why she probably came here in the first place."

We arrived at our new home on the outskirts of Seattle. We'd made it, but I wouldn't get to see the Space Needle that night. Oh well, I bet I'd get sick of the sight of it eventually. I did see the faint outline of Mount Rainier. I'd hike that in due time. Seattle the seaport; Seattle the rainy city; Seattle the technological center; Seattle the Star of the Pacific Northwest; and Seattle the birthplace of 'grunge' rock. I couldn't wait to meet the women.

The new place we'd stay in was impressive. It was in the forest and hills (location discretion for obvious reasons) and that's all I can tell you so we're all safe. This house also had a high iron barred wall all around it, and it was nestled deep into a very tough to find area from what I could tell. Deedra said there was like 2,000 owned acres that the place was sitting on, and the next few closest houses were miles away. The abrupt halting of urbanization around her area gave us all the solitude we'd ever need. The bought land was money well spent whenever it was bought.

The house itself was a fairly prodigiously-sized brick mansion. It even had one of those roundabout driveways along with a garage that looked like it could've held 10 cars. It sort of reminded me of a hotel or something it had so many rooms. Deedra said there were 20 of them.

"What for?" I said as we drove up front in the roundabout area. "I don't know. She wanted a big place, and got it, I guess. Joan's no architect, but knows what she wants it to look like. Hardly any of those rooms have been slept in anyway, I don't think. Can you sense her here?"

"I don't sense anyone. Where's our valet?"

"We don't get one," she said and drove into the garage. "Besides, it's like four in the morning."

There were half a dozen different kinds of Lexus and Mercedes Benz cars and jeeps throughout the garage. "Hmm. Nothing old school here, but still flashy selections. She's what you might call a 'baller.'"

"Why, do you want something older to drive? We can get something for you."

"Don't spoil me! I'm proud. At least make me earn my keep. She'd seriously get something for me? I mean, these cars in here are already way choice. Just at the thought of driving one...man!"

"Vulgar, but those also make dem hoes wet, as they say back in the 'hood where it's all good. Joan would give you one. She's so going to trip you out. She looks like nothing you'd expect."

"Why?"

"She's young looking." "Well, so are we."

"Yeah, but wait 'til you see her, dude!"

We went in and I inquired about our sleeping accommodations. I couldn't wait for the winter, when I wouldn't have to wake up then go to bed a few hours later. I felt like some bad kid getting sent to bed early every night, and sometimes even without any supper. But I'd fed well, couldn't complain, and the vista of hunting old Chief Seattle's land intrigued me.

After walking through the elegant marble and plush carpet floored house, we went to vault that was even deeper in the ground than the one that was in the cabin by my hometown. It was definitely a high- class area. I almost felt underdressed, even though a lot of the styling seemed hippy-like with its bead strings hanging from some of the doorways, psychedelic paintings, original

Andy Warhol prints, posters of Jim Morrison, Hendrix, Guns N Roses, and old movie stars. I naturally assumed Deedra did a lot of the interior decorating. There was an odd assortment of unconventional objects about, including a blow-up alien doll next to an authentic ancient Greek statue.

This house's vault was hidden behind a revolving fireplace door. "Nice. She's got that whole castle thing going," I said. "Say, did you find out where Joan is?"

"She left me a note saying she's in India. See?" she flashed me the note. "She hasn't fed in a few months and needs to fill up, I guess."

"Like a gas station. She has cool handwriting. Not so 'bubbly' like most chicks these days. My handwriting sucks."

"When you get her age, you don't have to drink that often. But she still has the blood lust, you know? That never goes away. In India, she likes to drink all of those young HIV infected prostitutes up. There's literally like a million of them. Well, I don't know the number, but it's out of hand. Then they have this twisted belief if a guy has AIDS, he can get rid of it by screwing a virgin. So then of course the very youngest girls, like ten-years-old or whatever, get it. And so on that goes like dominoes."

Our elegant sleeping quarters, with ornate maroon velvet draperies all around, gold lamps, billowy beds, Persian carpets, etc... looked like it was capable of holding half a dozen vampires as there was at least that many coffins, but I preferred the open beds. I mean, did it matter if I slept in a coffin aside from perhaps nostalgia's sake of being a vampire? But mostly, I was tired of especially claustrophobic places like dirt graves and slits in mountains.

We laid back and stretched out. Deedra explained something about us not even having to kill everyone every single time if you were good. That was a relief. I would need to be more confident, but it'd beat dragging people out into the woods every night like the rest of those serial monsters did.

If I saw one of those killers, I figured I'd probably study them a bit out of curiosity sake before permanently ridding the Earth of them.

Chapter 22—Rave D'oeuvre

IT FELT SO GOOD TO WAKE UP and be warm, shower, to comb my hair, whatever. It wasn't as if I'd never stayed outdoors for a period of time, it was just that I definitely needed some sort of reminder I was still a part of society during a very transmogrifying period of my life. Sleeping in the dirt of the forest, a cave in the mountains, and then killing for survival like a wild animal made me feel so inordinately primal. I would've forgotten I used to have been human after another week of living like that.

I had money, I was out of clothes, and I had to go shopping. Deedra was still dressed in a hooded sweatshirt (newer), and baggy cargo jeans. I was dressed the same. I finally got to see the city of Seattle in all its splendor as we rolled into town in a Lexus. I was driving for once too, though I shouldn't have been since I had no idea what the freeways or whatever were like. Screw it, it felt so good to drive with the windows down. We hit an independent mom and pop record and accessory shop, and I finally got some clothes. I bought a couple of new t-shirts, sunglasses, CDs, and one of the shirts that had the likeness of Jim Morrison on it. I put that one on as soon as we got outside. We went to a department store before it closed and I bought a few pairs of pants. After that, we were done shopping as most of the clothing stores were closed.

Deedra said she knew of an artist girl that I should meet who'd called earlier and invited us to a party. The address given was an old warehouse building a little ways from the city in a suburb. I couldn't tell if we were in a different town or Seattle still. We snuck ourselves in with our quickness, though we could've paid the somewhat cheap cover charge. But screw lines on our short time. Deedra had put on her stylish blue lens sunglasses again, and I put on my new ones, as well. Cool dude guys. There were all sorts of crazy lights going, neon glow-sticks glowing, and loud, hype-inducing, bumping techno music—albeit a little dark sounding—that made little sense to me. It was a swinging rave shindig, and I'd never been to one before. So many young energetic young people around with the scent of fresh sweat, incense, and even some pot in the air.

Some drunk girl named Kate gave Deedra a hug and asked where she'd been. The brown haired Kate seemed out of place in her neutral brown corduroy pants and long sleeve striped shirt. Most everyone else had gothic, extravagant, or zany attire for the occasion.

"Oh, a little vacation," Deedra yelled over the music. "A.D., this is Kate. Kate, this is A.D. You guys are both artists, you know!"

Kate said, "Oh, are you? Nice to meet you! You guys should come by and check out my new work sometime. I could use the extra money! You'll love it too, Deedra. I used that one idea you had. It turned out like way too cool!"

We walked around slowly, observing the scenery. It was alright, but it was driving me nuts since I was so used to the solitude of the forests and mountains. I needed to quell my rising irritability so I could mellow and get on the same plane as everyone else. A girl who looked supremely faded sat with her friend on a table by the wall. They were by far the most lethargic people in the room. "Her," Deedra said.

I went and stood next to her, and used my mind powers. It's cool, babe, I relayed to her. There's nothing wrong. Take a look up at him. He likes you.

She glanced up at me, I nodded, and plopped close

next to her.

"What's up?" she said with low eyes.

I leaned close to her ear and said, "I'm going to kiss you for a second, cool? Good."

I never even gave her a chance to answer the question. I lowered my mouth from her ear to her neck, and bit. She winced, and I saw Deedra off by the dancing commotion, waving a finger at me while smiling. 'No, no,' she mouthed, and then disappeared into the 'ravers' to dance.

The blood tasted a bit tainted since the girl had done heroin or powerful pain pills. I bit into my tongue, then licked the girls neck up and down. It was all healed in an instant. Anymore blood lost, and the girl would have probably slipped into a coma forever she was so wasted. Who goes to a rave or whatever all high on that shit? Funny. I considered the other blood tastes from all of the people I had drank from; this one tasted different because of the heroin, yet so did the Satan worshiper's blood compared to my earlier victims. Wait a minute, I thought, that's because the Satan worshipers weren't drunk like all the others! They were sober, and so it gave me a different kind of 'pure feeling' buzz. *Weird.*

I gave the young strung out girl a quick hug and peck on the cheek. "Gotta go!" I said.

She never knew what hit her. I wouldn't have been surprised if she fell over dead if she self-medicated with any more injections out of a needle later on. Oh well, she wasn't my problem although I bet I was quite the trip to her.

Deedra was in the middle of the dancers, and out of curiosity, I asked a young nerdy looking party person if he knew what music group was playing over the speakers.

"It's Wumpscut, dude! Haven't you ever heard of them? This DJ is from New York. I think his name's Jet. He's even got some new industrial shit I ain't ever heard, bro."

"'Wumpscut,' huh? No, I have not heard of them. It was quite the mystery. Much obliged." I nodded my head to the beat. "Actually I don't know any of this type of music. Sounds dark but with catchy beats though. Hey dude, check out my girlfriend with the angel chick!"

"Lucky!"

I was just happy to be having some dude conversation for the first time in a while.

Deedra was feeling up some seductively dressed chick that had fake angel wings attached to her. The rest of her attire consisted of a glittery, light blue, very see through silk wedding maiden looking dress that one could see the lingerie underneath. She was not very inconspicuous, and stood out like a beautiful, sexy sore thumb.

Deedra started giving her a 'hickey.'

Crazy shit, dude.

Chapter 23—Indecent Proposals

DURING THE COURSE of the week, we ended up feeding off of a few junkies, gang bangers, and more prostitutes along with a few stolen 'kisses' here and there from various people. Prostitutes were a staple. I didn't like killing teen and college girls if they were too young, but they were great to snack on—or 'make-out with.' It's not as if I were having sex with a minor. The hookers gave Deedra an idea: Why not let me be the prostitute? She wanted to use me as bait.

"No way!" I laughed at her. "You are not using me as queer bait."

"Oh yes, I am," Deedra said. "I'm making you my bitch, remember? Jokes. But seriously, all you have to do is go to this one spot I know in the city. It's where a lot of male prostitutes go for their drug money or whatever. Who knows, maybe you'll get lucky and find yourself a boyfriend or sugar daddy!"

"Dude, as if I'll do it now after you say that!"

"Please, do it for me? Don't be so homophobic. We're in a liberal bastion, you redneck! Live a little, and I'll do you a favor, too. We can't be simple serial killers, as in we keep picking on female whores, and besides, I want some variety."

"Some fruity flavor, eh? Hah hah! That has nothing to do with being liberal-minded, you know—the exact opposite, really as I am saving them!—and I'm not scared of homosexuals if that's what you mean by 'homophobic.'"

"Then do it! You can make some money, too. It's not

like they'll sodomize you—I won't let them, my pretty—
it's usually just older creepy guys who want to give you
blow jobs. Or you can do vice versa if it suits your 'taste.'
Hah!"

"Intriguing. Thank you for not letting them sodomize
me. Where do I sign up for this good paying, skillful job?
Gross! Screw that."

"Please? I said I'll do any favor you want."

I did have some lustful favors I would've liked
fulfilled, but I wanted something basic that lead to that
anyway. "All right, quit begging. I'll do it on one
condition," I said.

"Yes!"

"Dude, you're like really psyched to pimp me out,
aren't you? Anyway, my condition is simple: get dressed
up really hot in two days, and we go see a movie, and
have a date."

"It's done. I'mma dress *you* really hot."

I don't know why I even agreed with her, but it's not
like I had anything better to do. Oh wait, yeah I did:
anything else. But the night before I'd never even went
out. Aside from a brief walk, I just stayed in most of the
night and read in the big library Joan had. That library
had antique books that I was afraid of even opening lest I
damage them, yet I couldn't help but admire everything
from the jackets to the letter fonts to especially the dusty
smell on them. She had like virtually every classic book
that you could have in its first printed year. The craziest
book I saw was an old German and widely used *Malleus
Maleficarum*, dated 1486, the original year it was
printed. It was written in Latin, the official Holy
language of the Catholic Church, and its title translated
is, "The Witches Hammer."

Next to it was an original 1597 *The Daemonologie*, by
King James IV of Scotland, or the First of England; and
you guessed it, it was that King James of the Bible
version.

There was a couple of those 1611 King James Version Bibles laying around, not to mention some even older different versions that may have been biased in translation. The Geneva Bible, the unofficial first well-written study Bible that abruptly ended its popular printing run in 1644 after being introduced in the mid-sixteenth century, was also present. That was fun to read, as it was also the true first Protestant Bible as regular people could read and interpret the scriptures in their own language, and not just be fed what the Catholic-controlled Latin version told people.

There also was some German writing on paper inside of a cabinet in a leather case, and I could see the name Martin Luther labeled on a side note near it. Based on the format, I presumed it was his 95 point thesis which led to the bloody rebellion against the Catholic Church when it was written and first posted on a church door on October 31st, 1517. It looked printed, as Luther's ideas had the fortitude of having John Gutenberg's printing press out in full force by then. Otherwise, he would've perhaps suffered the same fate of the *Malleus Maleficarum* text's victims as a heretic and his reform ideas would've been forgotten as other similar reformist's ideas did prior.

The library was a bibliomaniac's wet dream come true.

The night after the rave we'd visited the Kate artist girl. She was a good-hearted person. Deedra had bought some of Kate's morbid work in the past, and now she was again trying to sell some to her even though she was saving up paintings to have an actual gallery. Deedra could've afforded it easily, but said she'd think about it as far as buying any new stuff went. Her work was almost too dark in nature, but nonetheless well-designed. It had a lot of shock value, but it also had a casual, eloquent beauty to it. Looking through her portfolio, I saw on oil and canvas a bluish image of a girl with a needle in her arm resting against a wall; an excavated mass grave with people about crying; a mushroom atomic cloud with ghosts in it; Holocaust victims; a monk burning; and other friendly images. I wanted to buy her seven part collection of Dante's *Inferno* paintings. That was Deedra's idea she'd mentioned at the rave, and it was really well done. Later, Deedra told me not to buy her stuff as she wanted Kate to get her own gallery. Let her starve and work for a bit, as it'd all be worth it and give her more insight to what she wanted to paint, Deedra reasoned. It sounded good to me. After all, I did some of my best writing and painting while under much duress. Making art is a good drug to alleviate emotional pain. I loaned Kate fifty dollars anyway for beer and food money, and gave her some weed.

Deedra dropped me off at the 'designated' area. There were other young males present who looked like they might want to kick my ass for stealing potential clientele, and they probably would've tried if not for the new silver luxury Cadillac that quickly pulled up and called to me.

"You," a middle-aged man said. That was annoyingly fast. I walked over to his car and scanned his thoughts. They were too perverted to echo. The guy was actually rubbing himself while looking at me. *Ugh! I hate you, Deedra.* He said, "Need a ride?"

"Sure," I said, and grudgingly went into the car.

"What is it?" he said after we pulled off. He meant the price.

I wanted to ask how much he had, but that would've been 'unprofessional,' or just gave me away as an informant or something. I knew nothing of male whoremongering. I skimmed his mind, and he had an assortment of prices picked out for various deeds, but wanted to pay around $200 since it was pretty me, and that would be for a while. "What do you want?" I said.

He told me something 'basic' at first, and I tripled the price. He was sort of perturbed, but I didn't care as I watched Deedra's car following us from a distance out the side of my eye. He started griping about usual prices and I noticed he had a wedding band on as well, but he *really* liked me, and I knew he'd pay whatever it took. I finally said, "Look, I'll make you a deal. Get a cheap room, and take that cost out of $350 and give me the rest. I'll give you an hour to do whatever you want."

"Two hours."

"Fine," I said, obviously planning on reneging anyway. Maybe part of it was narcissist pride in seeing how wanted I really was.

I didn't want to know what he was thinking, and I tried to make myself go away in my own head. It was not cool at all. He was babbling away about 'making this sort of arrangement in the future. We could make a schedule. *Your name is Abidan Drew. You are an artist and writer. You are still you, remember*. Perhaps next time could be longer, he said. He'll pay more tonight even. Maybe go to his home. He has a better setup. *You love to read. You want to write books yourself. Perhaps you'll make a fine author someday*. He was holding my leg, and moving his hand up too uncomfortably. I roughly swatted it away, and said, "Not...until...you pay."

We were finally in the motel room. *Anytime now, Deedra*. The guy asked me to "gently" take off my clothes, and turn slowly with my hands on the back of my neck so he could have a better look at me, but I of course stalled and said I had to use the bathroom to piss. I had to assure him it wouldn't be counted against his time.

I came out and Deedra was still not present. I figured she might be near and would come in at the appropriate time—if not, then it was her loss. The guy was getting impatient with me, and said he was paying a lot of good money.

Screw it, I thought as I walked to the guy and stood close to him. He was completely enamored, but I never looked him in the eyes—only his neck. Using both hands, he grabbed my arse, and then tried to kiss my mouth. *Alright, enough of that.*

I drank from the guy as I covered his mouth with my hand, calmly told him to 'shush,' and forgot all about the scenario I'd just gone through to get there. Was all that posing as a prostitute for this man—with perhaps a family of his own—really necessary? Maybe, maybe not, but it didn't matter then. There went my conscience. There was a quiet but rapid pounding on the door that I knew to be Deedra. I roughly shoved the guy down and opened the door. She came in, closed it, and started laughing hysterically. The guy on the ground, holding his neck, started to make some commotion and yelled a bit. Deedra shushed him as she rushed to finish him off on the floor. She fell back on the bed, and started to point and laugh at me some more.

"Har-dee frickin' har," I said. "So-o-o funny. Why don't you do that next time if it's so great?"

Deedra had a bad case of perma-laugh. "That..." Deedra could barely breath. "That...pederast, he wanted...he wanted to—"

"I know!" I said before I went and washed my hands.

***

WE WENT TO KATE'S apartment after that, leaving the Cadillac with the keys in it in a sort of gang-run neighborhood. They'd profit off it. We left the body in our trunk as a surprise and labor cost. It was cool to hang out at Kate's. It was near the busy Capitol Hill area that had a beatnik collegiate atmosphere about it. Kate wasn't as uncomfortably radical and judgmental as some of the young locals were wont to be. Not that it wasn't the same for conservatives, but some of them so-called liberals could be ironically un-liberal and even bigoted in not considering other viewpoints.

Tonight Kate was busy painting away, but there were some people in her den. They'd entertain us for a bit. They were stoned on weed and LSD, sipping beers, listening to some music from a band called London After Midnight, and sort of talking about vampires, oddly enough. *How typically gothtastic*, I sarcastically thought. A young twenty-something 'grunge kid' about my age named David knew a lot about Vlad 'The Impaler,' and was telling of his cruel deeds in defense against the Ottomans. It sounded like he studied it well, actually. Perhaps he did a paper on him. It was necessary psychological warfare, I chimed in, as "everyone just hated Turks." Someone had to thwart and stall the Ottoman Empire's Muslims from creating a gateway into Europe. We can't judge those times, places, or deeds given that motive—although I think dining in the middle of hundreds or more impaled men just to hear them in pain as if it were an orchestra as their bowels emptied was a bit extreme. It was also a theme from one of Kate's newer paintings, hence the conversation subject matter.

The other people—two girls and a dude—were what one would label as 'gothic.' One girl even had custom fake fangs on, and asked if we liked them before pulling them off and putting them in her purse. Of course we did. They were very pretty like her. She used them on Halloween once, and now just wore them whenever.

Deedra and I nodded as she told us this.

The girls said they sometimes sucked on each other's wrists after cutting themselves. I asked if I could try sucking on the one named Melissa who had the fangs, high boots, fishnet shirt, nylons, and a short black skirt, and black lipstick. The Woman In Black. I guess I wore black a lot too, because it was easier to keep clean. Her white and ghostly make-up made her look like more of the stereotypical vampire than me or Deedra ever did. We weren't pale because of the pervert we'd drank, otherwise I thought Deedra did look like a vampire too, 'if there was such a thing.'

She was very hesitant, but I peer pressured her. "Oh, come on," I said. "It'll be trippy. Plus, it'll totally like enhance your high. I don't have STD's, I promise."

"Yeah," Deedra said as she moved a spot towards her on the couch. "We want to know what it tastes like. We're thirsty."

Man, we were bad. She really wanted to be a vampire in a psychological sense, and with both me and Deedra conniving and doing our Jedi mind tricks, she couldn't resist, much to her redheaded female companion's dismay. For her friend it was a sort of private ritual, not something to be dragged out in front of whoever the hell we were. I got the vibe that her friend didn't like Deedra, and especially me. There was no need to read that in her mind as it was evident on her face. Oh well, at least she didn't become violently jealous, although she heavily pondered the notion.

She pulled out a razor that was probably used to cut her dope among other things, and I winced when she cut her lightly scarred forearm. "Let me try," Deedra said, grabbed her hand, and stopped the needless suspense. After a sip she commented, "It doesn't taste that bad, but it doesn't taste that good either."

What a liar! It was my turn to try and act like I hadn't drank blood before, but I sucked and drank the dribble of blood hard. It did not want to come out very well, and it was too much of a tease. I had the urge to just bite it. I think I frightened girl as she pulled her arm away. I had to quick think of a lie. I said, "I like that a lot." I could not tell a lie. "Anyone else want to donate?"

"Dude!" one of the guys said. "You have fangs, too! I didn't know that. Let me see 'em!"

That didn't work out too well. *Oh, shit.* Where did I get the fangs? I, uh, bought the fangs at...where did that girl get hers? Ah, yes, that's where I got mine, too. I'm an out-of-towner, and can't recall what specific places are called. I opened up to them a little more after that, and I think they were paranoid of me when we finally left. They also thought Deedra was weird too for some reason.

Perhaps it was their drugs. We had indeed left an indelible impression on them, as we were like the twilight zone portion of their psychedelic highs. All in all, it was a piquantly swell night.

Chapter 24—Date Rape

ON THE NIGHT of our planned date, Deedra came out from getting ready looking as bombshell as ever. A backless, black silk, evening gown with a long slit in the leg hugged her ravishing body like a glove. She said it was some Italian brand I didn't catch as I stared at legs that were highlighted by black-seamed, full-length nylons (with a small but deadly dagger attached to a leg band on the inside of her 'non-slit dress' leg), high stiletto heels with straps around the ankles that wound up her calf a little bit, arm-length opera gloves, diamond earrings, and a high collared platinum and diamond necklace. Her face was accentuated with gold eye shadow and dark, maroon lipstick. She was Helen of Troy to me, and would've easily made anyone's top fantasy. She said she also had 'special clothes' for after the date. Bonus!

She was being apologetic about her straight, plain hair with two, thin bang-braids on each side attached in the back, but I never let her finish apologizing as I kissed her, and told her how perfect she was. I liked the way her shiny hair matched up so well with the dress' black color. Deedra could play dress up exquisitely if the mood fancied her right. I really wished she would've have done it more often, as it was better than her baggy jeans with holes in them, or the local 'grunge' look. Whatever was convenient, I guess.

My clothes for the occasion? I was dressed sharp. There was a closet full of high priced suits of various sizes and styles, shoes, and even tuxedos. I didn't know whose they were, but I thought I'd borrow one. I found a dark gray, Armani suit that fit me. The dark blue one I liked was a bit short. I also had a dark blue tie with thin, maroon, slanted stripes. I looked very Wall Street and business-like instead of formal. Oh well, I didn't want to look like I was going to a wedding.

Deedra approvingly whistled. I'd even used gel in my hair. "My, oh my, love," she said. "Aren't we the handsome one?" To have a woman that ravishingly gorgeous sincerely call you her 'love' makes you very appreciative to be alive, or whatever. "So, where are you taking me tonight?"

I told her it was some theater called the Big Picture, and I had reservations for us in some sort of plush private "Living Room" area of the theater that let you smoke cigars. I had to pay a hefty price of a few hundred dollars per hour and that took a chunk of my spending money out, but that didn't matter. It was for her, and she was impressed. I could've also taken her to dinner, but who goes to the hooker strips or searches for heroin junkies on a date? Along with the homeless, those were vampire staple foods, and not really delicacies. I don't know why to a point, but wealthier people with more prestige tasted better. Anyway, we were well fed for the week. On average, all we needed was a few victims a week to sustain us. After that it was just gluttony. "I'd like to take you to an opera or a play or something classy, but I think we are a bit too late for that. You'll of course have to guide me to this place as I don't know where I'm going. This city and its funny streets. I'll be baffled for weeks to come, I'd wager."

"Joan is supposed to be in town sometime this week! Goody. And I sent that witch Kaitlyn an email telling her to get her butt up here and to write back to me so we could kill her. That was like two days ago though. I didn't say that in the email, 'we were going to kill her,' though!"

I didn't feel like discussing the politics of killing someone under a flag of truce, even if it was an evil bitch like Kaitlyn, so I wouldn't argue the point right then. I put my arm around Deedra's elbow and we walked out to the cars. We'd take the Mercedes Benz jeep. It felt so cool to have options like we did for vehicles. Life was perfect.

After our late night film and more conversation as I puffed on cigars, we randomly strolled the streets. We ended up veering towards Kate's place, and Deedra became a chatter box.

"You know, in the winter time it's easier to become more 'cultured,' and we can hit all of the theater stuff if you'd like, or that's what I do. I wasn't really into it until Jacen got me into it in New York. But when you go with him it's like, going with your grandfather or something. At least to me it was! I just couldn't help thinking about his actual age even though he was hot. Plus, he did keep treating me like I was his granddaughter or something. I'm going to have to tell you about my New York adventures sometime. Anyway, I was saying something about my hair, and I could get it more professionally styled and all, but it takes time, and that's something we don't have a lot of in the summer, but you get used to it. It hasn't even rained since we've been here. I think that the same storm we had while driving in was the last time it rained here. Maybe we should go to a bar. Would you like to go to some sort of night club? But it's kind of getting late for that."

"Maybe," I said. "We look so high class to waste it. I feel like we should be on our way to some VIP party or something."

"That takes a little planning, but I just throw around Joan's friends' names or whoever she donates financially to. There's this club around the other side of town, and maybe we can get ourselves a drink. There are a lot of yuppies there, and those chicks will adore you. They'll give you a drink from their neck, and not even know. They like graduate from preppy to yuppy. That's funny! Women are much easier to get than men, it always looks like to me, but you and Jacen are too smooth. Well, you're just bold, and he's smooth. It'd seem that men would be easier to drink because they have the higher sex-drive and will throw themselves at you. But you know, I think for me it's harder partly due to me not wanting to come on to men so much as to not be seen as a whore or tease. I know this Madame, and I could have a part-time courtesan job, you know! I did it once, but it wasn't that cool, really. I just can't do it cause I wasn't attracted to them, you know? You don't have to do them. You can just bite them and spank them and they love it. You said you wanted to make your own way. I respect that. You can be an escort!"

"Well, I don't know about all that, but I got to do something for my keep," I said. Deedra sounded like she was high on speed. "But I don't want to be an escort to some rich lonely old lady or a whatever. I'm not going to mooch off Joan forever, although I don't mind living there for obvious safety purposes. I just want to have my own respectable income I can be proud of and at least be able to tell my grandparents something. I'll start painting again tomorrow too, and work on getting some stuff published, too. I want a legacy, you know? With that library, I got some serious resources to write some good historical articles for some publisher. I'll just write and tell my grandparents I'm on a fishing boat in Alaska anyway. Beats saying, 'I rob and kill people.'"

"Legacy, makes sense. Money? Not so much, we're fucking loaded, and it's all yours too. Never feel bad, we're superfluous royal style. We could feed all the homeless forever instead of feeding off of them. Hah! Anyway, I wanted to go to Kate's house because I do feel I should help her out. I'm going to loan her some money. She's going to sell a couple of her paintings for dirt cheap just to pay her rent. That's not good. I'll pay it for her and tell her it's an advance for the 'Dante' picture. I'll let her keep it for the gallery showing though, let her get some prints off it before she sells it to me. That's her mark in this world. I love that one."

"Me too. It's amazing."

We got to Kate's, and Deedra said she was the only one there. I never went in, and just waited outside across the street in the dark. Deedra was sort of talking my ear off, and I wanted to smoke the rest of the cigar. I didn't mind her talking too much, because she was riding a high. Not a blood high or generic temporary high, but a high that she was genuinely content and proud to be walking next to me. I was so pleased for us. I knew this was likely the happiest Deedra had ever been in her life since it was probably her first date ever. I'd been feeling the same too since we started our road trip. Sure, the annoying necessities of being a vampire game me moments that nearly drove me mad, but I could just shut down, read away, and go back to my artistic endeavors when it all became too much. Then again, I didn't really have anything to be stressed about anymore compared to those living in the hustle and bustle of working life.

After being outside for about 10 minutes as Deedra did her business, I had a wonderful idea come to mind, and it was interrupted as a disturbance came about the atmosphere.

'Over here. Let me have a look at you,' a thought said to me. It was directly into my brain like an earphone. Very suspicious, I kept my mind closed, trying only to let that particular voice back in. *'It's okay, I'm one of you. Are you alone?'*

Reason told me not to trust this being, this being I knew to be a vampire, and shut off my mind completely, run away from the area, and tell Deedra about the voice later. But I couldn't risk having this thing track me to Deedra or Kate, however. I had to protect them. Deedra could probably handle her own, but Kate could not. I opened my mind again ever so slightly. Whoever spoke again. *'I'm alone. I just was in the area and saw you.*

Are you alone?'

I gave whoever my own question. *'Why the hell you care if I'm alone or not?'*

'I don't want you to hurt me.'

I thought to them, *'I have no reason to.'*

'Then...come here? I saw you smoking, and then went up three blocks. It's private here.'

'I don't know, it sounds like a trap to me. You come here.'

'Just come, please.'

I actually didn't want to meet whoever this was in front of Kate's apartment complex and have Deedra coming out, because then they'd know where Kate lived. A rocked skipped across the street, signaling to me where to go. I begrudgingly went.

The object of my infatuation in the nearly windowless alley turned out to be a wild looking, bleach-blonde female who looked like she was about 35 or so in human years, but she was far older in vampiric years. I could sense the power radiating off of her. I think she may have been showing that on purpose for a dramatic effect. I wasn't nervous at all then, but very curious.

"Hello," I said.

She turned her head slightly, as if it helped her observe me better. I looked at her clothes; a fur-lined long coat, a dark purple, very old school corset a black, leather mini-skirt, and heeled, thigh high, tan leather boots. Her hair was in some type of 1950's beehive style with braids going to each breast, accentuating her oval face with its fierce eyebrows. Her blue eyes gleamed and tried to impress me before she spoke. "Why, you're just a baby, aren't you?" she said in a brisk, British accent. I think it was British. "Isn't this the freakiest bechance? I was going to just dispose of you, but I'd like to keep you instead as I may need you, love. You look too unique. I can see why they chose you. Now, where's your maker?"

The hell she was keeping or needed me. She'd

probably functioned perfectly well without me before now and would continue to do so. "He's not here," I said. It looked like I had a fight or something coming on with this chick. The only other female I'd ever hit was Deedra the night she made me, oddly enough. "This is not your territory, and I'm not going with you."

"As you Yanks say, 'This is a free country.' I can go wherever I please."

"But I have American Indian ancestors," I said contemptibly and pointed to myself, "and I say get off Chief Mojo Rising's land, or we become what the government refers to as 'hostile.'"

She laughed. She found my feistiness amusing but annoying. "So I take it your maker is not present. No big deal, as it's probably best for them. Now you'd be wise to lose that haughty-naughty attitude, as I'm already going to make you apologize repeatedly for it. Now come along like a good little boy so I can spank you proper before bed time."

Funny. "Maybe another time...love," I said and winked.

Even though I knew she meant me harm as in kidnapping—the spanking was not what I was worried about—she was curiously tempting!

I sensed someone behind me, turned, and saw a large, overcoat wearing, hooded male vampire with a large chain draped on one shoulder and a machete at his side. I could barely see the outline of his square white face. *Fuck, me. Shoulda figured that fucking guy would show up!*

The lady said quite rapidly, "As you can see, you don't have an option unless you want to die right now, but I think I'd rather take you alive to be my slave since my other wore. Quite frankly, the only reason you're still breathing is because I like the way you look, and I want you to live just to call me 'Mistress.' Now just come along young lad, as we're running out of time and I'm losing my patience!"

"Quite frankly, piss the 'fook' off," I said, ready to make a break for it. So much for negotiating. She was stubborn. What was I, a magnet for psycho chicks?

Another female vampire dressed more plainly in a light-purple Colombia jacket and jeans hopped down from the roof, wielding a sword. I knew I was screwed as they enclosed their circle around me like wolves, waiting for me to go whichever direction so they could react. *Oh, man, I'm fucked.* They were too close and ready to strike.

"Wait, wait, wait!" I said. I had to buy time, but they weren't selling it. Deedra was still not around, but I figured she was going to come to my rescue—somehow. I dared not open my mind about her. "I'll go with you, okay? No need for the violence. I'm with you guys. The word is 'cool.'"

"Chain him up, and take him to the car," the leader lady said as she was on me and jerked me by my hair, and immediately took a good drink out of me so I'd be weakened. In another time I would've liked it, but not while a pair of rough dude hands grabbed my arms and pulled them back. "I'm going to enjoy running that rebel streak out of you as you grovel at my heels, and you will call me Mistress from now on." She grabbed my crotch roughly. "Got it?"

She had me by the balls, quite literally. I had no choice but say, "Yes...Mistress."

I was not content to be this wild woman's servant until perhaps she grew tired of me and killed me. Deedra knows for sure by now. Wait for the opportune time. The chains were tightly and deliberately wound around my arms, and I had to try something. "You don't have to chain me," I said. "Please, Mistress?"

"Oh, but I like you chained, it looks good on you. I have other ideas of what might look good on you, too, that's not that fancy suit," she said as she held my chin and licked my cheek. "Plus, I'd hate for you to try to escape."

Well, she's going to hate this too, I thought, and head-butted her nose my hardest, and dropped to the ground whilst doing a leg sweep as best as I could to the ones holding me to force them back. I'd knocked one male down, but it took me a second too long to shake the chain off and by then the sword wielding female had stabbed deep into my lungs as I rolled away on the ground. The blade tore all the way out of my side. The guy with the machete that I knocked down had reacted quickly enough while falling to nearly hack off my leg at the thigh. It was the worst physical pain I ever felt aside from maybe the night I died at the hands of Deedra. I heard a loud *ching*! noise and saw Deedra with a tire iron. She'd whacked the sword wielding female square on the forehead, and sliced and stabbed her up in deft blurring moves as she fell away. Then she started banging the hell out the other male one with rapid blur swings. She'd caught them totally off guard. The main 'Mistress' female was already on her hands and knees with most of the inside of the back of her neck exposed to me as her head was half cut-off, and a good puddle of blood lay on the ground before her. *Way to go, Deedra!* If that was a cat fight, then Deedra was a Saber-toothed tiger.

I looked at my wound, and knew I should've been dead. A hole sliced through me from my sternum, down through my ribs, and out by my kidney. That woman had almost cut me in half. I was fading out rapidly, too hurt, and didn't think I'd make it. There was only a small pool of blood around me as a result of being drained. Not good. I stood up, hardly being able to support myself from my injured leg. I looked at that too, and wished I hadn't. *Geez, I think he cut half-way through the bone.* I wanted to cry. *What to do?* Deedra stabbed the eye out of the one female would—be kidnapper down the street. The male kidnapper had ran away while carrying the

Mistress, his own face a bloody mess. *Everything...so fast.* I fell over. I heard shrieks of pain. *Was that me? It could be. No, I can't even really breathe. I want to say something. Is this how it all ends?* Deedra swept me away to the jeep as I faded more out than in. "Where we going?" I said while gaining temporary consciousness. "What're they doing?"

"Don't talk, just breath steady...easy," Deedra said as she put me in the back of the jeep. "They're helping what's her face out. They won't follow us now unless they don't want to save her. I'll fucking...fuck her!" I was completely out for a moment, then we were driving and Deedra was banging on the steering wheel. "Shit! Shit, shit, shit! This can't be happening. You're my best friend. No, I don't want you hurt! I love you too much, Abidan. God, I'm sorry. Forgive me, please. Please, don't die! I wouldn't do anything to ever get you hurt A.D.! God, I hate myself so much! I...I love you too much!"

She was crying, sobbing, and I wanted to tell her I was all right and she'd saved me. But I couldn't talk, and really didn't know if I was all right. I tried to say a redemption prayer just in case, but my consciousness went out like a dimming light again.

Chapter 25—Sweet Dreams Are Made of These

I WAS ON A BED in the vault area, and the pain was brutal as the initial physical shock and numbness of being attacked faded. I knew it was the next day. Or night. Deedra cut her wrists deep, and was draining herself over my severe torso wound. Everything was blurry, but I didn't want to fade out. Deedra's eyes were red, and her face was streaked with blood tears. She'd been crying hard. I have to comfort her. Morpheus beckoned, and I went away and dreamed instead.

Daylight. It was usually sunny daylight in my dreams, and there were these random righteous scruples pounding at me during the most peculiar times. I'm walking with my buddy Drew, and he's telling me something. We stop by a mountain creek we believe that no one else has even been to before aside from a mountain man or Native years ago. He just wants me to hear him out. He sits on a rock, takes a drink from his canteen, splashes water on himself. He says matter-of-fact like after getting up, then sitting back down, "She's troubled, you know? That's some good fucking water. But don't go her way. Show her the true way. Help her. Help each other. You've become rather amoral. Sure you messed up bad at the end of your life, but that doesn't mean you can't change now."

How does he know about Deedra? My dreams are interrupted, and I wake up briefly to feed on someone. I rudely don't even open my eyes to look at them. The smell of Lotus filled my imaginary air.

I'm at church and people are crying. I'm crying, too. I'm at a funeral, Drew's funeral, and this did happen. The urn is what's left of him. I stare at the urn until it becomes blurry with my tears, and a preacher is talking. I curse God. Someone taps me on the shoulder. I look up and Drew is standing there. "Good to see you again, brother," he says.

"Where are you, man?"

"I can't tell you, bro. I really can't tell you. They won't let me."

"Why did you die?"

"Why?" he says, then chuckles as if my question amuses him. "There is no 'why.' You know that. There just is."

"Please, at least tell me you're in a better place," I plead.

There is the faintest trace of a smile on his lips, yet there is sadness in his eyes, and I don't know what it means.

I say, "Will I ever see you again?"

He embraces me tightly, and I hold him back. I don't ever want to let go. He says, "I'm sorry I left you, bro, but I'm at where I'm at. You're a true person. That's what they say about you, and it's right. Don't ever forget who you really are."

And then he was gone.

***

"HERE, TAKE HER. WAKE UP." Deedra was shaking me. "You have to. You have a dearth of blood, and it's almost time to sleep again."

There was a scared, scrawny brown-skinned teenage girl in short cut-off jeans and a dirty halter top begging for her life. She kept saying she was only 16, and didn't want to die. She said she wanted to go back home. Back to Wyoming. She wanted me to care. Her family and tribe would report her. *Hmm.* We should please just let her go, she kept saying. Deedra should've at least told her some kind of white lie on what she was doing there, but what did it matter now? She wanted to know why we were in such a deep basement, and I think my gory appearance frightened her terribly. I lay there naked and wounded. The wounds must heal, Deedra said. I must have fresh, youthful, nourishment.

I raised my left arm, Deedra gave the girl's neck to my still strong grip, and I drank the sobbing girl.

I regained my consciousness a little bit after slaking my thirst. "Where's those other vampire people?" I asked tiredly. The girl slid limply to the floor.

Deedra was happy just to hear my voice, and she was rubbing her hand through my hair. "They're not in town," she said. "They might try and be back for revenge eventually, because we got them good. I hope they'll try. Joan will be here tonight. We'll have a good dust-up then. Don't worry about them."

Sleep.

***

I WAS STILL WEAK THE NEXT NIGHT. Deedra let me drink her as dry as possible, and then I relaxed as she went to get me yet another person, I figured. I was going through people pretty fast, I thought as I closed my eyes.

I figured I was dreaming as the blonde, glowing, porcelain-faced angelic creature stood by the doorway. Perhaps she'd come to take me away. An Angel of Death at last. Deedra came out from behind and I was happy to see her, although my eyes were more focused on the girl. She didn't look panicked by the sight of me at all, but she did look concerned. "Who's the child?" I asked. "Is she for me?"

The child laughed, and it sounded as if a chime echoed in her voice. She took several steps, floating briskly and ghostlike as she did, then was next to me as her dress settled. Not wanting to be vulgar, I made sure I was covered down below. I was. I studied her darling, alabaster, almost cherubic face with its large emerald eyes. I read somewhere on a sign that said Seattle was the 'Emerald City.' She had pouty lips, a refined and delicate nose, a wide forehead, and sophisticated sharp eyebrows that made me think of the word 'nobility' whilst trying to read her emotions. She was very short next to Deedra, and I judged her to be about 14. She leaned over and gave me a kiss on the lips before signaling to her neck, her blonde hair with curly locks caressing my face. I said to her, "You have a nice library."

"Why thank you," she said. "And welcome to my very humble abode."

Both her and Deedra laughed hard. I had to smile, because it hurt when I started laughing. "Humble!"

It got even better as I drank from Joan. Man, that stuff was potent. And of all things, she'd just gotten over a feeding frenzy or whatever in Asia, and I could feel that mixed-strength and freshness. Yeah, I felt bad for draining her, but she really hit the spot. I could actually witness my wounds healing better after I finished drinking from her. All of my tissues were connected and it wasn't open anymore; it was just the regular outer layer of scarred looking skin that needed healing, and perhaps the rib bones needed more mending together, as I felt an incredible soreness when they helped me to sit-up. I got to put my feet on the floor and be upright at last.

I looked at the blood stained sheets. "I'll change these if you want me to," I said. I couldn't focus well. I was going to say something else, but I forgot what it was.

"You'll do no such thing," Joan said, her voice sounding more like a teenager with a slight German accent than the angel she resembled. "So, Deedra tells me you like to start trouble? I jest! Don't worry, we'll get them for you."

"Can I come?" I asked, and then realized I'd only hinder them. "You just need rest," Joan said. "We've got to go feed soon. You've drained us both well. I just fed after months, too!"

"Sorry about that. I really am."

"Don't be," Joan said. "The important thing is that my daughter's love is okay."

I chuckled and said, "'Love.' That one chick...never mind. I'm out of it a bit."

I stood up, and the harsh sharp pain shook throughout my body, but I ignored it. I felt old. Deedra came over to assist me. I didn't know where I was going, aside from that I needed some good air. "What time is it?" I asked.

"It's like three," Deedra said. "Where do you want to go?"

"Outside. I need some air. I need to read some newspapers, too. It feels like I've been in a coma."

"You have been."

Joan assisted me, too. "Damn, you are young," I said and laughed. Ooh, that hurts!

Joan said, "Au contraire! Pardon my French, but you're just a baby. But I get that a lot. I must look good for my age. I was born only yesterday it seems. Jah. Yesterday and many centuries ago."

"Where were you born?" I said.

"Worry about your health first," Joan said as we made our way up the stairs. "My name's actually Gertrude, but I go by Joan if Deedra has not already told you. Oh, I'm from Bamberg, Germany, too. I was born in 1609. I sound like a chat room introduction now."

"Damn." I was shocked just to hear the fact. "You've lived awhile. Was Bamberg that town with all the witch burnings?"

"Yes, it was," Joan said. "Bad times. I'll tell you later. You seem to have an 'insatiable hunger for knowledge.' Deedra said something like that. She didn't speak all bad about you!"

I smiled. "She said 'insatiable,' too, right?"

"Jah! That was her word. You know her."

"Yup!"

We were outside, and Joan left Deedra and I to discuss our plans on the back patio that had a lot of statues among other pieces artwork. There was also an outdoor atrium in the center that we sometimes chilled at with a lot of plants in its garden. Deedra had also planted marijuana seeds in that garden, so there were like some nice looking very green, purple, and orange tinged plants right in with the regular plants and bonsai trees. *Weirdo*. To be fair, they were pretty plants. She also had all kinds of rare orchids and different mountain flowers. Deedra said they had some Oriental guy come buy every week or so to trim them and talk to them and whatnot.

"I'm going to go to with her to kill them," Deedra said, her eyes dead set and intense. "Those scum suckers won't get away with this."

"Dude, you already fucked them up pretty good from what I could tell," I said. The fresh air cleared my head. "But yeah, she was trying to steal 'your baby.'"

"Not good enough for me. And damn right, she can't take you from me. You're my bitch, not hers. Prison rules. Hah, hah! But seriously, I'm sorry I didn't come in earlier to assist you. I knew they were around, but I had to find a weapon and wait for the opportune time to strike."

"Hey, I was there. I know what happened. You did what you had to do, otherwise we both could've been injured bad. How are you anyway?"

"I'm okay. I got grazed on the shoulder by that machete, and sliced on the arm, it wasn't serious though. I'm healed already, but they ruined my favorite dress! I special ordered it."

"That's right," I laughed. "You were kicking ass in that dress! I barely remember seeing all of that."

She hugged and kissed me. "I know. I thought you were dead. Well, I don't know how us vampires cope in regards to wounds that severe, but I knew she drank you and you could've ran out. Don't ever do that again. You scared me."

"Yeah, I'll try to avoid activities that consist of people thrusting swords through me. It's a good thing I'm not fighting samurais. Anyway, aren't you guys going to get a bite to eat?"

"Nah, maybe tomorrow. She makes it seem like we're in a rush tonight, but being in rush for her is like a week. That's what I have I to tell you about. Tomorrow we're going to go hunt those fiends down. We're going to California and cleaning the whole coast all the way down. She's going to do most of the killing, I'm going to sort of observe and polish them off if need be. It'll probably be tedious work to even find them, but we got to send a message: Nobody fucks with us."

"Sounds good. Do what you have to do. But what makes you think they went to California?"

"Logic. They are too messed up to go anywhere else but south unless they have a plane—which is always possible. But they'll have to keep feeding if the leader woman is not already dead. Besides, that's the direction that they came from."

"Hmm. Did you get anything else out of them?"

"This is the part that will really trip you out: They heard about us through Kaitlyn."

"Kaitlyn?" I almost yelled. "What the hell were they doing talking to her?"

"They found her in Denver, that's all I know. It makes sense though, as she was probably naturally trying to search for more of our kind anyway and left herself vulnerable. I don't know what they did and got out of her, but they were already on the lookout for the two of us. They had to have heard about Joan though, and maybe assumed it was okay to whatever...'clean us out.' I don't care. I'm trying to find Kaitlyn too on this trip, though I have a feeling she'll try to find us now if they didn't kill her, which I don't think they did, apparently. They're stupid if they didn't."

"Damn. That's...complex."

I'd thought about Kaitlyn at least once on a nightly basis when I was more conscious. Truth be told, I was hoping she was still alive.

Deedra said, "Listen, you'll be safe here anyway. Just stick around the neighborhood until we come back. That could be a couple of weeks. Try to get ahold of Kaitlyn, see if she's alive if I bypass her. I'll check in periodically through email or phone, but we'll be busy. I don't mean only stay around the house—you can drive around town—just don't leave the Seattle area. I mean, we'll try to make sure the whole state is clean for sure, but just use precaution. You're probably still pretty weak."

"Yeah, I am. I might go check out Kate after I feed one of these nights."

"Dude, I'm sorry, but she's dead."

"What?"

"Bastards killed her. They drained her early the next night or something and left. I found her."

I was very perturbed. "Fucking hell! Cowards! How? I mean, why?" I was on the verge of angry tears. "The only reason why I confronted that vampire bitch in the first place was to make sure they stayed clear of her."

"Listen, I know how you feel. Trust me. One of them probably went back to see what we were doing in that neighborhood in the first place, and came across her and read her mind. They stuck a heroin needle in her arm to make matters worse, make it look like she killed herself. She'd never touch heroin, she's seen the worst of what that stuff can do. That's too bad, but we got to move on. We'll avenge her. That's partly the reason why I'm going with Joan and watching you: it's personal. Otherwise, she insisted she do it on her own."

"That is too bad. I hardly knew her, I wanted to, but I know you did, and I'm sorry about that. I tried."

"Thanks, man," Deedra's eyes welled up. "I know you

did. You're a good person. You would've died protecting her just because she was cool with me, and you just met her. Loyalty."

"And I almost did die."

"That's right. You almost did. You almost did."

Chapter 26—So Opiate!

I ASKED JOAN what her exact strategy was before they embarked upon their great mission of destroying those who would destroy artists like me and Kate. *Bastards.* Deedra had all of Kate's paintings at least, and promised her parents she'd get a gallery in her remembrance in the near future. Joan basically co-owned a gallery already so it wouldn't be hard to do. I was supposed to add in some paintings as well, and finish whatever Kate was working on. That sounded swell to me because although our styles differed, I was versatile enough to do it.

Joan explained in short detail that they'd clean out Washington State first, of course, then work their way through Oregon, and then down into California. She also said she had a pretty fancy lair in a forgotten, reinforced mineshaft in the mountains of California. I'd never been to California, and that sounded interesting as you generally didn't think of mountains in the same sentence with California, although I wasn't ignorant of them as I recalled the Donner Party that turned to cannibalism in the mid-1800's while attempting to travel through them in the winter.

"But I might go into Los Angeles alone once we start hitting the major cities starting from the Bay Area around San Francisco," Joan said. "I want to see if any of the elders there have seen them. I think I'm still on good terms with them. It's not really my call to crush jugend down there without asking at least."

"Or you can just go into San Francisco and ask if they've heard of anyone who goes by the name

'Mistress,'" I said. "You might be able to narrow it down to a thousand possible choices if you keep at it steady for a few weeks."

Joan laughed. "I'll ask the L.A. ones if there is an especially sadistic vampire Fräulein lurking about, though I think we all sometimes are, as it's hard to be a murderering masochist. I'll ask if there are any who go by that description you guys have given me. She'll be laying low if she's smart and that wounded, but we'll find her if I have to search the world over."

"Oh, I have another thing I must add if Deedra didn't already say it," I said. "Gosh, I'm an idiot for not mentioning this earlier. My brain's a little...humdrum still. I said she seemed to have a British accent, and she seemed to be powerful. She didn't have your type of radiance, but I could feel it, right? For some reason, in hindsight, however, I think she might've been Australian. Or picked up an Australian or New Zealand accent. It was very slight."

Joan pondered this. "I'll keep that in mind. Well, she won't be too powerful now as she's probably pretty wounded if not helpless. But she'll be protected."

"Deedra almost decapitated her!"

"I should've," Deedra said. "I only had my littler knife. Then I stuck that in that other one's eye."

"You say she sounded English, but maybe Aussie?" Joan said. "Yeah," I said. "Something like that. Who knows? It could've

been Aussie, but I'm presuming it was mostly English because of her word choice. See, she also called me a 'Yank,' and I doubt she's from the south. Bluh-ee fookin' English, anyway. Hah! It's a major hunch, too. Australian is the second choice, anyway."

"I have a couple of English friends," Joan said. "They're asking about it. That Aussie bit might help us out a little bit if she is older than 100 or so. We'll see about that. Nonetheless, we still have to burn up the coastline. I'm looking forward to it. I haven't drank vampire blood in many years. That was when someone else was 'cleaning house' and the world over it appeared, and I did a sweep of the area to make sure they didn't have to come up here to my cozy little corner. I saved them the work and they like me for it—so I heard. Whoever they were. But these young worthless ones popping up like weeds, they need to be pulled if they are going to be disrespectful like that, otherwise I'd maybe let them pass."

"'They,'" I said. "Always they."

"'They' are finished," Deedra said. She twirled, and then thrust her large dagger into an imaginary foe.

It was almost humorous watching and listening to Joan explain the politics, calculations, and the strategies of killing, which was essentially 'catch them off-guard' if possible. And decapitation worked well, followed by torching. Molotov cocktails were in fine order, and gunshots to the head area were perfect for temporarily paralyzing and stunning the enemy. It was no time to get cute, that's why they had also packed an Israeli made .50 caliber Desert Eagle for quick disablement. This girl looked like she should be studying for her driver's test, not planning genocide of powerful supernatural being! Woe to those who incurred her wrath, but perhaps that's how she survived for so many years.

After apologizing at least 20 times for having to leave, Deedra left with Joan. I told her, "You be safe. Don't worry about me sitting around and reading books."

I gave Deedra one last hug and kiss, she walked out the front door with Joan and just disappeared. I was kind of upset because I was going to watch them until they went out of sight. Plus, I knew Joan flew out of there holding Deedra, and I'd never even got to see it. I wanted to see her fly like Superman in the worst way. It was relaxing to have trivial complaints like that at last instead of wondering if I was going to die. I momentarily saw them flitting across the atmosphere due south like a dark satellite before disappearing in the clouds. Trippy.

***

A WEEK LATER I MADE MY WAY to the garage after a long shower. I put on a nice brimmed dress hat, and felt like I'd cashed out big at Monte Carlo I was in such good spirits. I drove downtown in a silver Audi. The Seattle skyline with its magnetic, phallic-like symbolic Space Needle building that everyone had to flock towards like it was some sort of North West ancient pyramidal tribute to the Gods never looked so good to me. It was a modern day totem pole.

I was out and about once again, but I didn't know where I was going, I was just going. The music in the car from Deedra's autographed Alice In Chains CD—a former local band—sounded invigorating, so I blasted it loud. I ended up in an area that had a lot of bars, and found a place to park. I wandered the crowded sidewalks of the sleepless Broadway Street that had been continually active at night for nearly a century due to generations of drunks. There were clubs and taverns with future rock stars of America jamming in them, eccentric shops that I'd checked-out with Deedra, countless cafes with coffee drinking geeks, and even gay bars. Unlike the previous older pederast who I'd killed at the motel who wanted me, I didn't find the licentious glances of these young 'hip' homosexuals offensive at all, but rather sort of flattering in a way. I tipped my hat to a group of them politely after one of them whistled teasingly, but I wasn't bi-curious and continued on my way towards the Asian Museum area.

I really wanted to kiss an Asian girl if one found me suitable, and perhaps I'd take her up to a hill or a lookout point that I'd never been to if she'd give me the chance. I imagined every hill was a huge heap of garbage and sawdust ever since I heard that's what a lot the city was built on. There were even entire underground, old-time streets and buildings under the current ones that were a tourist attraction. Deedra once showed me an even lower level of the underground city that she said was an old opium den. There was Chinese writing and oriental antiques strewn about. It looked like it'd been abandoned in a hurry, perhaps because of a police raid. Or more morbidly: Joan.

***

I FOUND HER IN A TAVERN, sitting alone in a booth twirling her little pink straw in a mixed whiskey drink. It was that Melissa girl who'd let me drink from her wrist that night at Kate's. She made me as libidinous as I was the last time I'd seen her. What was it about me and girls with dark hair? Actually, her hair was dyed black from blonde, but I still liked it.

I asked her who she was with, and she said her friend named Kip. That wasn't his real name, as it was a shortened version of his last name that he'd gotten from his football team.

"Where's he at?"

She shrugged. "I don't know. Some girl wanted him to go with her. I think he dogged me out."

She was sort of lying for whatever reasons—probably to make herself more pitiful sounding—as he'd actually left with some other dudes to party. I said, "Oh, that sucks! I'm sorry. Hey, do you wanna like go...about? Like, ride somewhere? I mean, do you wanna come to my place, or come somewhere? Blegh! I mean, would you like to chill out with me!"

I am so unsmooth sometimes.

"Sure!" she said and downed her drink without using the pink straw. She crunched a piece of ice. "I'd love to."

***

THERE ARE A LOT of people—mostly young females—that haven't been found in those deep woods of the Northwest from Oregon to Canada. But it's not just exclusively in the Northwest, as there are a lot of 'person missing' posters on bulletin boards throughout the U.S., and more young bodies than you'd believe always turn up in the morgue as 'John' or 'Jane Doe,' and are never claimed. Many come from all across the small towns and Indian reservations in the U.S., and flock to a hub city maelstrom like Seattle only to disappear forever while in search of that elusive American dream.

A lot of young females that stray towards Seattle naively seeking adventure get addicted to their drug of choice, get hungry, and they need a place to stay once their funds run out and it gets cold. A pimp will often accommodate these basic needs. Transients, gang members, addicts, and general lowlifes, it's really no big deal when they're dead. Everyone expects them to die anyway.

Melissa knew what I was, just as I knew she was a student at the Cornish College of Arts Kate had gone to. On the drive, she said she hadn't told anybody, but she had a distinct feeling that if there ever was a vampire, me and Deedra would have to be it—especially me. She said that she wanted me to drink more of her that night. She said that the only reason why she never asked was because the room was too crowded, plus her butch girlfriend was watching. She was 'punished' thoroughly for that scene, and had finally gotten off of her actual leash only because her girlfriend left town. She wasn't that much of a lesbian, really, and wanted a boyfriend more than a girlfriend. She just loved being submissive. She said, "Are you a domme or sub?"

"Both, I guess," I said. "Mostly sub though."

"I'm sorry I'm rambling like this," Melissa said. "You probably think I'm some sort of psycho now! I don't really mean all that about you being a vampire and all. It's just the way you compose yourself: walk, talk, look— everything. You probably don't even believe in them. I know it's stupid, but I do. But seriously, you haven't even said anything. Do you believe in vampires? Or do you just think I'm some kind of weirdo?"

Shit, this is odd. Play it cool.

We pulled through the gate and headed to the castle-like mansion.

"I don't think you're a weirdo," I said. It was so hard for me to lie but screw it, I figured, it could be unfortunately fun. "I've seen vampires before, in real life, dude."

She let me drink her that night over and over with the unspoken hope that maybe I could make her like me. She had a quixotic, romantic notion about vampires. I would've perhaps thought the same if I was ignorant of what I personally did to people on a near bi-weekly basis. Does carrying a cold, lifeless, often already decaying and stinking body into the woods in the middle of the night to become tree fertilizer sound poetic and glamorous? Some of those gargantuan trees undoubtedly ate those bodies up at a considerable rate in accordance with the region's heavy rainfall.

She could live forever she thought, but there was no such thing. A fountain of youth that one must sell their soul and remaining innocence for is all it was. Even then, I'd almost died right away anyway.

***

SHE WAS RUNNING OUT OF THE BLOOD sustaining her, and was still looking oh so alluring lounging on a desk chair. She'd taken her clothes off by then, and was wearing only a crucifix necklace along with a pentagram, fishnet leggings, high-cut dark blue panties, and a matching bra. Earlier, I'd shown her the library and explained to her the importance of some of the rare books. She was a good student, and really did like learning. Personally, although I wouldn't have the patience to teach those who wouldn't listen with actual interest, I thought I made a good teacher, too.

"Aside from the books of like John and Revelations, and the letters of Paul, the New Testament wasn't written by the authors whose names are on them—so the skeptic theory goes. They don't have any evidence though," I explained to her when we skimmed through a very old fourteenth century Bible with a regular King James Version, and noted the differences.

"So what's the theory then?" she said. "Is it like old Greek Hellenistic schools of thought, but just with Christian books instead?"

"Yes. You're very good! Very.... The New Testament as it is now was just the earliest version of many thoughts and beliefs of what Christ was said to have taught. Some of the later 'Gnostic' versions—and I use the term 'Gnostic' loosely, as in not centrist—although there was no real center of Christianity until later—do sound a bit pretentious to me. But I digress, I just think the authors and their 'schools' sound that way. Like, one book was supposedly written by Christ himself, or so we are led to believe.

"Anyway, the Gnostic stuff is an interesting read nonetheless, and contains legit Christian teachings—more or less in my humble opinion—from having browsed through it," I said.

I found the copy of a translated *The Nag Hammadi Library* book whose Coptic words were originally discovered in Upper (southern) Egypt in 1945. They were actually thought to have all been destroyed long ago. I handed it to Melissa.

Most Gnostic books were written a half-century or century after the selected Biblical books were written, proving the Christian Bible developed and evolved outside of what was eventually canonized.

"I can't verify what every book in there says, but the popular Gospels out of here like Thomas and Mary, they seem to fit the mold of what Paul would've agreed with—the teachings anyway. I don't know about the storylines. In fact, someone who obviously studied Paul in that Gnostic bible wrote a book called, 'Prayer of Paul.'"

"Cool," she said and skimmed through it. "Huh, 'The Dialogue of the Savior'?" I told her that was supposed to be Jesus' book I mentioned earlier, but that was probably written by an extremely bright, charismatic second century Christian scholar named Valentino, who had an outside chance of becoming a Pope, strangely. "Weird. What about the ones selected then for the 'real Bible,' what do you think of them?"

"The letters by Paul are always an impressive read. The Gospels, although they do give you a thorough and sound base for what Christ taught, are elongated 'Passion' stories, as one scholar said. He may have been biased, but think about it. He said they all lead to the Crucifixion, basically. Not that it's not very important, because it is. The reason I mention that is because, well, those other book versions not selected, they don't have the Crucifixion, coincidentally! Just supposed teachings. Aside from the timeline, it's that 'cross' symbolism that seemingly separates the versions.

"The cross is therefore an 'idol,' I dare say, without hoping to be deemed a blasphemer. But it's true, nonetheless. Where does it say in The Bible to pray a cross, or pray to Mary the Mother of God?"

"You heretic!" she joked. "I'm Catholic, by the way."

"Ah! I already noticed your spiffy crucifix. It's beautiful. 'Blasphemy' is wearing it next to that pentagram."

"I know! Sorry? Hah."

"Don't be. I'm not a priest. But anyway, the Gnostics on the other hand, they were more concerned to referring to what the 'living Christ' said while he was alive rather than the strong underlying point of 'why he died', which was for our sins, as everyone knows. They wanted their emphasis to be on the *living Jesus* as opposed to *his death*. I think they're right in a sense. People focus primarily on his death, and forget about the way he lived, the way we should strive to live. The Gnostics do sound kind of pretentious, as I said, if the books they came up with were written a half-century or more after the fact of the other main New Testament gospels, but then again—"

"—All of those New Testament books would be if they weren't written by the authors whose names are on them, and they added and edited what they deemed 'Christ-like.'"

"Theoretically. Impressive. I really like you. But the tone of what Jesus said in the Gospels is pretty consistent. 4 Gospels, 4 directions, etcetera, by some dude Marcion who didn't want more Gospels selected after 140 A.D., and deemed everything else 'blasphemy' essentially. He couldn't fuck with Paul, however, as he combined Judaism and Christianity perfectly. The guy went through a lot of personal trouble in promoting Christianity, and in doing so he became like the ultimate model for spirituality. But with each region, different sects seemed to develop, so there were many sects.

"But yeah, the fact that Gnostic versions came decades later is the main one difference one should consider in comparing the Christian books not selected. There's a lot to know, but that's a quick summary on a complex topic that not a lot of Christians bother to discover. Basically, that's all I've been doing all week. Trying to discover some religious roots. I may have discovered myself instead. There's a lot of books here, but I even ordered more books with express delivery."

***

I COULD BITE HER AGAIN ANYWHERE, she said. Then she asked where Deedra was. She could bite her, too. Her speech was starting to slur. I'd healed every wound so she wouldn't leak all over the nice leather furniture and rug in the den. I remembered an idea I had right before the 'Mistress' vampire had almost killed me. I explained this out loud to Melissa while I paced the room all buzzed up and she strived hard to pay attention.

"Those same vampires, they killed Kate you know," I

said. "They probably would've killed you too if you'd been at her house."

"They...did?"

She could barely keep her eyes open, and rubbed them. I should just stop prolonging it, I thought. I still had a few hours before daybreak. She wouldn't last until then, or she'd just pass out, unless I shared my own blood.

Though seeing her nearly naked was eye candy that made a wonderful decoration, I felt like telling and helping her put her clothes back on as it made me a bit abashed, seeing as we were both sort of hooked-up with other females, and technically Deedra could come at any time. She does look tasty, though. *Nice-a! Mmm!*

"Say...are you going to make me a vampire...or can I serve...serve you guys?" she said.

"Serve us? My 'goth,' you goth, that's funny! Sorry, I'm not laughing at you, it's just that the 'Mistress' chick maybe would've let you serve her! But I don't want to actually be the 'False Idol' and break that Commandment, too. I'm having a hard enough time with the other eight, as I don't really use the Lord's name in vain in like ever. But...about what you're saying, we'll see. But...I just told you what killed your friend—one of us— and you want to be that?" I asked rhetorically and shook my head with a smile I couldn't suppress with my blood high. "Oh, anyway, about that idea I had before I was so rudely interrupted by those other vampires who wanted to kidnap me: I was going to write a sort of autobiography about what happened to me so far. With me? Savvy?" I said.

"Yeah."

"All right. Just checking. But it would've had an inconclusive ending, however. Or maybe I did have a good ending...never mind! Back to the subject of the hour: He gave us free will, so it's not His fault if we fuck up. It's like, why does God let bad people do bad things?

The free will! 'Born without sin from our mother's pain and the desire of sin eventually controls our brain.' I wrote that lovely verse, by the way. Actually, my ending would've had a 'happily ever after ending,' but that would've been too gay. I don't mean that in a disparaging way, but in the 1930's way. Not that there's anything *wrong* with that—being gay. Classic. You know, you are a very beautiful girl, and I'd love to make you a vampire. You seem to have thought long and hard about it too, am I right?"

She looked up and said, "Yes-s-s. Please."

Deedra was right, there was a certain 'type' of consistent, harmonic, cold-bloodedness needed in order to be what we were functionally.

"You'd be content to be like me," I said. "You'd be so, 'happily ever after.' But it's just not the way of the world, as someone dear once told me. I'll tell you what I am going to do though. I'm going to give you one final demonstration of what 'vampire powers' are really about. I'm so sorry. I really do love you. Like a sister in God. Sort of. I don't know if that applies anymore."

She pled tearfully that I let her live before I took her. The 'overdose' practice with the syringe in the arm—like what those vampires did to Kate—was actually a good idea, especially in this particular area. I could put her in a public bathroom somewhere. Nah, I'd let her have the dignity of just disappearing. I'd bury her proper. Well, her parents wouldn't think it was dignified not knowing where she was but you couldn't please everyone when it came to death unless the person was a real jerk and the populace was happy to be rid of them.

I'd still have to try it with someone else, as it'd save me a trip into those particularly haunted woods. You keep thinking Bigfoot is going to grab you from behind while digging. I crept up on Deedra once, grabbed her ankles, growled, and she bashed my shoulder with the shovel, but it was worth seeing the look on her face.

Why did I kill another person I'd actually grown to know? It just sort of happened on a whim—I didn't even have the slightest inclination to kill her at first. I just wanted to hang out with someone for the night to break my studious, isolated monotony. She knew what I was even if she'd only romantically imagined it in her creative brain, but I couldn't chance her escaping with the real knowledge. Now both Melissa and Kate were dead simply for having crossed paths with me.

***

THERE WAS A COMPUTER in one of the rooms upstairs. It had a nice view of the moon, and you could see the treetops across the big lawn sway in the distance. I opened the window in hopes of hearing their song.

Ah, there it was—the voice of time that was nature. A steady, swirling wind swished the treetops as an incoming Puget Sound rainstorm gave me a random, orchestral concert before I'd eventually have to shut the window. They weren't lying. Everything does hold much more beauty when you've almost died.

I flipped on the computer.

The techno, in-your-face world that routed from Seattle to Silicon Valley had supposedly made everything faster, better, and more connected. But with that, a lot of people in this modern era had deprived themselves of life's simple yet greater pleasures—like connecting to the rest of Earth—without even realizing it until it was too late and it was gone.

I knew what would fill me with great elation, and I would not overlook it, not on that night. A sudden, swift breeze ran through the window, carrying with it a rainy mist that awoke me further. Take me away, to a dream state—the rest of my mind, yearns to be awake. I wanted to write, so I started typing out the best story I knew about a girl I met named Deedra.

THE END

About the Author

Adrian L. Jawort is a Northern Cheyenne writer based in Billings, Montana. A veteran freelance journalist and op-ed writer for various national and indie publications, she's also the curator and a contributor to the highly acclaimed *Off the Path* anthologies featuring American Indian and international Indigenous writers. A fearless and bold writer in both her non-fiction and fiction works, Jawort says, "Art must not circumvent truths."

www.ingramcontent.com/pod-product-compliance
Lightning Source LLC
Chambersburg PA
CBHW031058270626
47155CB00026B/698